Epiphany
THE
CRYSTALLING

BOOK 2

SONYA DEANNA TERRY

Print edition first published 2019

ISBN: 978-0-9942167-3-1

Published by Sonya D Terry

Structural edit by Deonie Fiford
Front cover image by Kim Dingwall and SelfPubBookCovers.com
Front, back cover and spine design by MiblArt
Additional elements by Vecteezy

To see a world in a grain of sand
And Heaven in a Wild Flower,
Hold Infinity in the palm of your hand
And Eternity in an hour.
WILLIAM BLAKE

The garden of Eden, this new promised land,
The time to set sail for will soon be at hand.
JOHN FREETH

EXCERPT OF 'BOTANY BAY' A 1786 CONVICT BALLAD
ROMANTICISING TRANSPORTATION TO AUSTRALIA

No act of kindness, no matter how small, is ever wasted.
AESOP

There is something perverse about more than enough.
When we have more, it is never enough. It is always somewhere
out there, just out of reach. The more we acquire, the more elusive
enough becomes.
UNKNOWN

Our birth is but a sleep and a forgetting
The Soul that rises with us—our life's Star
Hath had elsewhere its setting
And cometh from afar
WILLIAM WORDSWORTH

The measure of love is to love without measure.
SAINT AUGUSTINE

Someone stole all my credit cards, but I won't be reporting it.
The thief spends less than my wife did.
HENNY YOUNGMAN

The best things in life are not things.
AUTHOR UNKNOWN

Character List

18th-Century England

CORNWALL

Edward Lillibridge ....Documenter of *Our True Ancient History*

Prehistoric Norway
Portrayed as 'Norwegia' in Lillibridge's
Our True Ancient History

ELYSIUM GLADES

The elfin Brumlynd clan
Nature spirits of devic origin (sprites)

Maleika ....Clan Watcher

Pieter ....Maleika's firstborn son

Kloory ....Maleika's younger son

Croydee ....Maleika's nephew

Zhippe ....An adopted water sprite orphan

Carlonn ....Zhippe's twin

Forest creatures

Fripso
A young rabbit

Karee
Fripso's mother

Sluken
Croydee's dragon

THE GRUDELLAN PALACE

Gold's Kin
Known to the sprites as 'body kings'

Eidred ....Princess of Grudella

The Solen ....Gold's Kin Emperor/Eidred's father

Storlem ....Gold's Kin guard and Crystal Keeper

Rahwor ....Grudellan sorcerer

Zemelda ....Palace soothsayer/former bewitcher

Orahney .... An autumn faerie from the
Pre-Destruction Century

The Dream Sphere
A celestial dimension featured in Lillibridge's
Our True Ancient History

Alcor ....The Brumlynd clan's Dream Master

Modern Australia

SYDNEY

Rosetta Melki .... Friday Fortnight founder

Rosetta's Friday Fortnight book study group

Craig Delorey .... Lawyer/entrepreneur

Edith Derby (Eadie) .... Beauty Therapy student

Royston Leckie .... Youth Counsellor

Lena Morris .... Health foods shop proprietor

Darren Eddings .... Former Hairdresser

Izzie Redding .... Rosetta's daughter

Glorion Osterhoudt .... Izzie's crush

Charlotte Wallace .... Izzie's school friend

Diondra Wallace .... Charlotte's mother/Dette's friend

Dominic Wallace .... Charlotte's father

Molly Carr .... Maleika's visiting dream-self

Matthew P Weissler.........Former Investment Bank Trading Manager

Matthew's former work colleagues

Charlie Sanders................Trading Director

Adam Harrow..................Trading Manager

Celia Owens.....................Executive Assistant

Lila Donevski...................Administrative Assistant

Bernadette Weissler (Dette)............Matthew's wife

Sara Belfield....................................Dette's elder daughter/
Izzie's school friend

Laura Belfield.................................Dette's younger daughter

Grant Belfield.................................Dette's ex-husband/
Sara and Laura's father/
Rosetta's former neighbour

ALICE SPRINGS

Conan Dalesford....Author of *Thoughts on Tomorrow's Tycoon War*

Jannali Dalesford....Conan's Wife

Modern New Zealand

CHRISTCHURCH

Robert Bentley (Bobby).............Rosetta's half-brother

Tanya Bentley............................Rosetta's sister-in-law

Prologue

An excerpt of an email from
Glorion Osterhoudt to Izzie Redding
describing the heart-elixir crystals

...In ancient prehistoric times, Gold's Kin races involved in beauty-creation rituals sent crystals to 'uncivilized' Lemuria. As I told you when relating the story documented by Edward Lillibridge, the theft of faeries' manifestation powers turned these faeries into 'bewitchers', thus the term 'witches', a word initially used in Britain by druidic clans.

The power in these crystals was too kind and loving a frequency. Those of the empire could not tolerate a harmoniser such as this. It weakened them.

Contact with the heart-elixir crystals allowed the men and women of the court to become peaceful and sprite-like, and so, upon amassing amounts considered 'dangerous', Gold's Kin shipped this crystal-encased sprite magic to a far off land they would never inhabit.

Chapter One

A NOTE FROM THE PUBLISHER

Dear Readers,
If you are a first-time reader of the *Epiphany* series—welcome!
While Book-1 is naturally the best introduction, this second book is
also a great place to start. The <u>Character List</u> provides you with a
background on those who emerged in Book 1. A <u>Glossary</u> is
included as well, on the back pages, to help familiarise you with terms
used in the *Our True Ancient History* sections.

XXXV

Once at the door of Princess Eidred's chamber, Pieter smiled. After months of hiding within the Grudellan Palace, he was about to depart. He stood at the top of the Grand Hall stairway, feet twitching nervously.

The princess nodded to him. 'You will look the same as any of the men at court,' she said. His face was painted with dragon blood. 'Head down, now Pieter. And remember to bow to all who might pass you.'

The hooded cloaks of grey wool that he and Eidred now wore had arrived amongst many other garments in the basketful of cloth the princess was expected to scrub. Servants who wore these cloaks delivered and collected laundry.

Holding a basket of fresh linen on either side, he and Eidred made their slow descent to the Grand Hall. To Pieter, reaching the pyramid home of Zemelda in the palace grounds as lilac dusk crept into the golden sky was the longest walk he'd ever made, for it was fraught with the knowledge that if his disguise failed to convince, he would be slaughtered at sunrise.

An end to his life was not the worry. The effect of this on Eidred and Fripso posed greater concerns. The princess and Pieter's animal friend were vulnerable. He must protect them. He would learn to exercise pretence—as Eidred had advised—and become deceptive, although it would grate on his devic desire to remain perennially sincere.

And why were they taking this precarious journey from Eidred's chamber to Zemelda's dwelling in the palace grounds? Because a cushion had told them they should! Eidred had been seated at her loom earlier, having paused to watch rain outside her window, and she'd happened to look across at one of the square pillows adorning her canopied bed. She'd run to the elf and said, 'Pieter, look! Zemelda is heralding us.' There on the cushion had magically appeared the words:

Adahmos due upon the morrow!
From clothiers you must now borrow
Two hooded cloaks for you and he
Then hasten—both of you—to me

Pieter had blinked, and the words had dissolved and changed into new ones:

The elf must don what you have sewn
And once to me the elf has flown
I shall ensure the Solen hears
His guest has come—go now, my dears

They arrived unnoticed at a pyramidal structure, the soothsayer's quarters. Zemelda, a black-hooded woman with hair of white and skin as gnarled as birch bark, ushered them into a chilly dampness. Hanging upon every wall was a picture. Upon a small copper table, a paintbrush balanced atop a flat board daubed with various shades of green.

'Zemelda is an artist,' Eidred whispered, 'and a very skilled one too.' At Zemelda's stern warning to waste no time, Pieter flung off his woollen cloak and donned the headdress that Eidred had so cleverly constructed for him from flaxen cloth and golden twine. He did not pause to wonder whether he and the maiden he adored were the targets of trickery. He could not. He had to tell himself continually that Zemelda's intentions were good.

'Highness and Pieter,' Zemelda said in a voice that rasped growlingly like ocean waves in a storm, 'I wish to introduce you both to a friend.' She flitted to one corner of her strange, sloping-walled home and drew a rug from its place on the floor. There, within the wooden beams, lay a trapdoor.

Pieter eyed the steps that led into darkness. Were he and Eidred wise in going there? Could they be sure of Zemelda's loyalty? Pieter clasped Eidred's hand and descended the steps alongside her. While his faith in the former faerie might be dangerous, an even greater danger was refusing help. Presenting himself as a prince from afar was a prospect riddled with risk.

Beneath Zemelda's floor was a cavern. 'When did you discover a tunnel existed beneath this pyramid?' Eidred asked.

'I did not discover it,' Zemelda said. 'I created it. With this.' She held up what appeared to be a crystal on a staff.

'But Zemelda,' said Eidred aghast. 'Wands are only issued for the crystallings, our infant-naming ceremonies! And they're only ever given to the faerie concubines. You're no longer a bewitcher and yet you retain a wand. Why didn't a Crystal Keeper collect it from you?'

'I have an ally within the palace,' said the soothsayer with a secretive smile. 'He allowed me to retain one.' She led them to an arched door in the cavern. It swung open at their approach.

They found themselves within a sanctuary. Its walls were the colour of dawn, its floor a carpet of moss that sank spongily beneath their feet. Beyond was a stream, jewel-like in its radiance. On rocks edging the water sat tiny undines, chattering quietly to each other.

Zemelda's voice rose. *'Sluken,'* she called. 'I implore you to make yourself visible! I wish you to meet my guests.'

The air shimmered then, and expanded into ripples of light. The whirls subsided. In their place stood a dragon, elegantly humble, beaming shyly at the princess and the elf. The dazzle of the dragon's scales ignited a memory for Pieter, but he couldn't grasp whether it was an occurrence in the Dream Sphere or a distant childhood event. This dragon was not a wraith. He was as physically solid as the soothsayer.

'Sluken was hunted down in the forest when young,' Zemelda told them, 'and imprisoned in a dungeon for many season-cycles until he grew large enough to be slain for his golden blood. If they'd succeeded in killing him, they would have captured his spirit and trapped it in the Cave of Decay.' Zemelda ran a comforting hand over Sluken's neck. 'Moments before the Backwards-Winding, the eagle guards tied Sluken up in one of the courtyards. They were preparing to end his life. The quakes caused by the Backwards-Winding distracted the guards, and we seized the opportunity to rescue him.'

'We?' said Eidred. 'Who helped you, Zemelda?'

Pieter watched the soothsayer, awaiting the answer to Eidred's question.

'A companion,' Zemelda said. 'I was helped by my ally within the palace.'

The dragon addressed Pieter. 'You would not remember me, but when you were an infant, I played in the forest with your cousin.'

Pieter dashed across to Sluken and threw both arms around him. 'This explains my recognition of your scales! I remember a story Croydee told me once, about his dragon friend. I am deeply thankful, Sluken, that you've been saved.'

'The silver and the gold unite,' Sluken said to Eidred. 'Orahney has told me much.'

Orahney? Pieter spun round to Zemelda and said, 'The faerie Orahney is a friend of the Brumlynds. She is an autumn Clan Watcher and Dream Sphere dweller. Where would she be, good woman?'

The soothsayer bowed her head. As she did so, the hood casting shadows across her face fell away. The eyes that met Pieter's were dark and gentle. Could it be true? And yet it was. Right before Pieter, in the form of a bewitcher withered with age, was Orahney.

Eidred's voice was faint. 'I once heard the name Orahney. It is supposed to be the name of my faerie godmother...'

'Orahney is my own godmother, beloved.' Pieter gazed at the soothsayer in disbelief. 'How could...'

The former faerie held her wand high in the air. A silver glow appeared. The wand's crystal engulfed her in dazzling beams.

The princess grasped Pieter's arm. ''Tis all right, my beauty,' Pieter said to her. 'Silvery light is only ever benevolent.'

The wand returned Orahney to her true form. In place of her cloak was a flame-bright gown made up of leaves displaying all colours of the autumn: deep, dark red, clear orange and glowing amber. In place of her white and crinkled skin was a luminous complexion of deepest brown. Orahney's tresses, with their flecks of crimson and mulberry, fell about her shoulders like ropes of braided silk.

'*Orahney,*' said Pieter. 'It is really you!'

'Surely you do not know me.'

'You are my godmother,' said Pieter. 'You prophesied my birth! I've spoken to you many a time in the Dream Sphere. How did you ever maintain solidity in this world? And for so long? I have never seen this in a Dream Sphere dweller.'

'I am not a Dream Sphere dweller,' said Orahney. She appeared perplexed by Pieter's questions. 'I am from Earth. Elysium Glades. And I regret you've mistaken me for another faerie, for I am the godmother of no-one.'

Remembering then that Orahney in the Dream Sphere had once mentioned a life lived as a Clan Watcher in the Pre-Destruction Century, Pieter said no more. His godmother was the *future* Orahney, after she'd passed. He had to remind himself that he'd travelled back in time with the Grudellan Palace. Imagining the implications of telling Orahney he had met her ghost made Pieter blush. 'Perhaps I am mistaken,' he mumbled.

'You are Storlem's beloved,' cried Eidred. '*He* is the companion you speak of.'

Pieter thought back to Eidred's account of the forbidden lovers and Orahney's disturbing capture. During one of her walks in the forest of Elysium, the princess had overheard an affectionate conversation between an eagle-winged royal guard and the guard's true love who dwelt in the glades, a faerie woman clad in autumn tones. Courtiers in sprite-seeing cloaks had slashed through forest vines and stolen the faerie away to the palace. Eidred had explained at the time that she dreaded the poor faerie's fate. She was to be cruelly robbed of her magical powers in a ceremony, which altered faeries into bewitchers, and forced to live in the palace's concubine quarters. The heartbroken guard had mutated into his eagle form and hovered helplessly above the sword-wielders. *I will watch over you within the palace,* he'd told his lady. *I will always be there to protect you.*

Eidred was now telling Orahney that the memory had haunted her ever since. 'I was there in Elysium.'

'Indeed you were,' said Orahney, eyes downcast. 'What a terrifying evening. I was so afraid you might endanger yourself and try to defend me. Thank goodness you thought better of it.'

'Thank goodness you aren't a vacant-eyed slave. And you are not aged in the slightest!'

The faerie nodded serenely. 'My ageing, as you see, is a ruse. The rapid onset of maturity made me undesirable as a concubine.'

'A disguise achieved by magic.' Eidred was confused. 'The ceremony attendants were supposed to take all your powers!'

Orahney held her wand aloft. 'With the aid of this crystal, I continue to wield them.'

'Those powers might not be very obedient.' Eidred's words quivered with anxiety. 'Heart elixir belonging to another seldom complies with its user's will. My family's Crystal Keepers are careful to ensure they loan the bewitchers invited to crystallings heart-crystals that are not the wand-wielder's own. If faeries come into contact with their own beauty-creation, their strength is restored.'

'And what makes you think, my dear, that this crystal is not of my own heart? Our dragon friend has grown restless. He is eager to go.'

Sluken's wings unfurled into great, angular half-stars. 'I remain at your service,' he told Pieter and Eidred. 'Seek me out if ever you need assistance.' The scales upon the crest of his head flashed frenetically. He then vanished inside a fine wisp of smoke.

'We must hurry now,' Orahney told them as they left the cavern to make their way up the stairs. 'Eidred, Storlem is to escort you back to your chamber. He awaits you outside my door.'

'Storlem has kept his promise in protecting Orahney,' said a buoyant Eidred. 'He is watching over her within the palace. He has given her back her magical stolen heart.'

Upon returning through the trapdoor, the faerie addressed Pieter urgently. 'We must ready you for your introduction to the Solen. If it were safe, I would help both you and the princess escape. The time is not right, but you will extricate yourself from the palace one day. The dragon blood has altered your skin enough to emulate Prince Adahmos.'

'And yet I cannot mask my devic eyes.'

'The absence of genetically royal blue has already been explained to the Solen. He believes the reason for your *defective* brown eyes is a wicked spell cast upon you by a sprite.'

Pieter laughed at that, as did brown-eyed Orahney.

Blue-eyed royal Eidred, hastening towards the pyramid's exit where Storlem awaited her, turned and regarded them quizzically.

'Sprites do not cast spells,' Pieter explained. 'And our beauty-creation never works in ways that are wicked.'

'My family,' said Eidred frowning, 'are woefully misinformed.'

Storlem, Orahney's eagle-winged love, a wholesome warrior who looked upon the faerie with the romantic dreaminess of a besotted poet, was to march alongside Eidred. He assured Eidred he would create a distraction if they were stopped. 'Highness,' he said, 'would you allow me to hold your elbow as we walk?'

Eidred redonned the hood of her launderer's cloak, carefully concealing her golden hair, and set off across the palace grounds with Storlem. The sight of Eidred, a slight figure with head bowed, robed in unregal grey and locked in the firm clasp of one of the troopers, discomforted Pieter. He reminded himself that the guard had to appear as though he were taking a clothier away for punishment. Through his constant work as Crystal Collector at ceremonies, Storlem now resonated with kindness.

'My beloved possesses a sprite's temperament,' Orahney said, watching the trooper with eyes of pride. 'After he was silvered, he could no longer abide by the unfeeling ways of Gold's Kin.'

'This same marvel has occurred with my beautiful princess,' Pieter told Orahney. 'Eidred was silvered long before I met her. She has been in possession of a crystal since her naming ceremony. I'm still disbelieving of her wish to wed.'

'And yet it is true, for you are a good young man with a heart as pure as hers.' Orahney hesitated before adding, 'Gold-heritage infants are especially impressionable to heart-elixir crystals. As well as becoming silvered, they often reflect the traits of the faerie from whom the elixir is stolen.'

Eidred, Pieter thought, appeared to resemble Orahney in character. The faerie's voice, sweetly lilting now that she had shed her soothsayer form, was as soothing as sylvan bells and not unlike Eidred's dulcet tones. Pieter knew that the crystal Eidred owned was a small chunk from a wand. Eighteen-season cycles ago, when Eidred was but an infant, a bitter bewitcher stormed her crystalling and broke one of the crystal wands, a fragment of which young Eidred's nursery maid kept for her. Could the wand have been Orahney's?

Impossible! The faerie's capture and heart-elixir theft had occurred only within the last season-cycle. The silvering capacity of Eidred's crystal had probably been extracted from a faerie with similar graces.

Orahney handed Pieter a goblet. The liquid that bubbled within emanated curling blue steam. 'Drink this,' she said, 'and all will be well.'

'What will it do?'

'It will make you restful in readiness for your introduction. It will help you to evade the truth. I fear your kind-hearted elfin nature is *too* good for your *own* good.'

The potion tasted of forest fruits and bitter fern. When he drank the last drop, Pieter promptly became weary. 'My legs are almost unmovable,' he said, puzzled at the potion's effect. It hadn't differed much from the berry cider he drank with his clan, and yet the cider had never exhausted him.

He sank to the floor. He could neither open his eyes nor close them. His lids fluttered listlessly.

And then Orahney's hands, rough against his clothing, tore at his sleeves...scratched at the collar and headdress that Eidred had created for him.

Someone grasped his shoulders and dragged him towards the trapdoor. Any attempt to fight was in vain. Orahney's potion had rendered him motionless.

Water was flung over him, water from the cavern's stream. Beyond the haze he was locked in was the smell of salt and wet sand as the water chilled his skin. 'I have been tricked,' he murmured. 'This must not have been Orahney at all.'

Shortly after, he felt the brisk sweep of feathered wings on his shoulder. An eagle-winged trooper was lifting him from the cavern floor. Pieter tried to speak but failed. His senses were blurred and nightmarishly skewed, and his voice had become a pained croak. Again he attempted speech. 'Harm me if you have to,' he said in an opiated mumble, 'but you must never go near the princess or the rabbit.'

Then everything was swallowed by a deep, unforgiving silence.

After her teenaged daughter had retired to bed, Rosetta Melki curled up on a lounge chair to re-read the letter from a solicitor in New Zealand. A smooth sweep of her dark-brown hair obscured the page. She pushed the wayward strand behind her shoulder and pored over the subject line, half-listening to the rhythm of the rain as it pelted against the bungalow's lead-lit windows amidst flickers of playful lightning.

Robert Mark Bentley, a newly discovered half-brother. What would Robert be like? Would he be musical, like she was and have the same olive-toned skin? Maybe he'd be artistic like Izzie, and a snowy-skinned redhead as well, although Rosetta had always attributed Izzie's colouring to her ex. A typical Scot in appearance was Angus. Whether the titian was peppered with grey these days wasn't of much interest to Rosetta. Anyone capable of deserting a daughter and shirking the costs of child-raising was...but why think of Angus at a time like this? The letter had said she had a brother, a *blood relative* of her own.

She smoothed a hand over the crisp ivory page. The letter had provided her with another gift. The name of her mother.

According to our records, you are the biological half-sibling of our client and biological daughter of the late Mrs Daniela Sophia Bentley.

Daniela, the mother she'd never known, benevolent but not quite real, the smiling and receptive half of imagined conversations. Tonight those conjured talks ended in the words 'I'm sorry.' Rosetta was sorry she'd not made greater efforts to find her, sorry her mother's life had ended so early, sorry that she couldn't mend the past.

The buzzy anticipation of making an international call the next morning and speaking to Robert for the very first time had meant she'd absent-mindedly made tea without boiling the kettle, only noticing the coldness of it after a deep-in-thought sip. Would he be amenable to meeting her if she booked a flight to New Zealand? The word family was no longer an emotive word. 'Sibling' was a pseudonym for 'bully.' Sticking up for herself and others was never too much of a problem, but finding Robert Bentley to be just as aggressive as her foster brothers and sister would be a terrible disappointment. Rosetta took another sip of cold tea and smiled at the melodramatic mood she'd slipped into. The guy didn't have to match her jaundiced expectations.

'Another parent,' she whispered, shaking her head. 'I've lost another.' A different feeling, of course, to losing Mama and Baba. The Greek couple's passing had caused her to selfishly resent their desertion, but she'd been angry more with herself than with anyone else for not being a big enough reason to keep them here. Her Baba had been her one-man support team, and Mama...well, Mama had been a grump. Good-hearted, though, beneath all those crotchety words, and an ace with babies and toddlers, her love of them a major motivator for adopting newly born Rosetta so willingly. She'd imparted a lot of valuable knowledge when Izzie arrived in the world. The doting grandmother. A picture of practical nurturance.

Rosetta was pleased to settle down to sleep. She put to rest her desire for tomorrow to hurry up and arrive, along with worries concerning the house, the big-bellied cat and the prospect of phoning

Wall Street Golden Boy aspirant Adam Harrow to cancel Saturday's date, then submitted to an unusually restless slumber.

She dreamed she was diving through coral; frolicking with seals, delighting in the weightlessness of a world free of frenzy. She floated past a school of seahorses that bobbed through the water's turquoise haze like dewy-eyed kindergarten kids locked in an obedient march. She curled into a languid somersault and was stunned to find that her legs were no longer visible. In their place was a dolphin's tail, dappled with the fragments of a muted sunbeam.

And then she was back on land, running through the same magnificent forest that she and book-club buddy Royston had dreamt of previously, the forest described in Lillibridge's *Our True Ancient History*. The colours of the trees were fiery. Russet and yellow and crimson-red leaves fluttered about her. As well as the fiery tones were startling colours normally never seen in foliage. Electric blue. Lime. A deep hot-pink. A majestic night sky the colour of plums. The air was made Christmassy with the fragrance of pine needles. Added to that was the comforting aroma of smoke and hazelnuts.

She was running towards the most beautiful man she'd ever seen. He had the rippling physique of an athlete, skin that was golden, and calm eyes that were greenly blue. And feathered angel wings, which, rather than white, were a deep, dark brown. She went to throw her arms about the man, but he dissolved into the atmosphere as though he'd never been there at all. In his place was an eagle. The eagle blinked. To the sound of Rosetta's screams, the eagle turned to stone.

All that remained was a gold wedding band looped like a bangle around the stone eagle's leg. There came the sound of singers. Their voices were peculiar; screeching yet powerfully mesmeric. They chanted the words *We end your joy.*

The wedding band lit up as though struck by lightning and a foreboding voice shouted, 'All things golden!'

The dream tumbled into a memory of Matthew Weissler—at the bar Adam had taken her to—as he nodded across at his wife on the purple lounge. Again she felt the sudden intake of breath at discovering Matthew wasn't single as imagined. Looked down at his left hand where a golden ring glinted and wondered why she hadn't taken note of it earlier. And then Dette Weissler's voice, from

11

her phone call delivering Rosetta's interview result, replayed repeatedly in echoes. *You weren't successful.*

A car by the beach refusing to start.

The laundry intruder's taloned fingers clawing at the windscreen.

Icy, helpless terror.

Rosetta woke up shivering. She wasn't the only one to awaken with chills that morning. At the breakfast table, Izzie said, 'I was freezing when I woke up. Shivering all over.' The sixteen-year-old's face was damp with perspiration and an unhealthy shade of scarlet. 'But now it's boiling. Like summer.' By the time she was buttering her toast, she said, 'I'm freezing! Climate change sucks.'

'Honey, I think you might have a fever.' Rosetta retrieved from their first aid box a thermometer and packet of painkillers. Izzie's temperature was sky-high. She would not be attending school. Rosetta gave her two aspirins—the last in the packet—and a hot lemon drink, then sent her to bed before sprinting down the hallway to answer the meeping phone.

'Hey, Fornighter.' Craig. Friday Fortnight book-club regular and the friend whose career inspired Rosetta to take on the law degree she was yet to finish. Calling from Alice Springs on a mobile that kept cutting out. All Rosetta could hear was, 'Incredible...These crystals we discovered are...'

'Crystals? I didn't know you were into crystals all that much.'

'...Really amazing. We've started mining them. We've been...'

'A mine? A crystals mine? Sounds bizarre. Ooh, is this to do with that "secret project" of yours?'

Several bouts of soft, staccato chuckling emanated from the receiver. 'Yup. I didn't want to tell...and...off to Alice Springs again...drop my car across to you in the morn...A guy was...and his doc couldn't believe it either! How many people get to be cured of emphysema? Mining's now in progress. Company's nearly up-and-run...Can you hear me? Think my phone's out-of-range.'

'I can hear you okay, Craig, but you're breaking up.'

'That better?'

'Slightly. Looking forward to the loan of that gorgeous car of yours.'

'Rosetta, can you hear me?' The call cut out.

Rosetta tried calling Craig back, but his phone had switched itself off.

Izzie Redding woke from a fevered sleep. She wanted to be at school. Instead she was confined to her room, with nothing to listen to but the syrupy *chip-chip-chireeee* of a bird in the magnolia tree and nothing to look at but the bungalow's whirly ceiling cornices.

Dozing some more would have eased the aches, but an edgy restlessness kept Izzie conscious. It didn't help that her mind was circling around Glorion. She'd already known he lived in Brighton-Le-Sands but could never have imagined his home would be a narrow beachside shed or that he'd cook her a zesty birthday dinner, and without the need for electricity or gas.

Izzie checked her phone for texts. Apart from Jandy, Marla, Sara, Andrine and Rella, no-one from school had replied. She assessed the picture on the corkboard she'd sketched not so long ago, of the sun and moon locked in a kiss. She would re-do it one of these days, with brighter colours. Glorion's art was more vibrant than hers. His golden girl, silver boy painting was awash with the boldest of hues, both primary and pearlescent. *Adahmos and Eid* he called it, his very own portrayal of book characters he believed had existed in real life. It made sense, Izzie supposed. Why would the author name his book *Our True Ancient History* if it wasn't true? And how bizarre was it that Glorion voiced an interest in that particular book? He even knew of Rosetta's Lillibridge site. 'Rosetta Melki is your *mother?*' he'd said. 'But your surname's Redding!' and she'd had to explain that her mother returned to her maiden name after divorce.

Propping herself up against the pillow, Izzie eyed the dark-blue book-club novel on her bedside table, the edition her mother had borrowed from Royston. She'd loved Glorion's account of the book. She didn't doubt Adahmos and Eid were real people once, but Glorion's belief in the existence of sprites and a power-hungry race obsessed with gold had seemed *way* too way out. By the time she'd left for home, though, Izzie had wondered more about the theory.

Even wondered why Glorion knew so much about that apparent timeframe. Modern science deemed time-travel impossible, and yet...

Guess I'm not *too* giddy with this cold-virus to read, she thought.

She was eager to look over a few pages, if only to check that Glorion's retelling of the story was right.

A thin streak of light shone on the corkboard, setting aglow her sketch of a pink gem encased in lunar-gilt metal. She paused to remember the silver-pink crystal Glorion carried around, which appeared to have powers she couldn't explain. Izzie had never seen anything like that at the crystals shop her mother had worked at. None were known to generate the effects of electricity and gas. When she'd ribbed Glorion about it, he'd cosied-up on the couch and kissed her.

Izzie floated for a while in the memory of Glorion's kiss. *It's only you, Izzie,* he'd said. *I only like you.*

She grasped the cloth-covered novel with its tarnished title and pressed it open. Its yellow-edged pages held the familiar woodsy fragrance of antique books. Her eyes skimmed over the first page.

Our True Ancient History

A tale from the People of the Sea

Retold by Reverend Edward Lillibridge
In the Year of Our Lord, Seventeen-Seventy-one

Izzie turned to a random chapter, Chapter XXXVI, which began with the nocturnal Norwegian elf named Pieter dazzled by sunbeams streaming into a gilded room.

Realising she needed some sun herself to sharpen the faded words, Izzie opened the curtains behind her aching head, settled comfortably against the pillows and began to read...

XXXVI

'*Q*uite handsome, if it weren't for his brown irises.' The words hung ponderously in the stillness.

Piercing daylight stabbed at Pieter's half-closed eyes. He glimpsed the gleam of a gold ceiling etched with rose garlands and sun-faces.

'Ah, you are conscious now, Your Highness.' A servant woman curtsied, then exited the room.

Swimming through Pieter's bleared vision was a sallow face with cold eyes and the thinnest of smiles. A man of Gold's Kin, cloaked in fabric embellished with emeralds and amethysts, was towering imperiously over him. Rings on his nobbled fingers flashed in silver-white and azure bursts. From his neck hung a grotesque medallion representing the pterodactyl god, Grudas, a pendant Eidred had told him was only ever worn by the empire's solens. 'Highness,' he said. 'It is fortunate you survived the shipwreck. My men have salvaged some of the treasures you brought ashore in your ship's life boat.'

Vague memories filtered back to Pieter...a potion tasting of forest fruits and bitter fern, dozing drunkenly on damp sand, his ankles nudged by waves...callous hands dragging him along a beach...cries of 'Enemy! Shipwrecked invader! Kill him!'

The recollection of another voice, deep and commanding, returned to him. 'Release him at once. Do you wish to be clapped in irons? This is the Solen's most honoured guest: Prince Adahmos of Ehypte.'

He'd felt a feathered wing brush against his face...had heard the gallop of hooves...and then he'd been overcome by a stifling blackness.

The Solen continued. 'My vizier will explain what has happened. I expect to see you at the midday banquet tomorrow. It is to be held in your honour.'

'Er...Sire, I thank you. I ...'

The Solen swept out of the room.

Another man of Gold's Kin was soon before Pieter, explaining in a hurried, disinterested way that he had been discovered crazed with fever in the shallows of the Grudellan Sea. 'You will meet the Solen's daughter at the banquet tomorrow. Eidred of Grudella has all the qualities of a humble and obedient wife and is renowned throughout the land for her delicate beauty.'

Grateful now that Storlem's courage and Orahney's magic had protected him, that they'd had no intention of betrayal as he'd initially concluded, Pieter waved a careless hand in the air. 'I will judge her worthiness and decide for myself. You are dismissed.' The unfamiliar words had burst mechanically from Pieter's mouth. Orahney's potion had caused him to be arrogant!

The vizier bowed three times and backed out of the chamber.

A fanfare celebrating the princely visit preceded Pieter's first royal dinner: one hundred trumpeters upon a scarlet carpet, and a procession of fire-eaters, acrobatic jesters and pastel-hued forest unicorns, which, tragically, were kept imprisoned, locked into gilded cages beyond the pyramids.

And Eidred's body-king father, a man who subscribed to the illusion that he, as Solen of Grudella, was more important than anyone of lesser riches, a man who thought nothing of having his former wives murdered upon giving birth to daughters and not sons, greeted Pieter magnanimously, as he would a favourite nephew. Adahmos of Ehypte was known throughout the empire to be exceedingly affluent, in possession of a great deal more land than the Solen. The prince's fondness for Eidred of Grudella was to be encouraged. Like wheat basking in the benign rays of Sol, Adahmos was to be rewarded warmly by the Solen when interest was shown in the princess.

Their restriction in proximity was maddening in the extreme for Pieter. He and Eidred were not permitted to touch while courting, not even to clasp hands in greeting. Where once Eidred graced him with her presence on returning from schooling each day, now it was only at banquets that he'd got to speak with and look upon her. On the Sun's Days he was granted a walk around the grounds with his cherished lady, only to return to a cold, gold-filled room, aching for when next they would meet, and on those all-too-seldom saunters they were never completely alone. Two servants trailed behind them. Behind the servants, two of the Solen's eagle-winged guards.

Once Pieter officially proposed marriage, the Solen requested he visit Soothsayer Zemelda to hear how he might amass greater amounts of gold. Orahney certainly shared secrets with Pieter, but of quite a different nature. When Pieter discovered how deftly the autumn faerie had toiled in ensuring he and his beloved remained together safely, he was humbled with gratitude.

Feeling sleepy once more, Izzie set *Our True Ancient History* aside, wondering where Glorion was now. She could easily relate to Lillibridge's reference in that chapter to a restriction in proximity causing madness.

The bird in the magnolia tree began on another round of its *chip-chip-chiree* song, the shadow of its open-beak and scallop-edged feathers flickering gracefully across Izzie's quilt cover. Reminded of the feathery she-oaks she'd seen when emerging from the cavern beneath Glorion's boatshed, Izzie shrugged. Who had tried to break in? Who was Glorion escaping? She shook her head. What he'd told her just didn't add up. How could a quiet and respectable high-school student become a target for SAPO, the Swedish secret police? And Glorion wasn't a Swede. Or was he? The rumour sweeping the school that he faked his Dutch accent mightn't have been so crazy after all.

Something was not as it seemed. Izzie nestled back into the bed, fatigued by the woozy, prickly, clammy effect of her cold. How could she be sure that the guy she was head-over-heels for was actually who he said he was? Maybe Glorion was just a dreamy product of her imagination, someone too good to be true.

To:............Isobel Redding
From:..........Sara Belfield
Sent:............5 May 2008
Subject:........*urgent info*

Izzie!

Please reply as soon as you get this email. Today at school was mad. Two men, a reporter and a cameraman from *The Sydney Telegraph* hung around outside the gates and called out to some of the Year Tens that they needed to speak to friends of Glorion Osterhoudt.

Tyson told them he'd last seen him yesterday afternoon. Glorion was at his place watching the soccer and he told Tyson he was going to your birthday picnic. (Tyson couldn't go 'cos he got a respiratory virus—he wasn't ignoring us or anything). Around 5 p.m. Glorion said he'd join your party if it was still going and mumbled something about visiting the supermarket first to get you chocolates and flowers. Tyson warned him that you might have gone home, that this wasn't Europe where people partied hard. You're so lucky no buses were at the depot when you went to leave. You and Glorion would never have met up!

It was so exciting talking to everyone at school today about the group text you sent us last night. We all reckon you're a legend! Like I said in my reply, you just happened to choose the hottest guy in Year Ten.

What's with you dodging school on the most important day of your life? If you haven't seen the latest reports on Internet News, *do it now*. Since you haven't answered any of my calls or texts, I'm thinking it's possible you're in bed sick, totally unaware of the notoriety you're gaining throughout Australia and probably the world! If this is the case, I'll give you a rundown, just so you don't totally freak out when you see/hear the news. There's so much I want to talk to you about, but here's the more important stuff, and, I think, the most mindblowing information either of us will ever receive in our whole lives.

Glorion Osterhoudt is a prince. He seriously is! His real name and full-name is His Royal Highness Prince Nikolaus Kristofer Glorion Pieter Lars of Perelda. If you're wondering where Perelda is, it's an island off Sweden. His mother is Queen there. Can you believe it? Besides being the hottest guy in Year Ten, he's also a royal! And an escaped one! He *wasn't even allowed to be here.* How freaky is that? He came to Australia anonymously, at the beginning of the year. His parents, Queen Louisa and Prince Consort Wilfred, Duke of Norbury, sent him to an exclusive school in Adelaide called 'Fairmont School for Boys' so that he could experience life in another country. His parents somehow managed to engineer this in secret, without the media's knowledge, because they wanted him to concentrate on his education without having to deal with all the attention.

What I want to know is how did he end up in Sydney attending *Burwood High* of all places? He's been living on the beach in Brighton-Le-Sands, you said, and he's been at our school since beginning of term! This is so, so, sooo *freaky.*

Tyson took me across to see the reporters, kind of holding my arm as we walked, and, I'm really sorry, but somehow the men on the other side of the gates got it out of me, what your address is. I didn't tell them your name, only your address. Then Mr Putney, the Phys-Ed teacher who's also Tyson's rugby coach, spotted them and chased them off. Maybe I shouldn't have given your details without your permission, but think of this: you're now a celebrity! (And you have me to thank for helping you into the limelight). Someone else yelled out to them from one of the science classrooms and told them what your surname was. I think it was a friend of Andrine's.

I am honoured to be able to say you're in my group. My best, *best* friend, Isobel Redding, is a celebrity, and she's only just turned sixteen! You're even younger than Boyd Levanzi! I am so, *so* proud of you.

And if you and Glorion ever get married, say in 2021, (and from the romantic sound of Sunday night when he cooked you dinner and escorted you home in a taxi, I reckon you've got every chance of becoming his wife someday) just remember that out of all your friends, I would be the best ever bridesmaid to you. I've been

Bridesmaid five times now, well, Junior Bridesmaid at least, (Flower Girl) and kind of pretty much know the ropes about helping with bouquets, trains, a bride's wedding-day nerves, staying in the background and not upstaging the bride, etcetera. Plus I have light hair. Nearly all the other girls in our group, I realise, have dark hair, but your beautiful red hair looks best against a backdrop of hair that's blonde. Dark would dominate the wedding photos too much. Trust me. I've been there. I've witnessed heaps of weddings where the photos are ruined by contrasts in hair colour. For example: One of the brides had hair your colour and fair skin. She got two of her brunette, olive-skinned cousins to stand beside her during the photo session. The result? When she previewed the pics she said, 'I look like a corpse!' Anyway, that's just a bit of girly advice.

Have the two guys from the newspaper visited you yet? The reporter's really cute. He dresses well too. Silver tie and Jarmani suit and shoes that I reckon would look really cool on Tyson. Tyson's taste in clothing, as you know, is *so* last year.

I have so much to ask you but the PC I'm emailing you on is my stepdad's, and he's home from golf now and probably wants to use it. And for me it's absolutely *crucial* that Matthew (my stepdad) zooms through his emails quickly because he said this morning he's taking Laura and me ten-pin-bowling tonight at Skeetles (yep, your place of work. Pity you won't be there!) and we're leaving at eight. Don't want to leave any later than that. If I get home after ten I won't get the sleep I need, and I really want to avoid getting dark circles under my eyes. Mum always goes on at me about it, saying: 'Adequate sleep and under-eye concealer are our most valuable beauty enhancers. Guys don't like "tired".'

You're such an amazing girl, Izzie! Congratulations on the Glorion/Prince Nikolaus of Perelda, thing.

Reply soon okay? Can't wait to hear your thoughts on this discovery of a lifetime!

Hugs & Chocolate,

Sara

Chapter Two

XXXVII

The Devic Century of Ruin
Or 'The Century Of Progress'
to those of the Empire

Jolted back from her musings with the two undines' chatter, Maleika observed Zhippe and Carlonn as they scampered ahead of her.

'Pieter in love with a gold-skin? What a laugh,' said Zhippe, cartwheeling over the ferny bank.

Carlonn giggled in agreement.

Maleika, walking ahead of the two tiny undines, shook her head smilingly. 'Yet this has happened. We must do the best we can to find the palace of the present and tell Pieter we think no less of him.'

Carlonn, hastening up to Maleika, said, 'Perhaps a marriage between the two is meant to be. For the sake of all devas. Let's hope Pieter is instrumental in changing the body kings' ways.'

'Let's hope you are not being too idealistic,' called Zhippe. 'No-one, I believe, might change their obsession with themselves. Not even our Pieter. Ah, here we are at the cave.'

Maleika warned that the Grudellan Palace they viewed from the cave exit was merely a glimpse of another timeframe. Her dear nephew Croydee had not discovered the real Pieter, only a vague indication of his life since leaving the forest. The hologram of the palace's interior mapped events of either Pieter's past or future, but Maleika was filled with gratitude when Croydee reported that her son was alive and well.

As far as Croydee could see, Pieter had infiltrated the Grudellan Palace to rescue the rabbit Fripso and found himself trapped within its walls. A Solen's daughter had helped Pieter and Fripso into hiding from the guards and allowed them to live in the dressing-quarter of her chamber. 'Pieter's association with the fair-haired princess is companiable in the extreme,' Croydee had told her. 'I daresay he would propose marriage to Eidred if elves were permitted to wed royal maidens.'

Maleika and the undines would have no way of telling the accuracy of the timeframes. Gold-skins *counted* time and did so by means of the sun dials that assisted them in breaking their day into segments. Sprites relied on their own inner awareness. The devic clans' sensitivity to changes in winds, and to temperature and phases of the moon, allowed them to determine which day of each season it was, which part of the night they were in and the span of moments that remained before they retreated to the Dream Sphere.

'We are to explore a different hologram to the one Croydee discovered two sun-ups ago. This is the one Croydee and I first saw, through an exit over yonder. The palace displayed a birth flag when I saw it last. We must ensure Pieter is safe.'

Through the doorway in the cave they went. They slipped through the golden bars of jewel-encrusted gates. Faeries who dwelt in blades of grass, and pixies from the dell outside of the palace's projected images, called to them not to go.

''Tis not real,' Carlonn called in reply. 'It was real at one time, but the Grudellan Palace is now hidden. In its place is a harmless replica.'

The faeries gasped and, after tiptoeing with tentative glances at the pebbly road where the gates began, grew frightened and ran to the safety of their homes.

''Tis not real I tell you,' Carlonn called after them. 'You can visit as oft you like, and naught will happen to you.'

'Just yet I would not tell them that,' Maleika advised Carlonn. 'And if I say the word "*hark!*" both of you must run as fast as you can to the safety of the thicket.'

'Agreed,' said Zhippe.

A wide-eyed Carlonn crept on, visibly sobered by the responsibility. Soon they were outside the princess's room. She was nowhere in sight. The one who now inhabited it was a girl, perhaps five season-cycles her junior. 'Is this a younger Princess Eidred?' Maleika wondered. 'Have we returned to her childhood, before Pieter set foot in the palace?'

Maleika heard laughter in the hall. Turning, she saw the lady in question walking merrily along beside a gold-skin. The gold-skin wore a tall, pointed hat with intertwined snakes embroidered onto it and a tunic of flax stitched together with golden thread. He was darting at the princess, attempting to kiss her while she giggled and wriggled away from him. They joined hands and wove along the corridor.

The gold-skin's shoes were elongated sandals that curled into points beyond his toes. Eyes that were darkly sinister with their lining of black clay stared calmly ahead, then gazed upon radiant Eidred.

Eidred looked from left to right. Under the illusion that no-one could see her, she stood on tiptoes to receive his kiss. 'Then that should be all,' she said. 'It is most improper, Adahmos, for husband and wife of this court to exhibit any form of affection.'

⁘

Clutching each undine's hand, Maleika watched the palace's holographic scene in awe.

The princess was now looking joyously up at her glittering husband. 'Father is quite content for you to not attend our Sun's Day ceremony,' she told him. 'And it is just as well. I couldn't bear to again see the distress you go through in having to endure it.'

'And today is the day we succumb to the slumber.'

'Oh, Adahmos, to think the entire court is to fall into a hundred year sleep, and all on account of me.'

The prince's arm encircled the princess's waist. 'Everything will be the same when you awaken, Beauty. This is why your father and solens of other realms enforced the Backwards-Winding.'

'But Adahmos, I know that you grieve for your clan.'

Zhippe turned to Maleika. 'Gold-skins don't speak of clans. And the eyes! The eyes of the lady's prince are brown!'

'What sort of body king is this?' Carlonn said. The little creature gasped. 'This is no body king! This is a Brumlynd! Pieter no longer a boy but a man! Ye gods, he is changed. They have turned him into *them*. Heaven forbid!'

23

'Hush at once, Zhippe,' Maleika scolded. 'For we must listen in order to learn. And try not to call them body kings!'

'I will see my clan again though,' Pieter was saying to his royal wife, 'when we emerge from the hundred-year slumber. I'm comforted to know my only distance between them is a differing timeframe.'

Maleika, Zhippe and Carlonn turned to one another with sad smiles.

'Beloved, I apologise for not telling you earlier the reason for that awful journey back to another timeframe. I was afraid.'

'You say Grudellan sorcerers have moved this palace and other palaces throughout the world to another dimension of time and that all surrounding each Gold's Kin realm is now one hundred season-cycles in our past.'

'This is correct. They have done this so that when we awaken, we will have caught up again with the rest of the world. You already know of the Backwards-Winding and the distress it caused you and Fripso with its alarming quakes. The reason for the Backwards Winding was to deliver the Grudellan Palace to the Elysium of a hundred years ago, The Pre-Development Century.'

Pieter shook his head. 'I still marvel at the idea of Norwegia and the rest of the earthly world being a century younger now.'

Eidred lowered her voice. 'In effect, Adahmos, you have not yet arrived in this life. Thank goodness you infiltrated the palace one season before the Backwards-Winding took place. To think we might never have met!'

'A preposterous thing,' Pieter said, gravely, 'manipulating time frequencies.'

'It is fear that drove them. They believe the devic people will rise up in their absence. Within the hundred season-cycles that we are forced to sleep through, our empire risks loss of control. And now we reside in a part of history. And all on account of me!'

Maleika, astounded, shook her head. To Zhippe and Carlonn she said, 'They have left us. They now reside in The Pre-Destruction Century! No wonder we stand here inside a hologram! We are standing in a memory, my children, a memory of all that has gone before.'

'An echo,' whispered Carlonn.

'A remnant of energy,' agreed Zhippe. 'An accidental shadow of an image that is no more. Each of the palaces is a time-travel instrument!'

Pieter was speaking again. 'You are not to blame yourself, Beauty. Be grateful that the faerie concubine all those season-cycles ago blessed you and saved your life, at a cost to be sure, but would you rather be mortally wounded by piercing your finger?'

'I wouldn't rather it, although I know that the wicked old bewitcher at my naming ceremony would. Father did consider having me killed. If I were dead before my eight-and-tenth year, he and his court would not be spun into the century of sleep. But then, a daughter is better kept for the riches she gleans in marrying well. And so my father expects he will receive plenty of gold with the furthering of Ehyptian relations.' Eidred laughed. In a whisper she said, 'To think you know nothing of Ehypte!'

Pieter laughed in agreement, adding in a whisper also, 'Yet my wife has told me all I need to know.'

'And that is not much, my knowledge of the Ehyptian hierarchies being as it is.' She patted Pieter's chest. 'Despite our upsets, life still flows forward.'

'Little Lunara is proof of this.'

The princess lowered her tone again. 'Poor little gold-painted creature. I wish I did not have to disturb her so, in applying the dragon blood.' She gazed at the floor. 'I have found a way of getting the essence we talked of, Adahmos.'

'Eidred, I warned you not to.'

The princess's mouth had set into a determined line. 'Yet I did it anyway.'

'You've endangered yourself.' Pieter's whispered voice was hoarse with concern.

'I have stored this in the dressing-quarter of our chamber. When we awaken from the spell of repose you will be knowledgeable of all that has happened to you in the Dream Sphere. Imagine that, dearest, recalling one hundred season-cycles of an uninterrupted visit there!'

Pieter shook his head solemnly. His face broke into a reluctant grin. 'Well done, Eidred! But you must never retake that sort of risk.

Perhaps you will visit the Dream Sphere's devic realm. Perhaps you, also, will remember.'

'You know very well that those born to my family go little higher than the lower-astral plane.'

'But you?'

'I am no different. You and I are divided by frequencies in our sleep and never shall meet. Please do not ask me to remember my slumbering travels. I would only relive a gamut of horrors where monsters reign supreme. How I would love to visit your world of slumber.'

'Each moment of my hundred season-cycles will be spent paving the way for you,' Pieter said, eyes brimming with adoration. 'And despite your royal heritage, you certainly have something of the silver devic about you. You need not be restricted to golden habits.'

The two bade each other an ardent farewell and departed, Pieter up a flight of stone stairs to another floor of the palace, Eidred down a wide staircase and into the Grand Hall, where she was escorted by the Grudellans—evil, granite-eyed versions of dragon birds—out into the sun's unforgiving beams.

'Follow the princess,' Maleika instructed Zhippe and Carlonn. 'I will observe Pieter awhile.'

The two water sprites floated down the staircase. Carlonn's filmy moss-like tresses, and Zhippe's pointed flame-like ones, bobbed about, then disappeared entirely from view.

Maleika, following Pieter, climbed many circular staircases. Pieter arrived at a door at the top of the final spiral. Behind it was a hexagonal shaped room with a window cut out of its ceiling that channelled sunlight into the centre of the floor. So reflective was this floor, it could have competed quite admirably with the surface of a lake at dawn. The ceiling's gilded edges were fashioned into geometric shapes.

'Hello sweet Lunara,' Pieter said tenderly. By the window, and overseen by a nursery maid, was an elevated basket. Pieter peered into it and smiled.

Maleika rushed across to this basket. When she saw the creature it cradled, she sighed delightedly. There within was a babe of perhaps three seasons, golden-skinned and blue-eyed, with an aura of pearlescent hues. A mist of silver signified the infant's link with the devic realm. Also within this aura were the primary colours that gold-skins were known for, the faded reds and blues, and a particularly ugly metallic yellow. These appeared on the left side of the doe-eyed child's head. Only on the right were the swirls of light with which Maleika could empathise. She would possess both qualities of logic and intuition.

Tears of delight sprang to Maleika's eyes. Pieter had not only become mortal since living in the Grudellan Palace, he had become the father of an imperial child! His daughter's eyes were the temporary blue that all sprites displayed in their first few seasons of infancy. Lunara's eyes were darkening, an indication they would turn the same warm colour as Pieter's in the not-so-distant future. She had inherited the elf's skin tone, which, as Eidred had mentioned moments before, was now masked by golden dragon blood so that those of the court would accept her as royal.

Pieter, tall and strong, and handsome by gold-skin standards, sat himself down by the window to read a voluminous book, which Maleika supposed was the *Book of Rightitude*. According to Croydee, this compilation of Gold's Kin law was referred to much by Eidred's granite-eyed pterodactyl schoolmasters.

Realising there was little more to witness, Maleika looked lovingly upon her granddaughter one last time.

A memory fluttered back to her, of a Grudellan Palace crystalling many season-cycles earlier that the autumn faerie Orahney had insisted she attend. Disguised as a hooded bewitcher, crystal wand in hand, Maleika had methodically carried out all of the faerie's puzzling instructions. Her first task had been to move invisibly across to a line of wand-wielding bewitchers who were drifting blankly towards a temple in the palace grounds. With the rest of her Kindness Merits, Maleika had located the weariest of the former faeries and had granted her a restful slumber upon a hyacinth-perfumed cloud, along with invisibility so that her absence would go unnoticed. She'd then joined the line, in place of this bewitcher, just as her Kindness Merits dwindled and her visibleness returned.

With motherly pride Maleika smiled at the sight of her dutiful son, now a fine young man and parent himself. 'Thank goodness the maiden fell in love with him,' Maleika said to herself. Pieter's princely devotion to Eidred had allowed him to evade a dreadful fate.

She looked at the child again, and again she thought of the naming ceremony she had infiltrated all those season-cycles ago. A vicious woman had cast a frightening spell, something to do with a prickly demise upon reaching the age of eight-and-ten, and although the crystal wand that Orahney had told an oak's dryad to give her hadn't the strength to undo the spell entirely, its power was able to soften the nasty effects. What had Maleika uttered to lessen those cruel consequences? All such a long time ago! What had those significant words been? They had not made a great deal of sense to her. Ah! She remembered now. The words Orahney wished her to utter had appeared discreetly in the wand's crystal, and Maleika had said, 'The princess will not die. She will sleep. All of gold will sleep for one hundred years.'

Pieter's previous words to Eidred floated back to her. *Would you rather be mortally wounded by piercing your finger?*

Of course! How could she have not been reminded when the pair had moments ago spoken of the century of slumber? Time had faded the event from Maleika's consciousness, but the sight of Pieter and Eidred's small daughter had acted as a powerful memory prompt.

And now Maleika knew who she had gone to aid back then. She had rescued Pieter's young wife. The infant freed from the threat of death had been Eidred! 'How glad I am,' she murmured, 'that Orahney sent me to that crystalling.'

Monday rolled on, a stretch of glowing autumn haze. Rosetta made garlic soup and weeded around the lime tree, reflecting on last night's dream. It returned to her, frustratingly, in flashes. A gold ring shackling an eagle's leg...the long-haired intruder leering at her through a car window, kohl-rimmed eyes pale and crazed. She wished her fear of him would fade. It was ages since she'd moved from Punchbowl, and she had to remind herself that spotting him again on the night Izzie went missing didn't mean Izzie had been in any danger. The guy had been on the esplanade. Izzie had been a good kilometre away, over at Glorion's. Coincidental, yes, that he should reappear, but hopefully unintentional.

In the early afternoon she looked up budget flights to New Zealand. Not a single price her bank account would cover. Good thing she'd clarified that before telling her mysterious half-brother she'd travel to meet him.

When she checked in on Izzie, she found the girl tossing and turning, sheets twisted about her in white spirals.

'I forgot to tell you, Mum...'

Rosetta crossed the room and pressed her hand against Izzie's forehead. Still burning up. 'What did you forget to tell me, sweetie?'

'Glorion said...' Izzie rolled over and went to speak, but couldn't.

'You're exhausted, you poor thing.' She helped Izzie unravel the bedclothes and tucked in the edges. 'You need rest. Just go to sleep for the moment. You can tell me about what Glorion said when you're feeling more up to it.'

Izzie sat upright. Her eyes rolled towards the ceiling before focusing blearily on a spot above Rosetta's head. Delirious. Rosetta would get more painkillers at the corner shop. Now. She hastened to her feet.

'Glorion said you've got to keep away from that man,' Izzie called after her.

'Which man?'

'The man who's threatening to distract you from your life-path.'

'Doesn't sound like anyone I know. That's probably meant for another mother.' Pausing in the doorway, Rosetta added, 'Although, if Glorion intuited Adam, I'm already rid of him. You go to sleep now, Iz. I'm off to get you more aspirin. The ones I gave you this morning were the last in the packet.'

Izzie called out faintly, 'He just said that knowing this guy could be confusing.'

'Okay, gotcha.'

'And also...'

Rosetta returned.

Izzie stared ahead, eyes like muted blue glass. 'I had the weirdest dream. I dreamt Sara sent me a really bizarre email.'

'You did check your inbox earlier.'

Weakly, Izzie said, 'Did I?'

'About an hour ago. Around four I heard you get up to read your emails, and then you went back to bed.'

Izzie's shoulders slumped. She groaned, almost inaudibly, and fell back onto her mattress in the same way a limp marionette would, when freed from the puppeteer's strings.

Rosetta readied herself for the walk to the shop, briskly twisting her hair into a smooth ponytail, deciding as she did so that she'd phone the New Zealand law firm once she got back. What would it be like to speak to her own biological brother? While the idea was more than a little scary, the prospect of making his acquaintance intrigued her. How lovely it was, that she shared her late mother's middle name. She switched her iPod onto the whale song, slipped on her favourite sunnies—the multi-coloured reflective ones that Izzie often complained looked like the shells of Christmas beetles—and bolted down the hallway.

When she stopped to pop a stick of chewing gum in her mouth and check her pockets for the tenner she'd salvaged earlier, the doorbell chimed. She answered the door. Two men in their early twenties stood on the verandah. One was smartly dressed—suit and satin tie—the other less so. Tattered cargo trousers, a rucksack slung over his shoulder, alert and discomforting stare.

Just as she was about to plead Buddhism, her usual response with door-to-door spread-the-worders, the casually dressed guy produced a camera from his bag, lifted it to his face and stepped backwards. The guy in the tie shoved a voice recorder under her chin, babbling: 'How are you today? I'm Jason White from *The Sydney Telegraph*. I'd like to speak to you, if I may, about your association with a Swedish prince.'

Rosetta gaped at him. The man she'd been dating was blond and wealthy, but Adam Harrow was no Prince of Sweden. She pushed her tongue against the chewing gum, slid it to the side of her mouth and said, 'April Fools Day was *last* month.'

She wished them well and attempted to close the door. Jason White insisted on continuing with his assumptions. 'Would you happen to be the young lady who's romantically involved with him?'

A dozen thoughts flew through Rosetta's mind. Izzie's new boyfriend was Dutch. Could Izzie have got the country wrong? And forgotten to mention blue blood?

She needed to send these guys on their way. Cameras made her nervous, and this one had her head and shoulders in its sights. But how would she deter them? She lowered her flashy sunglasses and studied the journo's inquisitive eyebrows and determined jaw. When the journo caught sight of Rosetta's thirty-eight-year-old eyes, he blushed and mumbled, 'Sorry.'

'Don't be,' Rosetta said, stifling a laugh. 'Don't ruin it for me, Jason!'

Ignoring this, Jason White said, 'We believe a high-school girl lives at this address. She spent time with the prince last night. Do you know who this tenth grader from Burwood High might be?'

Rosetta tried to imagine her daughter dating a royal. Marrying into the boy's family...waving graciously to adoring crowds, head held regally high, red hair made sparkly with an antique tiara. A laughable notion. If Izzie did marry someone in the public eye, he'd be an athlete because of Izzie's sports reporter aspiration. A prominent artist even, but not a prince. A prince, for reasons of rarity, class and locality had naturally not occurred to Rosetta. The news boys had knocked on the wrong door. She had to deter them somehow.

A Nissan pulled up in the driveway. Marching towards the bungalow's verandah was a woman in an elegant frock, businesslike jacket and perilous heels, accompanied by a baseball-capped TV cameramen.

'Mrs Melki-Redding,' she called, and her march broke into a tap-tapping run. 'Do you mind if we have a word with you, Mrs Melki-Redding?'

Sidelta the cat, shaken from her stretched-out reverie on the verandah steps, folded herself into a tense crouch and watched the uninvited guests in alarm. Across the road, Ernie Dalfrey's wife, Eliza, was transplanting roses from big terracotta pots, her arms wrist-deep in soil. To Jason, Rosetta said brightly, 'Try across the road.' Eliza rose to her feet and dusted the potting mix from her fingers, her single plait of silvery-white taking on a golden sheen in the afternoon light.

'That her?' said the *Telegraph* journalist anxiously.

Rather than deny this and tell Jason White he could really do with a crash course in age estimation, Rosetta shrugged. Mistaking Eliza for a blonde and bejeaned sixteen-year-old was understandable. The senior woman had a remarkably youthful figure, and she did happen to be facing the other way.

Once the *Telegraph*'s journalist and cameraman bounded to the other side of the road, followed sharply by the TV reporter and cameraman, Rosetta shut the door hard and locked it. Only then did she feel a sense of guilt at having not put the reporter right about soft-voiced Eliza Dalfrey who had been going about her business uninterrupted until now.

What about the aspirin though? Remembering her ensuite cupboard had an assortment of barely used first-aid items, Rosetta ran to check it. A half-used packet of Fizzy-Relief tumbled out when she opened its doors.

She flicked two of the painkillers into some water and ambled back down the hall to deliver the glass to Izzie. Putting on her best squawky voice, she called, 'Oh Isobel, dearie!'

A voice called back weakly: 'Yo?'

'Did you...' Rosetta fought off giggles. 'Did you, by any chance, happen to be hanging out with a *prince* last night?'

XXXVIII

*M*aleika found the undines in the palace courtyard, fluttering after Eidred and her minders towards a domed temple. Once inside, she and the two undines watched as each member of the palace, including the princess, donned a headdress even more awful than the one worn by Pieter, or 'Adahmos', as Eidred now referred to him. The headdresses were of metal curving into a peak. Bovine horns protruded from either side.

At the end of the temple, with its high rounded ceilings of crystal, was a gold statue representing a being with the beak of a bird and, perversely, the body of a mortal. 'Half pterodactyl,' Maleika said to herself, aghast.

'Hail all kings of Norwegia,' a voice at the end of the temple boomed.

The royal worshippers raised their arms above their heads. 'Hail all kings of Norwegia.'

'Hail Grudas, God of all things Golden,' shouted the speaker.

'Hail Grudas, God of all things Golden,' the temple's crowd repeated.

The hail to Grudas accelerated. The crowd's cries resounded chillingly throughout the temple. A sound rose up sharply, like that of a wailing sea. High above the congregation, on a towering railed parapet, was a choir of broken mermaids, sirens who were sprites of the sea once, now pitifully wretched, evidently devoid of their power of the feminine. The facial expressions of these fishtailed choristers had lost all traces of devic gentleness. No emotion dwelt behind their dull-lidded soul windows. In screams they sang a song of destruction. Clever in pitch was the song, deplorable, though, to the hearing sense.

Maleika cast a worried glance towards Zhippe and Carlonn in the aisle ahead of her. They had covered their ears with their small hands in an effort to shut the screeches out. With sadness, Maleika watched the choristers whose blackened eyes lifted to stare, unseeingly, at the quartz ceiling. Mouths rounded to form perfect tones of ghastliness. Tails the colour of rotting seaweed flinched with freakish stops and starts. No longer were these people of the sea graceful, blissful, serene. Here within this sun worshippers' temple, they were nothing more than shells of bodies, once animated and aglow with the pristine souls they housed, bitter bewitchers who delighted in cancelling out purity so that they might revel in the furtherance of ugliness.

'Bring forth the fey women of the forest,' the voice at the altar commanded.

Upon the altar appeared hundreds of faeries. All were trembling like fallen leaves, their large eyes made larger with fright.

The sight of these victims of Grudella made Maleika want to weep. 'Please free them,' she murmured. Even though the timeframe she was observing had passed or was yet to come, she hoped that someone of influence in the Dream Sphere would hear her, that her panicked wish would be granted.

A high priest, resplendent in a cloak that echoed moonlight, was ushered to the altar by a bowing, obsequious youth. In a tuneless drone, the high priest addressed the royal crowd. 'We give thanks to our God, Grudas, whose benevolence ensures our ever-growing fortune. We thank him for those he brings to us who are ordained to become bewitchers and, once the radiance of youth has left them, soothsayers. We gladly receive these additions to the royal court that are proffered us and will, in the name of alchemic science, deplete them of all poison, their wicked life-force, which endangers the people of our empire.'

The gold-skins watched the faeries, not by looking upon the altar but by gazing up at a replica of them inside an oval on the ceiling. Maleika wondered why this was so. Was it their way of acknowledging their god? But no! The oval must have conveyed some sort of reflection, a mirror like a window into another world, connected by beams of solar fusion to the spy-lights that Croydee had described so vividly. Within the mirror was an image of the scene upon the altar, of the poor, helpless faeries cowering and clinging to each other while sobbing uncontrollably. Why did all in the temple gaze at this reflection of the altar instead of the altar itself? And was it indeed a mirror? Maleika observed it further. No, it was a spy-light projection. 'Of course,' Maleika breathed. 'I almost forgot gold-skins were blind to sprites.' Without the shining oval they were powerless to perceive them.

Eidred's sight, of course, was an exception. Pieter was no longer entirely devic at this point in time, so was therefore visible to not only his princess but to all at court. How clever of Eidred to allow him to live freely within the palace. Pieter posing as an Ehyptian gold-skin! Maleika would never have warranted it.

The high priest's cloak sparkled like starlit water. 'A sprite-seeing garment,' Maleika said warily. The enchanted robe enabled him to discern the unfortunate creatures on the altar. Apart from Maleika and her undine children and the Princess of Grudella, the priest was the only one present who looked directly at the captives. Maleika recalled the gold-skin who had peered at her clan through an oak's glistening branches, the one who had secretly listened to Pieter's dream recollection of a saviour named Det-ah-Wise-la. He, too, had worn a fluid and luminous garment.

Ropes of plaited copper were now being tied about each faerie and were secured in a knot below the base of each of their throats. Beneath this knot, a shard of hollow crystal was placed.

Zhippe and Carlonn, who had up until now been beside holographic Eidred, joined Maleika at the back of the temple. They were shuddering almost as much as their ill-fated kin.

Each crystal projected a stream of light that glimmered firstly like molten metal, then solidified. 'The devic silver cord,' Maleika said to the undines. The normally invisible cord, which both anchored sprites to Earth and connected them from their heart chakras to the Dream Sphere, was precious. It allowed sprites access to beauty-creation and was responsible for their manifestation of nature's loveliness, including the seasons and sunsets, the breezes and mists.

'All those of Gold's Kin, raise your sonic axes,' cried the man on the altar.

Maleika watched Eidred. She was looking about uncertainly. 'Don't do this!' Maleika raised her voice to a shout. 'Don't do this, child!'

Carlonn, in a voice soft with understanding, said, 'Maleika, you forget that all you see is a replica of the time-travelled Grudellan Palace. We might as well be ghosts.'

'And ghosts from the future,' Zhippe pointed out. 'They are all now residing in the Pre-Destruction Century.'

Maleika conceded she couldn't contain herself. 'Whyever would you think I'd forget such a thing,' she said, wringing her shaking hands. 'Knowing the horrid ceremony has already passed does little to stop me wishing I could halt it.'

A gold-skin robed in a cloak of rubies glided past Maleika. The urn he waved about emanated smoke plumes of green, curling and serpentine.

'Thank goodness we cannot breathe the vapours from that urn,' Maleika remarked to the undines. 'The potion is no doubt hallucinogenic in its effect.' She kept a careful eye on Eidred's bovine helmet, only to observe it swaying. When Eidred turned, Maleika saw that the eyes of Pieter's young wife were half-closed. She was smiling dully.

Zhippe waved his fist about in anger. 'How dare they opiate their people!'

Each gold-skin had taken up an axe and was now marching across the aisle to align with the crystal-solidified cord extending from each faerie's heart chakra.

'*Power to us,*' screamed the high priest.

'Power to us!' screamed the axe-wielders.

The choristers' voices rose up. The sirens' heads were bowed over the alchemic spell books they held. Words they uttered gained pace feverishly, then lifted in pitch and swirled in frenetic unison into trills that were as terrifying as they were inharmonious.

The spell-words of the song concluded in a chant that taunted hauntingly. Although spoken in a guttural language, the final section sounded similar to the words: *We end your joy*, and was sung in a single tone that repeated with sickening regularity.

The axes rose up.

Each gold-skin within the temple, all except for Eidred, began to change form.

Beaks protruded from golden countenances. Eyes blackened. Claws sprouted.

Jagged wings, bony and menacing, flapped with powerful ferocity.

The pterodactyls, which the gold-skins had become, lunged towards the faeries and squealed ghoulishly, causing Zhippe and Carlonn to wince, then sob.

The faeries screamed. The heart-chakra crystals illuminated as though infused with flame and quivered rapidly from the intensity of feeling that the faeries exuded through fear.

The axes went down, the silver cords were severed, and the gold-skins shrank back to their mortal form.

The crystals, now silver-pink, were retrieved by eagle-winged guards, placed in baskets embossed with sun-faced images whose guileless smiles mocked the savagery inflicted moments before.

The faeries appeared to be dead. Upon the silent altar, black-hooded witches were anointing the faeries' arms with oils, muttering incantations in rasping whispers.

It was then that Maleika noticed a subtle form of movement amongst the faeries. Some fluttered their wings, dazed and blinking. Others raised themselves listlessly from the temple's floor. They were conscious! Frightened and numbed with shock, certainly, but in no way physically harmed by the atrocious gold-skins.

Maleika dashed to the altar, praying they hadn't been too traumatised by the unforgivable ritual. She sighed woefully, however, at the sight that met her. The faeries' demeanours were no livelier than those of the shrieking sea women. Their inner beauty had vanished. The faeries' outer beauty: smooth complexions, shining tresses, dainty facial features, finely formed hands and feet, looked incongruous now that their higher intelligence had dissolved. When the axe-wielders severed the faeries' Dream-Sphere-linking silver cords, grace and innate kindness had been snatched away.

'Take our new bewitchers to the Solen's harem,' the high priest instructed.

The faeries rose to their feet. They formed a sedate line and followed the twelve hooded women into the palace grounds.

Dabbing away at tears, Maleika turned to Zhippe and Carlonn. 'Let us return to the glades,' she said. The scene felt like a memory, although she couldn't determine why.

The former beauty-creators were now slaves to the men of court. Their birthright had been torn from their very souls. That body king monster, whose name was greed, had devoured the magic within their hearts.

⊰⊹⊱

Dette Weissler reached across the table of the Port Vila restaurant and clutched Adam Harrow's hand. 'You okay?' she asked.

'Hm.'

She watched him gingerly. 'I'll admit the food's not so great tonight.'

Adam shifted in his seat. Lowered his lids. 'I disagree.' The red lantern on their table lent his face a weird glow. Despite the unkind light, Dette liked how it gave Adam a sinister edge: her golden-haired god seated calmly by the carmine fires of Hades. 'The food's as good as ever, Dette. That's what I love about Vanuatu: the French cuisine.'

'Sure.' Dette withdrew her hand and glanced down at the winking jewels on her fingers, a grotesque scarlet in the lantern's flicker. Again he'd disagreed with her. Could she *never* say anything right? She gazed out of the open grass hut that made up the darkened eatery. The lush tangle of hibiscus shrubs next to the hut creaked in the breeze.

A tallish man, all silhouette, paused at the exit opposite their table, apparently peering in. Surprised by a coldness settling across her spine, Dette shivered. She only ever got that sensation when she sensed someone watching her. She'd felt the same coldness earlier in the evening, on her way back from the restaurant's outdoor restrooms.

She grasped Adam's hand. He took hold of her thumb and wiggled it half-heartedly. Like he was bored. Maybe just dozy from all the sun and sex. 'Do you ever get the feeling someone has their eyes on you?'

'Tootles,' Adam's neon smile flashed. 'You're getting intense again. Just lighten up, okay?'

Dette lowered her voice to a hiss. 'I'm *not* getting too intense! I'm just asking you a serious question.' She tried again. 'Answer me please, Adam. Do you ever get the feeling of being watched?'

'Like now?' His green eyes met hers briefly.

He was feeling it too! 'Yes,' she said. 'Yes, like now!' She looked once more at the exit. Lowered her voice to a whisper. 'Who do you think it is?'

Adam stared down at his dessert spoon and harrumphed out a laugh. 'Well, *you* of course. Your eyes are boring into my soul.'

'That's not what I meant!' Giggling, Dette snatched up her napkin and swiped at his hair. He ducked, grinning back.

There. They'd shared a joke. That had to be a good thing.

She glanced back at the restaurant's exit. In place of the stranger were three waitresses, frangipani flowers in their hair, weaving se-renely around the tables. Dette hated those women. Two had already thrown Adam coy and conniving smiles, and Adam had flirted tastelessly with the waitress who showed them to their seats. For reasons she couldn't explain, Dette was glad the silhouetted man had left. Or maybe he'd taken a seat. She eyed Adam once more. He was signalling the same waitress he'd chuckled with when they'd arrived.

Not wanting to witness a second nauseating exchange of lingering eye contact and Adam's rumbling laughter, not wanting to hear Adam purr with sensuous approval when the waitress asked him if he'd like anything else, she busied herself with her Gabbianacci handbag and phone. What did that silly little waitress have, anyway, that Dette didn't have? Irritably, Dette regarded the girl. Her hand movements were quite graceful, she supposed. Probably doubled up as one of the traditional dancers to support her parents, grandparents and sixteen or so children. Probably lived in a tent. These people's lives were so painfully primitive! Graceful and feminine. That would have been it.

Dette gazed blankly down at her phone. Perhaps Adam didn't consider her feminine enough. She sighed. It wouldn't have been the first time she'd suffered punishment for a lack of ladylike qualities. Her attempt in kindergarten at painting a picture of the colonel inside a rocket ship above a grinning moon had only resulted in horrified shrieks from her great-aunt. 'Look at those black marks on your dress,' she'd scolded. 'You've practically ruined it! You're no lady, Bernadette. No lady at all.' Dette's five-year-old heart had heaved with shame. *Not a lady...*

In hindsight Dette saw the pointlessness of her aunt's blame. And she'd resolved to treat Sara and Laura differently. She would never put her daughters through that sort of humiliation. She'd sewn them their florally smocks before they'd shown any interest in art and had encouraged them to make as much mess as they liked on the back porch. Within reason of course. When Sara enrolled in the same art elective as her school friend, the former Punchbowl girl Izzie Redding—often mentioned but yet to visit—Dette had amply rewarded her with an easel to use in the basement. Sara had loved the little fluffy beret Dette had strung over the top, and Dette had joked that nothing would stop Sara now from becoming a modern-day Tamara de Lempicka.

She would have to remember to be witty around Adam like she was with Laura and Sara. Serious conversations just didn't appeal to him.

The silly waitress had now delivered the dessert menu with her silly flourishy fingers and cleared the table.

'So how are you going, Tootles,' Adam crooned, warming to her again. 'Any more phantoms lurking in the shadows?' He clasped up her wrist, kissed her palm and lowered her hand to the table. 'Or is it a bad case of paranoia 'cos Whatzizface suspects you're cheating on him? Can't imagine Matthew P Weissler hiring an investigator to check on you.' He tubed his fists and brought them to his eyes binocular-style, lips pushed out cartoonishly.

Dette laughed until her shoulders shook, although if she were honest with herself, most of the laughter was forced. 'Stop your kidding,' she said. 'Let's skip dessert and go back to the cabin.'

Chapter Three

XXXIX

Sitting at the edge of the dragon fountain, Pieter watched with wistful interest the small summer faeries tending the thorn thicket's rosebuds. It amazed him that within the entirety of the Grudellan Palace only his bride could see these very real people. How sad it was that all the others—apart from ill-intentioned courtiers who donned mesmeric cloaks—were blind to sprites and ignorant of devic lore.

An eagle-winged servant bowed to him. 'Highness, might I bring you a cup of dragon-gold?'

Pieter stared at the ground in an effort to mask his horror at the suggestion of drinking a creature's remnants. 'No,' he replied, deliberately omitting the word thank you. Gold's Kin princes, Eidred had instructed, did not waste their manners on anyone lower in fortune. The servant nodded, bowed again and moved away.

Pieter leaned on the edge of the dragon font and closed his eyes against the searing sun that he was yet to feel comfortable under. One and a half season-cycles had passed, and they were still no closer to escaping the Grudellan Palace.

He returned indoors and climbed the Grand Hall stairway in search of his wife. She was in their chamber, gazing down at their little daughter while humming a devic lullaby Pieter had taught her.

He greeted her with a kiss. 'I feel as though we will never leave.' Finally, he was admitting to Eidred the concerns that haunted him from dawn to dusk.

'We will, Adahmos,' said Eidred smiling. 'We will. They see it as their responsibility to return you. Our ship will be such a helpful wedding gift! 'Tis fortunate for us that they won't hear of your family sending another. Imagine being face-to-face with a shipful of Ehyptians who discover you to be an imposter! I only wish our ships didn't take two season-cycles to construct. How irresponsible of you, my prince, to have lost your boat at sea.'

The two smiled at the irony then fell into affable silence. Their daughter relented to slumber, but not until after they'd sung her three lullabies.

'I think I shall go and visit the gallery,' Pieter said.

'Enjoy yourself, Adahmos,' said Eidred with a yawn. 'I shall rest now, along with little Lunara.'

Pieter strolled down the vast halls of the palace. Besides his and Eidred's chamber and the flat manicured grounds, the gallery was the only other place in which he felt at ease. Much of Gold's Kin art, Pieter felt, was dark and foreboding, but some of the portraits interested him, especially the ones of a certain Ehyptian prince.

Today Pieter was anxious about Orahney. Two suns prior she had attended dinner in her usual Soothsayer Zemelda disguise. Eidred had noticed something odd. When they were alone Eidred had told him, 'I do not know what has happened to Orahney. Her eyes have altered in colour. They are no longer brown.'

'Why would she change the colour of her eyes?' Pieter had said. 'Perhaps she is conjuring a new disguise.'

Eidred had shrugged and agreed.

On the evenings that had followed, Pieter and Eidred were made aware of a definite change in the faerie's demeanour. Examples of cruelty uttered at dinner caused Orahney to screech with laughter. She had cackled in rasps, for no apparent reason, and the sound made Eidred shiver. Certainly in her pretence as a Palace Soothsayer, the faerie—renamed Zemelda by an official courtier as was customary for involuntary concubines—was sensible in conveying to the court a quiet, weather-beaten bitterness. Reacting with relish to ghoulish tales, however, was a disturbing new aspect to her pretence.

Pieter located the gallery's gilded open doorway and stepped in. Opposite was the Solen's counting house. Pieter could not help overhearing the Solen. He was speaking with one of the courtiers, his gravelly demands reverberating in the grand hallway. 'And what have you learnt from this oracle you speak of, Rahwor?'

'The oracle I have created, Sire, in the name of alchemic science, tells of the exact date in the future when Gold's Kin will face the gravest of threats. A threat to the empire's governing powers.'

'In *my* lifetime?'

'Indeed no, Sire. The wheel of reincarnation continues, however. You might well have an earthly life at this crucial time in the future, although it lies thousands of years ahead of us.'

'Time means nothing.' The Solen's voice rose to a scream. 'Nothing!'

Pieter studied four of the gallery's portraits before him. Two of them depicted Prince Adahmos as a child. Apart from the blueness of his eyes, the subject in each of these paintings so greatly emulated Pieter, he might as well have been opposite the looking glass in his marital chamber.

He'd been unsettled when he'd first seen these, deeming it odd that he would have a twin in appearance from somewhere in Ehypte who resembled him both as a child and grown man. 'Now dead,' Eidred had told him. It was all too much of a coincidence. And, as Pieter had learnt, Orahney had manipulated events. 'Contrary to what you've been led to believe,' Orahney had told him secretly, 'the portrait isn't of Prince Adahmos. It's of you. And the artist is no other than me. The Solen has never met the prince and is under the impression that the prince's likenesses were shipped from Ehypte.' The faerie had learnt in the Dream Sphere that an Elysium Glades elf was in love with one of the Solen's daughters but was confined within a chamber of the palace. 'And so I did something rather devious to free you,' Orahney admitted. 'Relying on my Dream Sphere recollection of your looks, Pieter, I immortalised you in paint. I then penned letters in a style resembling that of an Ehyptian solen, the father of recently deceased Adahmos. The prince was similar in age to you, but not, as you've discovered, in any way similar in appearance. Forgive me for making you an imposter, my dear. I could see no other way to get you accepted as Eidred's husband than to arrange a false voyage and subsequent shipwreck on one of Norwegia's beaches.'

Pieter smiled sorrowfully at the gallery's portrait. The portrait's cornflower eyes stared impassively into the distance. 'Poor Adahmos,' he whispered. 'Fatally disturbed a marsh monster. I have Gold's Kin pride to thank, with the Ehyptian solen's refusal to announce his son's sad error and his court's pretence that the unfortunate fellow is still alive.'

The Solen's voice rumbled irritably from the counting house. As far as Pieter could gather, the Solen was at this point expressing a veiled brand of concern at the prospect of his empire overthrown aeons ahead in the future. 'We are to rule *eternally.* All that we have fought for must not be in vain. Tell me, Rahwor, who do you see to be the primary instigator of this revolt against us?'

'It is a woman, Sire, a woman who encourages the earth to listen to harmonies of the fey.'

'Then I shall, from here on, and in each life I am born into thereafter, have every woman in communication with the fey burnt at the stake.'

'And mostly, Sire, you will succeed in eliminating them. Until the emergence of *this* individual. With the aid of others such as herself, she will return the planetary population to their senses, their original senses, which Gold's Kin have thus far cancelled out.'

'Magic? They will draw upon their magic and fuller senses? Then I shall increase our heart-elixir theft so that no fey woman is left with the capacity to create or breed, and I shall ensure in further lives that their creations are pulled apart. Forests will be felled to render the extinction of dryads. Rivers will be blackened to do away with undines. Air will be made impure to dissolve all sylphs who have not yet been seduced. And did you find the answer, with the help of this cleverly constructed oracle of yours?'

'Indeed, Sire, I did. I have consulted for many suns with fellow magicians. We have discovered a way of transportation into this future time. The magician who transported us to the Elysium of the past, the century we now reside in, has developed this wondrous technique.'

Transportation into a future time! With machinery, no doubt, which was outside of them and separate from their physical and dream bodies. Pieter shook his head. In the Dream Sphere, sprites took for granted travelling to other timeframes.

'And who will go into this future time?'

'I have volunteered, Sire. With your bidding I shall seek the woman out.'

'You're yet to prove yourself as a loyal servant.'

'I concede this, Sire. And for any consternation I might have caused you, Sire, I remain deeply apologetic.'

'All in the court are most discomfited by that scurrilous incident in your past.'

'As am I, Sire. As am I.'

'To think you might have considered yourself worthy of inclusion in our family! What insolence! Given, however, that you appear to be suitably regretful of the conceit you displayed eighteen season-cycles ago, I shall be generous. I am prepared to forget your misdemeanour for now, although I warn you, Rahwor, it will never be forgiven. You are granted this permission.'

The ensuing silence suggested to Pieter that Rahwor had stooped into a grateful bow.

The Solen's voice echoed through the gallery once more. 'What do you plan to do when you arrive in this time?'

'Confuse. Distract. Destroy.'

Ruthless laughter rippled across the hall. 'Splendid'.

'I intend to make my acquaintance with the woman slowly, softly, through those who surround her. I shall capture her heart, for it is an indiscriminate heart that loves with sickening ease, and I shall twist and shatter this heart and fold the mind in half into proper logic. Her thoughts will swim in one direction only. She will become a servant of Gold's Kin. She will carry out the furtherance of our doctrines. Hail the Empire of Grudella!'

'Hail the Empire of Grudella!' The Solen paused. 'And what is the name of the wretch who believes she can meddle with the likes of us?'

'The name the oracle provides is highly unusual. The name is Det-ah-Wise-la.'

'Liar,' said Pieter under his breath. An oracle had not been the reason for this Sonic Unity Gathering attendant becoming known to Rahwor. The knowledge had been stolen from Pieter's own Dream Sphere recollections, a private conversation with Maleika, snatched without warning by the hooded one spying on them. Pieter had been shown in the Dream Sphere a crystal dome and a leader in the future addressing a large number of people. The gathering was to celebrate a return to the Currency of Kindness. The leader announced that a woman named Det-ah-Wise-la was mostly responsible for this.

'I look forward to hearing of your travels through time,' the Solen was saying. 'I look forward to hearing of the demise of little Det-ah-Wise-la. I shall ask the gods that you have success in seeking, enticing and attacking her. I await your return, Rahwor, with interest.'

'I, Sire, am forever your willing servant.'

The magician who went by the name of Rahwor: the spell caster who imprisoned an eagle within a stony shell of ignorance...what sort of appearance did he possess?

An individual with waist-length hair stepped out of the counting-house doorway and into the corridor. Pieter turned from the painting he was pretending to peruse and observed the Gold's Kin courtier. Eyes like an arctic sea slid furtively side to side. With the sly determination of a beast hunting its prey, Rahwor crept past Pieter in the gallery and slunk towards the stairs.

Pieter recognised those eyes. This servant of the Solen had glared up at Eidred's tower-room window after killing a poktador. Rahwor had been the one to devour the animal!

When Pieter returned from the gallery, he said to his wife, 'What do you know of the sorcerer named Rahwor?'

Eidred looked up from her loom. 'I do not care much for his ways,' she said. 'Although he is probably no different to any other courtier. He is known to have little control over his temper.'

'In what way, Eidred?'

Eidred searched her jewelled sewing basket and retrieved a skein of violet silk. Her hands moved swiftly as she wove the colour through her loom. 'According to my former nursery maid, Rahwor asked my father for the hand in marriage of one of my older sisters. She was nine-and-ten at the time, and Rahwor perceived himself to be an admirable suitor.'

'When did this occur?'

'A good many season-cycles ago. 'Twas perhaps one season before my birth.'

'Evidently he did not succeed.'

'As a mere courtier, he was never in possession of enough gold. In his vanity, he had expected my father's regard for his powers of sorcery to outweigh material requirements. My father is known to have said, "Leave my sight at once you pathetic, blundering fool!" and although Rahwor made a meek retreat, rumour has it that he did not take kindly to the humiliation. My nursery maid's fellow servants suspected he had dangerous intentions. Amongst them was speculation on what Rahwor would do in retaliation. One mentioned she'd overheard a conversation in which he said, "The Solen will be harmed. I shall wreak havoc on the family of Grudella." '

'I see,' said Pieter. 'This explains much.' And now Rahwor planned to harm another hapless individual, a future saviour of the sprites. Sadly, as with Rahwor's attack on the poktador, Pieter was unable to intervene.

Perhaps there was a way of warning the woman named Det-ah-Wise-la in the Dream Sphere. Although he could not retrieve his Dream Sphere memories, Pieter vowed he would do all he could to prevent Rahwor from succeeding.

⋙⋰⋇⋱⋘

High on life, elated at having her golden-skinned, super-toned dreamboat all to herself on an idyllic tropical island, Dette weaved her way through the market's wafting palm shadows.

She'd bought a few pairs of pretty knickers—from a local dressmaker who excelled at producing elegant lingerie for discerning tourists—and had prior to that done something rare while in town: she'd had breakfast, a croissant and latte rather than her usual skinny tea, at one of the provincial-type cafes overlooking the sun-tinged beach.

Now she was buying souvenirs for Laura and Sara. So far she'd found oodles of coral necklaces and shimmering shell bracelets in colours they would adore.

The parasol-shaded woman at the market stall looked up from the gifts she was wrapping in pale mint-green paper and nodded to two kids at the coconut juice stand. 'They are your daughters?'

'No, my daughters are back home. In Australia.'

'How long you been away?'

'Almost two weeks.' With any luck, the woman would bloody-well tire of asking private questions and would bloody-well get on with wrapping the last of Sara's and Laura's gifts.

'*Mon dieu.* You must miss them much.'

'I do,' Dette said. 'Very much. Thank you. The wrapping is very pretty.' She hurried from the market and made her way back to the holiday apartment via the beach.

Hips forward catwalk-style to set off her new sarong to advantage, she quickened her pace, pleased at the idea of returning to Honeymooner Haven. He'd be restless with anticipation when she saw him again, eager to get amorously entangled. The man was insatiable!

Dette gulped. A memory had emerged when she'd purchased the souvenirs, an uncomfortable memory of Grandma Carmody. The grandmother had brought back from one of her many trips a Tahitian conch shell for six-year-old Dette, and a lipstick that magically altered from green to fuchsia when applied. Dette's great-aunt had been sour-mouthed and silent throughout Grandma Carmody's visit, and Colonel Doulton had made himself scarce with the excuse of having to weed around his rose bushes. After the bright and funny golden-haired lady had left, Dette's aunt snatched up the lipstick, which young Dette was smearing on in lavish streaks, and threw it in the bin. '*Scarlet,*' she'd said in disgust.

'It's pink,' Dette had said with a sinking heart, but the lipstick remained in the bin.

Later that afternoon she'd overheard her great-aunt tell the colonel that Grandma Carmody was *a scarlet woman.* 'Paid for a younger man's airfares and accommodation so that he'd accompany her to the islands,' her aunt had spat. 'I'm ashamed to call her my sister. No thought of settling into a proper marriage, just purely self-indulgent. One love affair after another!'

And Dette had resolved back then to be the opposite of her frowned-upon grandmother. Today she realised she'd failed to achieve that.

Perhaps it's hereditary, she thought glumly on her way back to Honeymooner Haven. Perhaps I have more in common with Grandma Carmody than I'd like to admit.

Adam was sprawled out on a single lounge chair when she returned. He stretched back, hands behind his head, and greeted her with that enticingly wordless up-and-down stare. 'What's your middle name?' he said.

Dette blinked and turned to face him. Adam wanted to know her middle name, a sign, perhaps, of his increasing fascination with her! 'It's Raelene,' she told him.

'Hm!' he said. 'Dette R Weissler.'

His rapid emphasis on each syllable gave the uncomfortable impression of a robot sputtering one giant first name. Det-ah-wise-la. He leaned back in the armchair with an enigmatic smile.

'And what's *your* middle name, Mr Harrow, now that we're trading secrets,' sang Dette, putting on her best pouty face.

'Haven't got one.' Adam turned away and moodily contemplated the fernery outside the window. He was still upset about the karaoke night having been cancelled. Honeymooner Haven wasn't consistent with its brochure. Dette had already presented the desk clerk with her letter of complaint.

'Are you sure you haven't got a middle name?' Perhaps Adam had been given an old-fashioned one that he was too ashamed to reveal. Kind of cute in a way, him worrying about what she thought.

Dette withdrew one of the newly purchased pairs of knickers from its beribboned box. The satin piping and candy-coloured embroidered daisies now reminded her of the decorated birthday cake Matthew had ordered for Grandma Carmody's 80th some months earlier. With distaste Dette deleted the association. She waved her purchase in the air like a cheerleader brandishing a banner, folded it into four, then blew him a kiss. 'It's what I'm planning to wear beneath my dinner frock this evening.' She settled the lingerie back into its tissue-wrap and smoothed it down with indulgent care.

Adam startled her then. He rushed across, snatched up this gossamer collection of silk and lace, then held it to his cheek as a child might when snuggling against a battered and beloved teddy bear.

He slumped into an odd sort of hunch and then scuttled down the hall to the bedroom, holding fast to the new knickers. The door closed with a thud and a click.

Giggling, Dette banged on the locked door. 'Joke's over, Georgie Porgie,' she called. 'No need to run away.' She shivered. This uncharacteristic descent into comedy was rather embarrassing. Funniness wasn't exactly Adam's forte. Matthew wouldn't have been seen dead doing something like that, not even in jest. He might have hollered 'woo-hoo' if she'd shown them to him, then he would probably have carried on with stacking the dishwasher, not altogether intrigued unless he'd seen them on her.

But then, wasn't that what she loved about Adam? His unpredictability?

To:..........Isobel Redding
From:.......Rosetta Melki
Sent:........16 May 2008
Subject:....Skyping 8.30 Tonite!

Hi Sweetie,

This email is to let you know I've arrived safely in New Zealand and that my brother and his family are gorgeous. I wish you were here to meet them. You would love them as much as I do.

We all ate dinner at Bobby and Tanya's place and, wow, Izzie! Your little cousins, Chrissie (the five-year-old) and Jayden (the three-year-old) remind me of two baby deer. They have massive brown long-lashed eyes, and Jayden has one of those adorable gurgling giggles that little kids are noted for. I'll send you the photos I took of the family as soon as your Uncle Bobby shows me how to upload them.

So this is just a quick email—Bobby and Tanya are at present stacking the dishwasher and won't hear of me helping them. They've insisted I relax and unpack in my room! And I'm free to use the laptop they've thoughtfully set up in here for me. Their house is amazing. Large, modern, light and bright. It has a pretty little barbecue area out the back with a greenhouse overflowing with pink and white orchids. I'm feeling thoroughly pampered, I have to say. Airfare generously covered. (Bobby has since said my return flight is a gift and not a loan). Huge comfy bed. Bobby's going to show me later how to use Skype and then you and I can speak face-to-face. It should be around 8.30 p.m. your time, Iz, so here's letting you know that I'll be calling around then.

Because I want Bobby and Tanya to sit in on my call to you, I'm emailing beforehand, to tell you some of my more private thoughts on all that's happened since my arrival here.

On the way back from the airport, Bobby drove us past a magnificent three-storey home. Its walls were wreathed in bougainvillea, which is a vibrant, purpley flowered vine. (The Dalfreys across the road have one on the left-hand side of their lattice trellis. If you look out our sitting room window on the hallway side, you'll see it easily enough.) The windows of this house were amazing. It had a fishpond out the front with a waterfall and a stunning glassed-in verandah. The place took my breath away. Just as I was about to thank Bobby for showing me the cream of Christchurch's mansions, he said, 'That's Mum's home, Rosetta. This is our estate.'

It's been such a bittersweet meeting. This poor man who happens to be my brother is grieving terribly, and it makes me feel so helpless. I'm joyful for having found him and for having also found a sister-in-law, *and* a niece and nephew, yet this is tempered by the sadness surrounding Bobby's grief. Tanya loved our mum as well and is naturally very broken up.

To be honest, I don't feel I'm grieving for Daniela, and I feel so bad about this, but Daniela was Bobby's mother more than she was mine. Bobby's wife, for God's sake, was more of a daughter to her than I ever was. I told myself I wouldn't be self-punishing, but I can't help feeling guilty that I never tried hard enough to find her while she was still alive.

That chance has passed now, and the person I'm learning about is only a memory. A beautiful memory, though, and her legacy is the people left behind who adored her, but I feel I've missed out. And I'm furious with myself about it. I can't bear to think that she and Bobby tried to contact me. If you and I hadn't lived such transient lives, they could have located us. I would have known my mother. You would have known your grandmother.

There's a box of tissues in here (Tanya thinks of everything) on the dressing table next to a vase of the most amazing flowers I've ever seen. These tissues are making themselves useful now as I'm getting quite emotional.

Tanya told me how Daniela loved walking in the mountains. She cherished going to the theatre and dance concerts, and her favourite ballet was 'Swan Lake'. It's made me wonder whether this was the inspiration for my original name, the name Daniela gave me. I came to a decision on the plane, Izzie, that if I felt right about it once I met Bobby, I'd change my first name back to Odetta to honour the woman who brought me into the world.

Bobby and I went for a wander around his neighbourhood (while Tanya cooked our dinner). He told me that Daniela was the patron of an animal rights group. While he was telling me, I broke down. It was too close to home, her love of animals. I thought of how Mama used to chase cats out of the front garden with a broom, and I sobbed and sobbed, angry that I'd never got to meet Daniela. Then I told Bobby my decision to change my name, and he and I hugged and cried, both of us stock still, clinging to each other in the middle of a footpath, immobilised by our sense of loss. He said something so lovely, Izzie. He said, 'Wherever Mum is right now, I feel sure she's delighted with you doing this.'

We walked some more, and I admired the towering pine trees and lush manicured lawns that many of the front yards displayed, then Bobby said softly, 'Okay, Odetta, let's get back home. It's probably time to eat.'

By the way, I neglected to mention this before I left: I've discovered something that may be of interest to you. Craig Delorey has been in contact lately with his old friend, an author named Conan Dalesford, the guy whose book launch I arranged on Craig's recommendation. Conan is based in the Northern Territory, and Craig, as you know, is up there at the moment.

Remember how I told you what Conan Dalesford told Royston? About a kind of guardian angel declaring that the people characterised in *Our True Ancient History* are supposed to be incarnated in today's world? The 'Silv'ring' poem at the front of the book is apparently an indication of certain letters that their new names will contain in the life they're living now.

Well, since then, Royston has had a really amazing dream. He dreamt Maleika (from the book!) visited him and said that she, and the other people Lillibridge wrote about, are reincarnated as Conan Dalesford suggests and that while some have returned to their original earthly home of Scandinavia, the majority now reside in Australia.

Royston has been mulling over Conan Dalesford's blog comment on my Lillibridge site. In the comment, Conan takes the 'Silv'ring' poem a step further and suggests that *lexigrams* within names might play a part in identifying incarnated sprites (people in the world today who were one of the Lillibridge-described sprites in another life). I'm not sure if you know what lexigrams are—you might have learnt about them at school. If not, I think Conan Dalesford described them best when he wrote:

A lexigram is a word, name or phrase hidden in other words, names or phrases. Lexigrams are similar to anagrams in that they involve word jumbling, but the difference is anagrams contain all letters (in the word/name/phrase) whereas lexigrams contain only some.

For example:

Assuming Eidred is incarnated in this world today, her first, middle and second names, this time round, might read something like:

'Lindy Maree Fields'

L I N D Y   M A R E E   F I E L D S = **EIDRED**

Pieter might now be known as: 'Terence Kieran Dunlop.'

T E R E N C E   K I E R A N   D U N L O P = **PIETER**

Royston's now getting great mileage out of his full name having the exact letters of Kloory's name in it. Have you got up to the bit about Kloory? He's Pieter's younger brother, but he doesn't emerge much throughout the book. I tend to get him muddled with Croydee and have to remind myself that Croydee is Maleika's nephew: the cute, large-eyed, dimpled kid who clothes himself in spiky chestnut husks.

Anyway, when Craig and I were on the phone the other night, we played around with the letters in our names—just for fun. Craig came up with the name Croydee and, how hilarious is this? One of the Brumlynds' names was hidden in my own as well. Maleika! Can you believe it? While I was wondering how many people walking the earth right now would also appear to have starred in Lillibridge's story due to certain letters in their names, Craig asked me about my true name, the name Daniela gave me. I scribbled down Odetta Sophia Ryland and came up with *yet another* sprite from *Our True Ancient History*. Orahney! Crazy, huh? Who do you think I should pretend I was in a past life? The elf woman or the faerie?

Even more bizarre is the fact that I've worked out a person from the book hidden in *your* name. You have Eidred in your name, Izzie! But then, so does Edith (Eadie) Derby—Sorry!! In case you haven't read the 'Silv'ring' rhyme at the beginning of the book, this is it here:

> The silv'ring link
> 'Tween he and she
> Is little more than 'i' and 'e'
>
> If not as such
> Then 'o' and 'r'
> Within each name these rascals are

Everyone who started our Sydney Friday Fortnight group: Eadie Derby, Royston Leckie, Lena Morris, Craig Delorey, and even me, have either an 'e' and an 'i' side-by-side in our names or an 'o' and an 'r'. Such a silly coincidence! Fascinating all the same, although my Odetta full name (unlike the name my foster parents gave me) contains neither an 'e' and 'i' pairing, nor an 'o' and 'r' side-by-side, and so in truth I could never have been Orahney. (I was cheating a bit when I suggested this two paragraphs back.)

As you can probably tell, I've become addicted to jumbling around people's names. Personally, I think it's some kind of impish joke that an enlightened Lillibridge has played on all his future readers to endear them to his story and to cause them to wander around muttering to themselves: 'I reckon *I'm* in that book. I was definitely one of the characters in another life.' As for the dream Royston had, it's more likely than not the result of wishful thinking.

Just discovered why having these flowers here in the vase feels so comforting. I have a childhood memory of blossoms in a tree that I've never seen in Australia, and this is what they are—a flower native to New Zealand! I must ask Tanya what it's called. And the bird with the curved beak was that other distant memory! I've realised just at this moment that the bird would have been NZ's kiwi! I wonder whether it's typical for kiwis to wander around residential areas?! Don't know whether you remember me telling you this, but I was three years old when my foster family moved to Australia, so it's a very early memory.

Ooh, and another thing. Royston isn't the only one to have had unusual dreams lately. On the plane trip over, I dreamt I was walking through emerald-toned grass and when I looked down, I saw I was wearing a long dress with an apron. The dress and apron were kind of cinched with a bodice, a bit like that wide brown belt with the criss-cross lacing that I reserve for evenings out, the one Eadie bequeathed to me that goes with my Spanish-dancer-style skirt.

Then I was inside a tiny little comfortably furnished hut where a lean, attractive man, who happened to look a bit like a man I was speaking to at a bar a few weeks back, was sitting at a table made of oak, writing with a quill. He looked up from his work and said in this beautifully adoring tone, 'Lucy!'

And then I was running through a meadow, and the meadow was studded with dandelions and buttercups and little red flowers that might have been tulips. On every flower was a dear little faerie. And when I looked around, I noticed that the meadow was *filled* with faeries. And elves and pixies. They were wearing such vividly bright colours, and their movements were so amazingly quick. They were greeting me with smiles. Looked like children who were both innocent and wise at the same time, and I loved them absolutely. I wish you could paint this dream of mine, Izzie. Words fail me when I try to describe the beauty in it, or the essence of rapture that I felt when the man called me 'Lucy'.

I'm wishing you a dream as lovely as that tonight. When you were little you used to dream of faeries and elves all the time. I believe I now truly understand the wonder you must have experienced in recalling those very magical 'Dream Sphere visits' (to borrow a term from Reverend Edward Lillibridge!!)

I think they might be finishing up in the kitchen now, honey, so I'd better sign off. I'll be giving you some *amazing* news tonight. Can't wait for you to hear what I have to say! You couldn't possibly guess what I'm going to tell you over Skype, but it's got something to do with *who* your late grandmother actually *was*.

So that's all for now until 8.30. Please share this email with Lena, and make sure you help her around the house. She's such a gem.

Love and kisses,

Mum

Dette waited an hour for Adam to emerge. What the *frack* was he doing with her underwear? The memory of Dominic Wallace and his artificially red lips floated back. Shuddering slightly, she marched to the bathroom at the end of the hall and retrieved her cosmetics case from the vanity. How could she have ever slept with someone as insecure as Dominic? Unprompted insanity attack? And what was it about men with green eyes that always drew her in? Matthew...Adam. Dominic's were more towards brown, but green all the same. His jarring interruption to a private call invaded her thoughts. *Hullo, Dette! If you're needing a lift to the airport, I'll be happy to oblige.*

Dominic had no right to hijack her phone conversation with Diondra. How deluded he was, to believe he could win her back by offering to play chauffeur.

She would have preferred to forget Dominic. That was the second time she'd thought of him during the holiday. The first had been yesterday when she and Adam were sunbathing on the beach. She'd reached for the magazine in her duffle bag and, despite the warmth of the day, had felt a chill trickle over her spine. When she'd checked the clouds in the west, a figure on the other side of the coconut grove caught her attention. A dark-haired man. Watching her from the shadows. She placed a fierce hand on Adam's arm. The man turned sharply away. Normally she would have been flattered. He was attractive, after all. Like Dominic. And that was just it. Whoever he was looked too much like Dominic, from a distance at least. Ugh! She'd made a point of kissing Adam, elaborately, and glanced up to ensure the stranger registered she had a protector. She needn't have worried. He had gone.

Still no sign of Adam. Dette dabbed at the chips in her toenail polish with the dainty travel bottle of Volatile Violet that Tina at Luscious had supplied and flicked through the winter edition of *Stylish*. Gypsy was still in, and '60s hair and make-up showed no sign of waning. Loose-weave bohemian shawls were a must-have, as were gold hoop earrings. She would buy a white peasant blouse. Nicer in design than the one Rosetta Melki wore the night of Matthew's work send-off, but with similar three-quarter sleeves. On second thoughts, she'd be best to buy seven of them, in varying shades and styles. Maybe even ten.

Bored with waiting, Dette gathered up her duffle bag, crossed the front garden to get to the beach, then went for a swim. Adam had been refreshingly agreeable during the holiday, but his initial congeniality had dulled. Was this latest behaviour a prelude to another of his sulks? Throughout their romance he'd vacillated between hotly passionate and bleakly distant. She didn't like how Adam often made her feel; didn't like that he seemed to be punishing her for not living up to his stringent expectations.

But then, she had to remember to be light, bright and funny. The idea, though, of being openly madcap always unearthed a memory that made Dette squirm. Age seven, lying in front of *Hey Hey It's Saturday* one morning, rolling around laughing at a joke Ossie Ostrich had told. In a rare moment of impulsiveness, she'd run stompingly onto the verandah where the Doultons were taking tea. 'I say, I say, I *say*,' she'd said courageously, before proceeding to tell a joke that failed to make her great-aunt and great-uncle smile.

That was when the colonel, his faded eyes clouding with disapproval, had given the first of many instructions on how to behave. *You must be pretty and amusing, but never a jokester.* Young Dette's heart had heaved with shame, just as it had when her great-aunt accused her of not being 'a lady'.

The swim soothed her unnerved state. Dette slathered on a generous dollop of Zaffarelli Shea Butter Crème After-Sun Body

Gleam Gelee, launched into a mini-jog along the beach, then made her way back towards their romantic hideaway, careful to avoid the coconut grove. What if the lurking Dominic Wallace lookalike in dark glasses had actually been the man himself? Dette shook her head, shocked at herself for having dreamt up something so improbable. Diondra would have mentioned it if Dominic had scheduled a Vanuatu getaway, and even if he'd arranged a trip after Dette was offshore, what reason would he have to come here on business? As far as Dette knew, Dominic sold Sydney properties only. She clutched her duffle bag closer. Jumped at the sound of guttural laughter.

Two raucous, chuckling children and a rangy dog bounded past her, nearly toppling her sideways. 'Easy now, boys,' she warned. One of them called out a flippant apology, in French.

She turned into Honeymooner Haven's gazania-lined garden path. A flicker of shadows and thud of footsteps caused her to halt. She glanced over her shoulder. Nothing behind her. And the side garden was fenced off from the front. Nothing to worry about. Just a bout of jumpiness.

She stepped up to the porch, her footsteps brisk, and flipped off her flip-flops, pressing them at perfect right-angles against the honeysuckle-strewn wall. She entered the cabin and called out to him. No answer. The door at the end of the hallway was still locked. Dette pummelled on the door and called out again. Why was he refusing to answer her?

Adam had never joked like this before. It wasn't like Adam to spend this much time away from her. Admittedly there'd been the six-day freeze-out when he hadn't picked up the phone, leaving the impersonal answer-service to instruct Dette he wasn't available. Thankfully, they'd sorted things out, and the bond between them had become as strong as Fatally Female Fortifying Finish, a substance well-known for its ability to repair broken fingernails.

He'd apologised with a bouquet of pink-edged white roses, and the card had read: *Am I forgiven?*

The choice of florist left a lot to be desired. Budget in favour of quality. If Diondra hadn't been there when the Floral Fiesta van with its orange and maroon daisy motif had rocketed onto the driveway and bashed against Dette's fishpond trellis, Dette wouldn't have suffered such hideous humiliation. Had Adam never heard of Parisienne? Matthew, at least, displayed taste when it came to sending flowers.

She went to the bedroom door one last time and tried once more to open it. 'Adam, can you answer me, please? You've been sleeping for ages.'

Ignoring her! How *dare* he! Dette sped out of the cabin and around to the outside window, anxious to spot Adam through a gap in the green and white curtains so that she could yell at him. Adam had not drawn the curtains fully the night before. They had laughed at those curtains, lots, the night they arrived, at the gaudy outdated-ness of them.

He wasn't on the bed. The ensuite door was open. Dette could see from where she stood that he was neither in the shower nor at the basin.

'Wha...?' Ice cold shock raced through Dette's heart.

At the other end of the room was a creature with waist-length hair.

What had it done with Adam?

Where was Adam?

It was seated at the dressing-table, its back to Dette, inspecting its clawlike nails.

Definitely the hand and forearm of a man. Dette choked back a gasp. But the fingernails! They were witches' talons.

She stepped back from the window. Drew in a sharp breath.

She had to run. She had to observe this person, though, for Adam's sake. Had to watch for clues to Adam's disappearance. But she had to run! She needed to get help.

The intruder was strangely still. The hair snaking down his back ended in a mass of matted black ringlets.

He jolted into motion then, rising from the dressing table and shoving the seat aside.

Dette's hand flew to her mouth. *Don't scream*, she told herself. *Don't make him turn around.*

She tried to discern the face in the mirror. Glittery, squinting, kohl-edged eyes locked firmly with hers.

Dette screamed.

The intruder spun round.

Dette flew from the window, frantic for somewhere to hide. Her knees gave out. She grasped at the nearest tree trunk. Clung to avoid a quivering collapse.

And then the flyscreen of the window was smashed away. A single strike of the intruder's boot had sent it flying into the garden, floating as though in slow-motion. Up...up...up in the air and then down. Down upon a flowered vine, tilting rockily back and forth until settling into stillness.

And then everything sped up.

The intruder was lumbering out of the window. The intruder was glaring at her with a grin.

She was unable to run. Could not even *walk*. It had to be a dream. A nightmare. The ghoul stomping towards her through snapping shrubbery was just imagination. The concrete sensation of her arms and legs was...but then a strange shadow blotted out the sun, and darkness descended in a sickly haze.

Chapter Four

Matthew P Weissler, lean-bordering-on-lanky mid-thirties former banker blessed with the Midas touch, grinned at his competitors. He was engrossed in ruthless property accumulation, having bought up every house and hotel on the Monopoly board. His stepchildren were far from impressed. Young teen Sara was languishing in jail. Six-year old Laura, not particularly interested in the game at this stage, was counting and re-counting her 'colours', cards she'd accumulated by purchasing anything either hot-pink or green.

Matthew punched the air. 'I win,' he yelled.

Sara thumped her fist down. *'Nooooo,'* she wailed, before adding quickly, 'I'm second,' and then glumly, 'although Laura's bought up pretty big. Maybe I'm third.'

The phone in Matthew's study rang. He jumped to his feet. 'You still might be second, Sara,' he called, walking backwards. 'Count up the dollars you and your sister have remaining.'

His eldest stepdaughter's eyes lit up. She dived at the paper money and sorted it zealously into piles.

Matthew crossed Bernadette's elegant sitting room, scooted down the marble hallway and seized up the phone on his desk.

A high, breathy voice said, 'Hello, Matth-yooo.'

'Howdy, Diondra! Everything all right?'

'Yeah, not so bad. With me that is.'

'Everything all right with Dominic?'

'He's fine. Um...'

'Glad to hear it. I'm afraid Dette's still in Vanuatu.'

'Did she say she was there with someone?'

'She went with her cousin, Marguerite.'

'Hmmph! Okaaaaay.'

'She's there until Friday, but I'll let her know you called.'

'Great! Listen...uh...' Diondra's voice grew soft. 'Matthew, do you think we could meet up sometime? I have something I need to tell you.'

Surprised by this, Matthew said, 'It's not something you can tell me now?'

'Hmm, not really. What I have to say is pretty big, Matt. I'd rather tell you in person.' Diondra was half-whispering now, in a purry sort of drawl. 'Are you okay for Thursday night? Because I'm free to meet up around seven.'

Matthew made arrangements to meet and ended the call, puzzled at Diondra's mysteriousness.

He took up the photograph on his desk, the one he'd snapped of Dette and the girls in California, their teacups raised in salute to him—an image that always made him smile—and was seized with a feeling of regret. It was natural, of course, to grieve over a marriage ending. He was bound to feel sad over the next few months.

Did he want to feel miserable though? Did he want to sit alone of an evening, wishing he'd summoned up the extra effort to build an enduring partnership?

No chance of recapturing the magic now. He'd once thought Bernadette to be lovely. Hypnotically feminine, sweetly unpredictable; a skilled tennis partner and smart skiing companion; a woman who put her whole heart into everything she did.

She was still that woman. Perhaps he was the one in need of a reality check. Perhaps his yearning for peace had made him irrational. If true, if he had unintentionally punished Dette for his own discontent, then the rift in their relationship was more his fault than hers. For someone as sensitive as Dette, living up to the expectations of a husband suffering from work-related stress and a stifling sense of confinement would have been irksome at best. Was it any wonder her moods had become so changeable?

He placed the photograph back on the desk. 'Hm,' he said. 'Maybe.' They'd agreed to be a family hadn't they, five years previously? And good families stuck together.

Maybe he should attempt to save his marriage rather than continually despise it. Giving the relationship a chance to revive didn't mean he and Dette would be stuck with each other for good. A number of considered conversations might well result in a mutual decision to move on, certainly a fairer way of breaking up than springing the news on someone after their return from a holiday.

Maybe he was acting too rashly. Maybe, just maybe, he should pause to consider alternatives.

XL

Pieter observed the Grudellan Palace grounds. It was nearly time. The shadows had grown long, but whether the bewitcher's spell would unfold while the sun still roamed the sky or once Luna graced the darkness was a wondering fraught with restless despair. This day, the anniversary of Eidred's birth eight-and-ten season-cycles prior, was the day they were all to fall under the spell of slumber.

Pieter yawned, weary still from a masquerade ball held the evening before to herald the autumn season. The Grudellan Palace's clever mask maker had crafted uncannily lifelike creations, imbued with sorcery that ensured the mask adhered to the face until dampened with dragon blood. Except for the misfortune of death, this was the only known remover of these fantastical faces. Pieter and Eidred had worn rabbit masks, much to Fripso's amusement. 'If it weren't for the rest of you,' he'd said, nodding towards their torsos, 'I would have sworn you were my brother and sister.'

Others of the court had presented as unicorns, mango eaters, lions, tigers. Some had worn masks of kings from history. One had dared to imitate the Solen. So alike was this courtier's disguise, many at the ball had bowed when he'd passed. Enraged by this, the Solen had sent the unfortunate courtier to his death and ordered the pterodactyls to throw the mask maker into a dungeon until the next Sun's day. 'He,' the Solen had announced, 'is at least of some use to us, scoundrel though he is. The mask maker is fortunate his work is a valued requirement at each season-commencement gathering. Let this be a lesson to all at court. If any of you are to be disloyal, impudent, or mocking of a superior, you will be slain without further ado.'

Pieter breathed in the cool air. The Grudellan empire's idolised sun was soon to make way for dusk. He sauntered down one of the many paths, puzzled by the groundsmen's obsession with turning evergreens into geometric oddities.

When were they all to fall into slumber? The aged bewitcher and caster of that bitter spell at Eidred's naming ceremony all those season-cycles ago said Eidred was to pierce her finger. But how? And at which part of her birthday? According to Orahney, all under the sleeping spell would be preserved within their current states of youth and would awaken untouched by the hands of time.

Thanks to Eidred, he would recall his hundred-year Dream-Sphere sojourn. Despite his insistence that she avoid danger, Eidred had managed to obtain from the sorcerers' workshop a flagon of Wondalobs water, stolen by courtiers to examine its properties. She had accomplished this through bribery, offering her jewelled sewing basket to one of the more corruptible sorcerers. She had then activated, with the crystal she kept under her pillow, the water's remembrance properties.

His first intention once he reached the Dream Sphere was to visit Maleika before she entered the earthly plane as her infant self. He was certain he would have already told her by now of the time-crossing phenomenon known to Gold's Kin as the Backwards-Winding. Now he would be free to remember their conversations.

Crossing the vast grounds, Pieter found Eidred seated near the dragon fountain, attending to Lunara, who was nestled in a basket. No doubt Fripso was in the basket too, wrapped in the small invisibility blanket Orahney had gifted Eidred, a shield against the invasive spy-lights. Eidred, diligent in ensuring the rabbit had his take of fresh air, would most days hide their long-eared friend beneath Lunara's blankets when taking a turn out of doors.

Eidred's voice was faint through the rippling of the fountain. 'Ah look, sweet Lunara,' she said. 'Behold these lovely flowers,' and yet she looked as though she were addressing the basket only.

Pieter thought back to the day he first encountered her when she'd talked to a construction of cane quite similar to this one. Back then he'd thought Eidred to be a basket worshipper. He hadn't known that it had encaged his rabbit friend, or that he, Pieter, would ultimately grow to adore a maiden whose family tyrannised his own clan and others.

He thought of their union's violent beginning and chuckled. Eidred had marched towards him with an axe when he'd hidden in her room beside the basket. She'd since said she had seen a monster in place of Pieter, the same monster that appeared at the Solen's despicable magic-robbing ceremonies. Their callous severing of devic silver cords required aiming golden hatchets at the frightful hallucinations emanating from crystals they'd attached to the faerie victims. Pieter had concluded that the faerie victims' terror manifested fear-feasting monsters from the Nightmare Realms, which only Gold's Kin could perceive. One of these negative spirits must have been lurking around Pieter after the distress of witnessing a poktador's demise.

Since that evening, when Pieter's life had looked as though it were soon to be dissolved, the hoity-toity maiden of hideous heritage had become, in his eyes, an angel of beauty. And now she was to fall unconscious against her will.

Pieter felt he should be grateful for the unknown faerie's act of grace in softening a bewitcher's spell when Eidred, as an infant, had been crystalled. All he could feel, though, was sadness. Knowing that the entire palace resided in the Norwegia of yore had instilled within Pieter a fear of loss.

The beginning of Pieter's life, his welcoming into the Brumlynd clan, was no longer nine-and-ten season-cycles ago. It was now enmeshed in the future. This return to a previous century—commanded by the self-protective Solen and invoked by the empire's magicians who cared not for the disruption to life cycles their dimensional tampering caused—meant Pieter was, in effect, yet to be born. He felt sure he was soon to cease his physical existence as Pieter of the Brumlynds, or, as he was referred to now, Adahmos, Prince of Ehypte, husband to Eidred, Princess of Grudella, and father of Terra, Princess of Dorweldior. Eidred favoured the secret devic name he'd given their child, but Rightitude law decreed that a royal daughter's name asserted the territory her so-called Ehyptian paternity allowed her.

The laws of nature would not permit Pieter to lead the same life twice, in two overlapping timeframes. Of this he felt certain. He would need to delete a loop that threatened to repeat continuously. Time dictated that during the century of slumber he was to begin his life as an elfin fledgeling in Elysium Glades. He could not exist in two places at once.

Alcor, Pieter's Dream Master, would no doubt advise him during his forthcoming Dream Sphere visit to cancel out the entirety of this earthly existence. It had gone wrong. Pieter should never have fallen in love with a princess.

He had not yet caught up with Eidred. She was by the thorn thicket, dotingly holding their infant up to the pale pink roses that bloomed within an entanglement of leaves and shadows. He smiled when he saw her nod delightedly at the cries of astonishment their daughter relayed in gurgles.

The hundred-year slumber might act as amnesia for Eidred. If fate were to be kind to the princess, she would awaken without husband and child and would begin her life afresh, unburdened by the memory of having ever known Pieter. But what of Lunara? What would become of their little Lunara?

Pieter, of course, would return to the Dream Sphere permanently, his heart heavy with the knowledge that a gap in the fabric of time had forced them to part. Relinquishing a life he treasured, and ensuring no trace of its occurrence remained, was a task he would undertake with mournful reluctance.

Crossing the grounds also, although venturing from the marble pyramids on Pieter's left, was one of the soothsayers. Her hooded head was bowed. The cloak that flickered and flared about her suggested a raven with outspread wings. This image struck Pieter as ominous, although when searching for a reason, he was at a loss. All former bewitchers wore black cloaks, and none were a threat to Gold's Kin. As she glided across the western side of the court, where clouds as softly pink as the garden's roses festooned a setting sun, the soothsayer in form appeared no different to a jagged strip, a streak of darkness tainting the radiant sky.

The soothsayer marched across to Eidred. Pieter recognised her now. She was none other than their faerie friend Orahney, now different in colouring to a former bewitcher. Not so long ago she had changed her eyes to blue, as with royalty, overlaid with a glow of yellow, though, which lent them the hue of sun-drenched sour-grass.

Her hands, too, were changed, no longer plump and modestly dainty. Today they were taloned and treacherous.

Orahney greeted Eidred with, 'Hello my pretty.'

'Hello, good dame, Zemelda.' Pieter's wife was careful to use Orahney's empire-assigned name.

My pretty! Not 'my princess' or 'Highness'. The term did not seem fitting for a soothsayer to utter, even less so for Orahney. Eidred, smiling down at little Lunara, seemed not to have noticed. Other than it being disrespectful, defiant even, the greeting had a vengeful artifice about it, as though hissed by a cobra hypnotising its prey.

A bestowal of Kindness Merits must have showered upon Pieter from the Dream Sphere then, for he suddenly saw the soothsayer through his soul's eyes. For a second her heart chakra became apparent. No longer did it glimmer silver and deep-pink as it had in the days she'd taken leave of the Dream Sphere and visited the Brumlynds. Orahney's heart chakra emanated greyness.

Pieter dashed towards Eidred. The presence of grey across this chakra was evidence of malicious intent. His wife and child were in danger. He must protect them from the autumn faerie who was peering at the princess with eyes as cold as glass.

XLI

Before Pieter had time to intervene, Orahney straightened from her hunch, lifted her eyes to the sky and bellowed, 'The Princess of Grudella is a traitor!' To the troopers guarding the gates, she cried, 'Tell the Solen his daughter has failed him!'

This could not be! Orahney was supposed to be their ally. Pieter wrapped himself around both his wife and daughter to shield them. Eidred was clutching Lunara protectively. He moved her away from the former faerie they had foolishly grown to trust and ushered her back towards the palace. Their traumatised daughter screamed.

Pieter called to troopers stationed by the fountain. 'Guards!' Using Gold's Kin terms to which he had become accustomed, he commanded, 'Attend to the woman by the thorn thicket at once. Her nonsensical riddles indicate a fever.' He had to prevent Orahney from revealing his heritage. He had to eliminate threats to his little family. The Solen's councillors might condemn Pieter to the dungeons or slavery, but they must never incriminate Eidred and Lunara for his deceptions.

'It is no use running away,' Orahney said in a purr. Pieter turned back. 'I have proof of your trickeries, elf.' She produced from inside her cloak a rolled canvas, a half-complete portrait of Pieter in Ehyptian regalia. 'My evidence against you,' she declared with a sneer. 'The Solen's daughter will fall to her death this day, and her imposter husband will be punished.'

'Orahney,' Eidred wailed. 'Why do you do this to us?' And with that, she dissolved into tears.

'Hush, beloved,' Pieter whispered. For the benefit of other courtiers who heard her utter the betrayer's devic name, he added, 'This soothsayer is Zemelda.'

Orahney rolled her green eyes to the sky where troopers, now in eagle form, were circling the palace's golden and bronze spires. She pointed to one of the eagles. 'I shall turn that traitor to stone!' She raised a hand and stabbed at the air with taloned fingers. Still gazing heavenward she roared, 'That eagle-guard is a traitor!'

Lightning raced from Orahney's fingertips.

Eidred shrieked and drew Lunara closer to her. Pieter hugged the two to his chest.

The lightning zigzagged upwards into the dusk. It wound sharply around one of the airborne eagles and disrupted its flight in a spectacular dazzle. The bird's beak and wings blazed a rusted red. Helplessly, the eagle plummeted.

Down and down. Flailing and thrashing to no avail.

Pieter melded with his etheric self and sent all the beauty-creation he had to the bewitcher's floundering victim. With no awareness of the number of Kindness Merits due to him, he could only hope he'd earned enough to soothe this sting of malice. Sadly, the powers used to identify Orahney's true intent had drained him of most of his merits. The magic he sent at least allowed the eagle a degree of returned strength. Its motionless wings revived, and its tumble whirled into a wobbling float, enough to enable an unsteady landing. The eagle perched on a towering granite obelisk.

Eidred squealed and looked away.

The eagle had fused with the obelisk's greyness. The eagle was turning to stone.

'You have disabled one of our guards,' Eidred shouted. 'The Solen will punish you for this!'

'On the contrary,' said Orahney, her voice oddly low. 'I shall be rewarded. I shall be hailed as a truth bearer.'

Clasping a sobbing Eidred, Pieter guided her away, pausing only to ensure the troopers he'd summoned were near in their approach. The eagle-winged men rushing towards them were still a small distance away.

On the ground before Orahney was a pale shape that resembled a raincloud. The shape moved then stretched upwards. Fripso had escaped from the basket and was confronting the sorceress!

'What do we have here? An animal? A live, uncaged animal within the court?'

Eidred spun round. Pieter tried to coax her to look away from their dear rabbit friend and to hurry onwards, but the princess remained frozen. 'Fripso,' she screamed. 'Fripso, run! You must escape her!'

The soothsayer lifted thin arms into the air and threw herself at the rabbit.

Fripso dodged her narrowly.

In a fury, the soothsayer struck her curling clawed hands against the ground.

With careful haste, Eidred placed Lunara in Pieter's arms. She flew towards the thicket where Fripso stood quivering. Pieter, holding tightly to his precious daughter, dashed after Eidred. Orahney lunged again at the rabbit. Eidred leapt in front of Fripso. In so doing, she lost balance. To steady herself, she clung to the brambles that made up the thicket.

Orahney raised a twisted hand and pointed to Pieter. 'There is no Adahmos!' She shook with laughter, savage screeches that caused small Lunara to howl uncontrollably. 'The true prince is *dead*. And our Solen knows not of his tragic fate. Never has an Ehyptian prince set foot on Norwegian soil.' With an icy smile, she added, 'Guilty of sending letters to our Solen. Letters, from Ehypte, supposedly, penned with your own hand. You will rue your wickedness, elf, when all here learn of your true name and origins.'

'No!' Pieter's voice rose. 'We shall not tolerate your insolent lies!' How could he keep this malevolent woman from disclosing his elfin identity?

XLII

The rabbit was lost within the thicket. Eidred had stooped to look for him and was now on her knees, searching feverishly within the rose thorns.

Pieter, holding Lunara firmly against his chest, reached for Eidred's wrist and hauled her away from the soothsayer.

'These thorns are poisonous,' Eidred said in a squeal. 'These thorns might harm Fripso!'

At last they saw him, a small heap of white fur burrowing into the ground beneath the thicket. Here was the answer! The rabbit had a chance of escaping the palace before the troopers arrived. 'Hurry my friend,' Pieter said beneath his breath.

Alas, Orahney's gaze fell upon the poor, terrified animal. She clawed at the brambles to get to him. Against the brambles she struggled.

There came a piercing cry. The soothsayer collapsed to her knees and held her hands aloft. Both palms were marked with blood. 'I am poisoned,' she shrilled. She had come into contact with the fatal thorns. 'I am poisoned and near to death!' She glowered at Eidred. 'It was meant to be you! I meant it to be *you*. The Princess of Grudella was to pierce her finger and die.'

Fripso was now far beneath the ground, well on his way to the other side of the thorn thicket. The devic side. The side of freedom. 'Well done, Fripso,' Pieter whispered with a sigh. 'You have escaped the gold-tainted illusion.'

While Fripso would never reunite with his family—they were one hundred years ahead of him in the future—he would make a life for himself within the glades. This was of little comfort to Pieter. He had lost one of his dearest companions. Devastating, too, for Eidred. She was now weeping bitterly.

Beside the toxic, bloom-abundant thicket, the soothsayer lay motionless. Two rose petals floated down to her, followed by tiny flower faeries who whispered their last respects.

The infant in Pieter's arms, having ceased her wails some time ago, was now cooing like a dove. She rested her downy head against her father's shoulder and patted his neck with a fragile fist.

Pieter looked with pity upon the wretch of a soothsayer, once a gentle and goodly forest dweller. 'She is dead.'

Eidred raised her hands in the air. Her fingers, like those of the soothsayer's, were awash with blood. 'Oh, beloved,' she said in a groan, 'I am poisoned too! I clasped the brambles when I tried to protect Fripso.'

XLIII

Pieter's wife was kneeling by the thorn thicket, gazing at her blood-streaked palm. 'Poisoned,' she said, shaking her head in despair.

Pieter lifted her other hand and kissed the back of it. 'Remember, Beauty,' he whispered. 'It is *meant* that you pierce your finger this day. You are saved from death. Instead you will sleep.'

Already, Eidred's eyelids had grown heavy. The hundred-year slumber was soon to commence. 'She said she meant me to die.' Eidred nodded towards the dead woman. 'It's almost as though Orahney had been the one by my cradle at the crystalling, the wicked bewitcher who wished the death on me. Impossible, of course. Orahney hails from the Pre-Glory Century and has only been with us since the Backwards-Winding took place.'

The hood had fallen away from the woman to reveal hair that was long and ringleted.

Pieter drew back and breathed in sharply. 'Eidred, look!' Hanging loosely from a face that had altered to smoothly sallow, was a mask. The mask resembled an aged Orahney.

Before them was not a sorceress the Grudellans referred to as Zemelda. Here lay a sorcerer, the time traveller, Rahwor.

'Orahney has *not* betrayed us,' Eidred said with a grateful sigh.

Pieter recalled the conversation in the Solen's counting house, overheard when he'd visited the gallery: a fawning commitment to destroy a woman Pieter had observed in the Dream Sphere. No travelling into the future would be achieved now. The woman whose name was Det-ah-Wise-la, wherever she lived in that distant timeframe, was saved from Rahwor's hateful intentions. Rahwor, no doubt, would evolve with each new life.

Det-ah-Wise-la would be safe, for Rahwor's desire to stop her returning the earth to its rightful state would have ended when his life did on this very day since memories of past lives were, as enforced by body kings, forgotten soon after they ended. It was doubtful their paths would ever cross. Unless, of course, the sorcerer had travelled forward in time after his meeting with the Solen that fateful morning. It was possible, Pieter supposed, and an unsavoury idea he wished not to entertain. He didn't care to imagine the frightening effect Rahwor's black talons and sneer might have on a woman unacquainted with body-king magicians.

Pieter preferred to think, however, that Rahwor was too taken up with finding clues of deception in Orahney's pyramid home. The mask that now lay by the thorn thicket, the replica of Orahney's face when she played the role of withered Zemelda, would have allowed him to slip past the pterodactyls guarding the former bewitchers' dwellings. Pieter could only hope that Orahney fled to the magical cavern beneath her home. He prayed she'd remained undiscovered.

Eidred shook her weary head. 'Of course it should be Rahwor. The servants believed this green-eyed courtier had a vendetta against my family when refused marriage to my eldest sister. I see this is true now. My crystalling allowed him the perfect opportunity to take revenge on my father. Rahwor would have adopted a bewitcher's disguise, just as he has today, with that soothsayer's clothing and mask.'

Pieter recalled the words Rahwor had uttered moments earlier: *The Solen's daughter will fall to her death this day, and the imposter will be punished.* 'Rahwor was devious, that is for sure,' he told Eidred. 'And the reason Rahwor believed you would die from those poisonous rose thorns is he didn't remain at your crystalling long enough to witness the twelfth bewitcher lessen the sting of the spell. He had no knowledge of her decree that you fall asleep instead, followed by all in the empire. He did not anticipate that any bewitcher present might possess enough magic to alter a spell as powerful as his.'

'How very fortunate the twelfth faerie's blessing was never discussed at court,' Eidred said. 'My father had no way of knowing whether the wicked sorceress was one of the palace bewitchers or someone from afar. His swearing the attendees to secrecy has resulted in our lives being spared this day.'

Pieter closed his eyes in contemplation. 'This has me wondering whether the bewitcher who rescued you was indeed a bewitcher. The palace's wands, you have said, have limited powers because the elixirs inside their crystals are *not* of the wielder's own heart. Undoing a spell would certainly require a great deal of beauty-creation, and an accumulation of Kindness Merits. Perhaps the modifier of the spell was a sprite from the glades, one empowered with Kindness Merits.'

Eidred was kneeling over their daughter, settling her into the basket, smoothing silken blankets across the child's small shoulders. 'Adahmos,' she said drowsily, 'I am concerned about Orahney.'

Already the eagle guards had arrived. One lifted Rahwor's body and carried it away. Pieter sent a plea to the angels for Rahwor's future—in the world his soul now dwelt—and made a wish that Rahwor's heart chakra would return to a state in which love could be effortlessly given and received.

The two sat side-by-side as the hush of darkness descended, gazing at their daughter sleeping soundly in her infant basket. Pieter valued these last few moments of wakefulness. He now had the opportunity to convey the truth Rahwor discovered about Orahney. And so he told Eidred Orahney's secret. He talked with Eidred about the time shortly after he infiltrated the palace, when the Backwards-Winding sent them back through time to the Pre-Destruction Century—Pre-Glory Century to Gold's Kin who were oh-so-proud of ending the lives of plants, animals and sprites. This was the century Orahney dwelt in.

Eidred smilingly recalled their secret courtship, when Pieter's acceptance into the palace as an Ehyptian prince was aided by their faerie friend and the eagle-winged trooper Storlem. Before the trooper and faerie had ever encountered each other, Storlem was a man possessing of little more than the unemotional logic and chilled heart shared by all Gold's Kin eagle hybrids.

'Even before I was formally introduced to Storlem, I knew he was one of my father's chief messengers,' Eidred told Pieter. 'As we now know, amongst Storlem's many tasks was the gathering together of beauty-creation crystals, the precious gems in the south, beloved, that you and I speculated on. Storlem also arranged their exportation to that lush wilderness across the seas.'

'Lemuria,' said Pieter.

A land uninhabited by Gold's Kin and far enough away for the crystals to lose their effect. Solens did not wish their descendants to be 'infected' with devic qualities. As Orahney had told Pieter when he'd visited her pyramid home, the messenger trooper was silvered through exposure to these crystals. Storlem's silvering gave him compassion for all earthly creatures, and the magical ability to perceive sprites.

After the backwards-winding, when the Grudellan Palace materialised in the Pre-Destruction Century, Storlem happened upon Orahney on one of his Sun's Day roams, and the two fell deeply in love. Orahney would emerge from each slumber when the sun was setting, in joyful anticipation of seeing her lover again.

At dusk Storlem would take on his eagle form, as all guards did, for each eagle would circle the towering spires after daylight vanished, to ensure the palace was free of intruders.

Once returned to his true form, Storlem would retreat to the forest to seek out his cherished faerie. Their time together was precious, marred always by the trooper's obligation to the Solen. Both Orahney and he were burdened by the knowledge that any suspicion concerning his whereabouts, or his silvering, might result in their deaths.

'I prayed she wasn't hurt when the courtiers took her away to the palace.'

'She was not,' said Pieter. 'She told me she fell into an enthralled trance, an effect of the enchanted cloaks. As soon as they embarked on their return to the palace, they set her back down, and she followed them to the palace gates.'

'Such conniving creatures,' said Eidred in disgust. 'How dare they corrupt the sprites!'

'And yet Orahney was fortunate,' said Pieter. 'Storlem returned all of her goodly powers via the wand. Other faeries robbed of their heart radiance are enslaved.'

'And she was able to reside near to her beloved.'

Pieter looked back towards the palace, grimly eyeing the eagle Rawhor had turned to stone.

Echoing his thoughts, Eidred whispered, 'Perhaps Rahwor was mistaken. Perhaps that eagle was another guard and not Storlem.'

'Whoever it is, I feel certain he would be suffering terribly.' Pieter's heart was heavy with sorrow. 'Trapped in a gloomy eternity unless he is freed from the spell.'

Eidred nodded tearily.

He remembered then, an eagle from the Dream Sphere visiting him in Elysium Glades. Hearing the echo of the eagle's lament about a spell caster named Rahwor, Pieter covered his eyes with his hand. 'I have been warned of this previously. I have failed, again, to help.'

As Orahney had explained to them when they'd visited the cavern beneath her dwelling, all beauty-creation she possessed was drained from her during the Gold's Kin ritual that altered faeries into bewitchers. A portion of the crystal storing her heart magic was fashioned into a bewitcher's wand. Although troopers were given strict instructions to lock away all wands in reserve for infant naming ceremonies, Storlem concealed one of these wands and then took it to his lover. It was the wand whose crystal contained her own magical heart.

Pieter returned to his tale of Orahney's secret, and Eidred listened with interest, her normally luminous expression clouded with sombre pensiveness. Orahney's regained heart powers allowed her to remain connected to the Dream Sphere. In one of her slumbering travels, she was shown both present and future events, of an elf from a future century hiding in the palace, removed from his clan and timeframe because of the Backwards-Winding, and she learnt that the elf and princess had fallen in love.

Orahney and Storlem contrived a plan that would allow Pieter's acceptance into the Grudellan Palace. It was decided that Orahney would manufacture a correspondence between herself and the Solen. First she penned an artificial letter of introduction, adopting the writing persona of the Solen of Deweldior, an Ehyptian emperor whose youngest son was of similar age to Pieter. Storlem had provided her with a letter the man wrote to their own Grudellan Solen, the handwriting of which Orahney copied meticulously.

Storlem did not carry out the command of delivering replies to ships bound for Ehypte. Instead he took each of his royal master's letters back to Orahney.

More elaborate means of establishing good relations were instigated. Orahney painted portraits of the elf she knew only from images she'd seen in the Dream Sphere, portraying Pieter as one of royal heritage, with skin and hair of gold, and eyes of blue. She wrapped each artwork in velvet and addressed these to the Solen, who proudly displayed them in his gallery.

The Solen of Grudella, delighted at the opportunity of building relations with a king of great influence, was eager to arrange a marriage between the Adahmos referred to in Orahney's letters and his youngest daughter.

It was within the following season-cycle that Orahney used her heart-elixir wand to disguise herself as rapidly aged, and was thereafter not of interest to licentious courtiers. That was when she was given the dubious title of Zemelda, Palace Soothsayer and expected to tell the fortunes of Gold's Kin.

'...And this is why you and I have been so carefully protected,' said Pieter once he'd told all this to Eidred.

'Orahney has been my guardian,' Eidred said, her lashes damp with tears. 'She has allowed me to love one of devic heritage. She, too, has experienced forbidden love, and she's suffered for it.'

To:.........Isobel Redding
From:......Glorion Osterhoudt
Sent:.......16 May 2008
Subject:...about my heritage

Hello Izzie,

Yeah, I have your email address. And it's not intuition—my learning of your address in the cab was only telepathy. I knew you were about to say it, so I saved you the trouble by saying it for you.

I got your email address from the birthday invitation you left in my locker. I know. I lied. I lied because I was too late and got embarrassed about saying I knew about it 'cos your official starting time had been Noon. Lame, hey? I was planning on visiting your picnic, but Tyson's aura indicated bronchitis heading towards a bad lot of lung-scarring pneumonia that would ruin his opportunity of becoming a professional rugby player. I didn't tell him I see auras. Just stayed and watched the soccer, switched the crystal onto healing mode and directed it at Tyson once he dozed off in his chair.

The cab ride home with you was cool, especially because the driver somehow got it wrong and took us almost to Wollongong. Crazy us! We were too absorbed in talking to notice!

But I gotta tell you, Izzie, what I meant to tell you before we said goodbye. I'm not a Lemurian like you suspect. Have you heard of a writer called Alcor? He's a famous psychic who's regarded as a fully realised being because he doesn't forget anything: neither his visits (in spirit) to the Dream Sphere every night nor any of his incarnations. Alcor claims that an individual's lives can be lived in places other than the third dimensional Earth plane of existence and that after a life has been lived, the individual always returns (in spirit) to its home base, the Dream Sphere / Heaven / Nirvana / The Other Side (whatever you want to call it.) He wrote a book a while back called *Thoughts on Tomorrow's Tycoon War* under the name of Conan Dalesford. (The name he uses on his intuitive readings website is Alcor, a derivative of his given names.) What I want to say to you is there are plenty of people on Earth with an uninterrupted memory like Conan/Alcor. Myself included.

Yes, I have lived in Lemuria. In a previous life. So have many people. The difference is I'm able to remember. I recall the technology we used like it was yesterday. That's why it's so easy for me to construct things with crystals. I learn a lot in the Dream Sphere each night. Everyone goes to the Dream Sphere when they sleep, but for most people, mental garbage messes with the remembrance process and corrupts nearly every recollection of visiting that awesome world. I'm lucky my nightly dreams are remembered in such detail. Upon waking, I recall many of the choices I've made during the seven or so hours spent in my 'dream body'. Remembering leads to making better sense of the 3D incarnation I'm living in now and grants me a broader perspective.

By the way, I guess you've seen the news headlines. I hope my being a prince doesn't make you think any less of me. It's something that's always made me feel ashamed, having a royal title. In previous incarnations I was totally averse to Gold's Kin, and yet look at the lineage I chose to descend from this time round! I used to say to myself: *What were you thinking?? !!* But you know what? I have to allow myself credit for thinking things through pretty well. The fact is, Izzie, pure undiluted Gold's Kin genetics aren't found in anyone these days, not even royalty. If it hadn't been for the descendants of the elf and princess, Earth's entire population would be very nasty indeed. I doubt there'd be anyone left here—everyone would have slaughtered each other, I imagine, in competition for riches.

I can hear you asking yourself something now, Izzie, so I will answer what I anticipate will be your query. It's to do with the cataclysm that destroyed nearly all of Earth's plant life and inhabitants (an effect of the laser-missile war I told you about when we dined in my hideaway). Your question is likely to be: *How could the bloodline of Adahmos and Eid carry on when their descendants would have been killed in the blast along with everyone else?* The answer is this. Some had access to tunnels that led to underground cities. Human clans, or tribes, had been warned of the cataclysm by Dream Sphere beings. They prepared for centuries, building subterranean refuges with the help of crystal lasers that sliced through layers of rock. Plenty survived, Gold's Kin included. Their monsters as well: the pterodactyls and other dinosaurs that were descended from peaceful dragons like Sluken. Dark magicians modified them genetically into giant toothy freaks. All who remained on the surface of the earth expired. And so history began again.

I have been drawn to Australia because it happens to be the site of the ancient Land of Mu. Asia (including India, of course) was a part of Lemuria, as was Australia, New Zealand and the Pacific Islands: basically whatever makes up the Asia Pacific region. All these countries were joined and made one island, the continent of Lemuria, where dreaming was seen to be on an equal par with prophecy. Lemuria has since been referred to in old English as 'The Garden of Eid and Adahmos' but over millenniums, this broke down and the Adahmos part of the term fell away so that it then became 'The Garden of Eid And ... ' only to wind up as the one your timeframe is familiar with: The Garden of Eden.

Their children, once grown, travelled throughout the world and settled where devas weren't oppressed by Gold's Kin: parts of the British Isles, areas in Africa, locations around the Mediterranean, and regions of South America. In their new environments, each met and partnered-up with those of devic heritage.

The sons and daughters of Adahmos and Eid, 'the first humans' according to Lillibridge, possessed both Gold's Kin's dispassionate logic (the capacity for clinical assessment that operated from the brain rather than the heart) and devic powers of compassion and creativity, which dwelt in the heart, the 'higher mind'.

In ancient prehistoric times, Gold's Kin races involved in beauty-creation rituals sent crystals to 'uncivilized' Lemuria. As I told you when relating the story documented by Edward Lillibridge, the theft of faeries' manifestation powers turned these faeries into 'bewitchers', thus the term 'witches', a word initially used in Britain by druidic clans.

The power in these crystals was too kind and loving a frequency. Those of the empire could not tolerate a harmoniser such as this. It weakened them.

Contact with the heart-elixir crystals allowed the men and women of the court to become peaceful and sprite-like, and so, upon amassing amounts considered 'dangerous', Gold's Kin shipped this crystal-encased sprite magic to a far off land they would never inhabit.

By the time the 1700s arrived, when your nation was invaded by white people, Australia's mixed population was diffident to the crystal energy. Just about everyone by then had enough of a balance of devic amongst their Gold's Kin genes to not be worried by this frequency. And it's true of all humanity, Izzie. The majority of us are basically a mixture of silver and gold, sun and moon. Some may be a little more 'body king' in the way they live their lives, others a little more devic.

Now that you know who I truly am and where I'm truly from, you'll understand why a relationship didn't develop. The auric colours surrounding us were of romance. Sadly, I couldn't allow this to deepen. I meant it when I said that you and I going out would do you no good. Getting together amid all the formalities I endure on a daily basis (one of the myriad delights of being royal!!) would place undue pressure on you, Izzie.

You are too young to get involved with someone in my unenviable position. Sure, I could invite you to the Palace, and we could start going out in Perelda, if that was what you wanted, but the media attention would be crazy beyond belief, too much for a cool, sweet girl who only turned sixteen a few days ago. So I don't want you to fall in love with someone as 'notorious' as me at present. Finish your education, live life to the full, heal your poor heart chakra, (which I've noticed is geared to repeat patterns of abandonment—Maybe your father left when you were young?) and go out with whoever you fancy.

And reclaim your goddess energy! Poor Izzie. You were so anxious and apologetic and afraid to be offensive around me. I notice this in a lot of women inhabiting the earth in this timeframe. They defer to men. They are wrongly led to believe they are powerless—a direct result of the Gold's Kin patriarchal influence where the sun /the yang/ the masculine, is seen to be the most powerful.

During The Silvering women will be encouraged to take the lead a lot more. And there will be a great deal of harmony between men and women, more than ever before. On a much larger scale than now, the feminine will appreciate the masculine for its powers of outer strength and protectiveness, and the masculine will appreciate the feminine for its inner strength and nurturing qualities.

So what I'm saying, Izzie, is value yourself completely, and always remember that you are worthy of admiration and that you do not have to twist yourself into knots to impress guys you are interested in. They have to impress you, to win *your* favour.

I was told in the Dream Sphere last night that your mother Rosetta has planned to move on from the potential partner who might hold her back in the future. This is great news! She will be very influential one day. She and the man who was once Reverend Edward Lillibridge have a lot of good work ahead of them.

Your mother is actually the reason I escaped to the area of Sydney you live in. As I told you on Sunday, I'd found out about her book club on the internet. I was impressed with the Friday Fortnight *Our True Ancient History* reading groups she initiated throughout the world. I planned to attend your mother's Sydney group while still in Australia and was eager to meet this originator of a growing worldwide interest in Lillibridge's book. As you know, thanks to SAPO (the Swedish secret police) my hopes of becoming a Burwood Friday Fortnighter were officially 'snaffled' as you guys say in Oz.

Remember how I said in the taxi that there's a prediction about to come true? (The prediction mentioned a few millenniums back by a guy named Isaiah.) Just like all texts treasured by whole populations throughout millenniums, *The Book of Isaiah* seems to have stood the test of time. Anyway the prophecy I'm talking about is:

Öknen och ödemarken skola glädja sig, och fröjdas och blomstra såsom en lilja hedmarken skall.

The non-Swedish version is:

...the desert shall rejoice, and blossom as the rose.

I'll send you an email in another hour or so, Izzie. Bjorn (my father's valet) has just knocked on my study door. My father didn't greet me when I arrived back from Australia, but now he wants to talk — in the south wing drawing room. Doesn't sound good. I can bet you he's right now pacing by the fire, tapping his fingers on the mantelpiece. You can almost hear the war drums.

Glorion

To:.........Isobel Redding
From:......Glorion Osterhoudt
Sent:.......16 May 2008
Subject:...Obamos and Weed

Hello again, Izzie!

Woo, am I in trouble! I've never seen my father so angry. He even seized up a candle from one of the candelabras and threw it into the fire, and I'm like 'Papa, what was the point in that?' but I have no regrets about escaping to Sydney.

I won't linger any longer on that though, because I'd like to talk more about the verse I mentioned. Africa is the heart of Mother Earth and, with the help of innovative new agricultural methods and massive community input, its central barrenness will soon be made fertile. From then on, other nations will follow suit. Deserts, I am pleased to say, are soon to become history! I'm glad to know you have such a noble parent. Rosetta will be influential in restoring various nations into lands abundant in health-giving plant life. When the deserts bloom, the planet will benefit from oxygenation, increased food supply and liveable space for the good hardworking citizens pushed out of their birthplace nations because of bombs and gunfights.

Here is some interesting trivia. Amongst the ancient Celts, many had a large percentage of devic influence in their genetics and were considered to be the 'druids', but Gold's Kin Roman emperors started some damning rumours about these people (who harmed nothing and no-one and were gentle in the extreme). They claimed druids killed people and animals to offer to certain 'gods'. Complete baloney! Druids lived good, honest lives and took care of, honoured in fact, flora and fauna. I remember your mistaken reference, Izzie, to Eid being 'Weed'. Interestingly, the word druid is derived from the word *deru* meaning 'to be solid form' and *weid* being 'to see'. Eid was an intuitive *seer* 'cos she possessed faerie sight. Lillibridge mentions Pieter/Adahmos took on solidity or solid form when he became more like a mortal within the Grudellan Palace's frequencies. And so your 'Weed' name for Eidred suggests she was one of the original druids: A mortal in harmony with nature and seer of sprites.

By the time the 1600's ended, nearly all druids—seers branded witches—had been slain. The pain forced upon them was because of Gold's Kin: the Cycle of Suffering their sorcerers inflicted upon the world long before. Sadly, these witch hunts eradicated a strongly devic bloodline, which stemmed from the ancestry of Adahmos and Eid.

I will go now, Izzie. You won't be able to contact me, probably not for a lot of years. This is my school email address. I will cancel it before it becomes a hacker's triumph. The last thing we want is these private words I'm sending you plastered all over the headlines.

If, in the future (say in fifteen or sixteen years) you feel like getting in contact with me, the way will be paved for you. If not, that's fine too. You might be married by then. In the meantime, hold no candle for me. Instead, hold a candle for your future and let it guide you to every conceivable happiness. I don't recommend you throw the aformentioned candle into the fire. Candle-hurling is only reserved for pompous Pereldans whose sons wag school in Australia.

I'm sending you healing from my crystal because I'm sensing heat. I think you might have a viral fever.

Goodbye...is never forever. The Dream Sphere unites us all in the end.

I am your willing servant, my beauty.

All my love,

Glorion

Chapter Five

To:.........Glorion Osterhoudt
From:......Isobel Redding
Sent:........17 May 2008
Subject:....a few last words

Hey Glorion,

I know you would prefer I didn't reply, but I'll write this email anyway. Probably when I go to press 'Send', it'll be blocked. Some weird dialogue box will nastily dominate the screen, and I'll know without needing to read it that your email address is from that moment forward defunct.

Whatever happens, I don't care. I'm writing this because I've *got* to speak to you one last time. If even the 'essence' of what I'm saying reaches you in spirit, then that's good enough. Regardless of whether my inbox's mailing status reads 'Sent' or 'Delivery Cancelled', I reckon that if I at least attempt to contact you, your intuition will do the rest.

I'm at the moment using a smooth-functioning computer outside of school. Usually I do all my homework on one of the laptops at the After-School Studies Centre (you know the one. It's between the library and the quadrangle). I do have a computer at home, but the monitor's about 15 years old (we found it disposed of on someone's nature-strip) and it goes blank every three or four minutes, so you have to bang the back of it to get the picture up again. It does my head in, so I try to only use it for email. Since I'm staying at my mother's friend's place, I'm able to use the one in the study as much as I like. It's got a huge flat-screen monitor. Cool, hey?

There are two reasons I'm staying at Lena's. Every time my mother and I stepped out of the house, we risked getting photographed. The Monday following my birthday I was home from school with a virus—thanks for your 'get well' wishes. Can't believe you sensed that, but then, there's not much about you that isn't unbelievable!!

When I had to leave the house the next morning, the dash from the verandah to the car got really hairy. As it turned out I was chauffeured to school. Craig (another friend of my mother's) devised a way of pulling up at the backyard end of the driveway after first phoning me to say he'd toot when turning into Ashbury Avenue as a warning to stand by. Once I heard the car, I leapt out of the back door and jumped in before any of the photographers in the front yard could catch up with us. That evening I was featured on the six o'clock news. How embarrassing—a five second shot of me and Craig looking deadly serious! The report showed us lurching out of the driveway with both our heads bobbing in unison when Craig swerved to dodge the news crew and bumped us over the gutter.

I just know news viewers all around the country will be going, '*She's* had a prince cook dinner for her?' in this really disparaging way, and then anyone my age and female will say, 'Even *I'm* better looking than that! Why don't *I* get to meet Swedish princes?' My top-knot was such a bright orange through the windscreen it could have been mistaken for a mandarine.

Don't worry, Glorion. This isn't me having a go at myself—I respect the goddess within. I've actually been having a laugh at it all. So has my mum. She got caught on the news zooming out of the driveway too and says she definitely has to ditch those multi-coloured sunglasses of hers 'cos they make her look like a mafia queen. Being on TV does us all good occasionally. Provides the reality check we think we don't need. I'm going to blonde my hair from now on. I'd much rather be a Princess Eidred than a Pippi Longstocking.

Don't apologise about being a prince, Glorion. It explains so much. I feel sorry for you getting hunted down by SAPO, but I'm guessing you gave up evading them once the cab dropped me home, and allowed them to catch you. By now you might have gotten homesick, so I'm glad you're back with your family and, apart from that crazed bout of candle hurling, I get the impression from the 'Duke of Norbury' page on the Perelda Palace website that your dad's a reasonable guy.

It's mind-boggling to think someone from your walk of life went to my school and befriended me, but it doesn't make my opinion of you any better. It's already ridiculously high and can't climb any higher. (Maybe *that's* why they call you 'Highness'!!) Highness, Lowness, Broadness, Cuteness, whatever! Someone's place in society has never actually interested me. How can anyone be proud of what was already there before they existed? Being born into wealth or poverty, a certain 'class', is all just luck, if you ask me. And like it says in a book I once read on reincarnation:

A prince may become a pauper.
A pauper may become a prince.

So I guess we've all had turns at being either rich or poor. Not that I'm suggesting, Glorion, that you reincarnate poor. Trust me, not having an obedient computer monitor when you wish you did is crap. But then, as my mother continually reminds me: although by Australian standards we'd be considered 'battlers', she and I are rich in contrast with the rest of the world. It's tragic that the majority of our planet's people endure poverty.

Lena has just told me we're all to sit down to dinner, so I'd better go. I'll send this now in the hope of you receiving it before you cancel your email address, and then I'll put the rest of what I want to tell you into another email later tonight.

Sincerest regards,
Izzie

To..........Glorion Osterhoudt
From:.......Isobel Redding
Sent:.......17 May 2008
Subject:...a few last words II

Hey again Glorion,
Here's the sequel to that last email.
By the way, thank you for the encouraging words about my mum helping restore developing nations to their former glory. She was totally overjoyed to hear that. Her life's ambition is to be jointly responsible for eliminating world poverty in our lifetime. It's a pretty noble aim, I guess.

Mine isn't humanitarian. I want to be a sports reporter. I want to interview gold medallists at the Rio Olympics in 2016.

I mentioned in my last email the first reason I'm staying at Lena's but not the second. The second reason is my mum went on an impromptu trip to New Zealand. She got a letter about an inheritance she is to share with her half-brother, and she only met this brother of hers (Bobby) a few days ago.

To make a long story short, it turns out my grandmother was a well-known singer! Have you heard of Danna Nolan? She sang stuff in the '70s and '80s. Not creepy stuff, like Doctor Cyanide sang. That dude's 'Gimme' video clip still terrifies me! You may not have heard of him—he was banned in Sweden. I know this 'cos I saw an interview with Doctor Cyanide on a retro replay of *Countdown* last Sunday, and he laughed pretty meanly about how stuck-up he thought your nation was. You might remember 'Gimme'. All he says in the whole song is either 'give me' and 'more' and he looks totally gruesome while he sings it. His face drips blood, then he turns into a gorgon from Greek mythology. (Long hair turning into worms or eels. Or maybe they're snakes. I've tried to un-see that image for years 'cos it gave me nightmares through primary school.) Danna Nolan's music, on the other hand, was pretty mellow: ('I am a Woman in Love' 'My Moonlight Prince' etc.)

It's weird how things can change so suddenly. I think I've spent the past four days with only one expression on my face. A surprised one. Here's why:

- I concluded you were a Lemurian time-traveller and then found out...
- ...that you're actually not. A bit far-fetched anyway :/
- Conan Dalesford is one of those cool fully realised beings.
- My mother and I (and my cat Sidelta) have to move.
- Sidelta is about to have kittens (can't wait!)
- My mother is about to inherit from a well-loved musician parent she never knew.

All of the above has been more than a little astonishing. It's a wonder my face isn't frozen with amazement: Mouth like an 'o'. Both eyebrows nudging my hairline. My foster grandmother always warned me when I got upset over things that 'the wind would change' and that I'd be stuck with one look forever. My foster-grandmother wasn't a very grandmotherly person. She didn't really like kids. I know for a fact she did love babies, but children over the age of two tended to bore and disgruntle her. She might have been nicer to adults, maybe. I don't know. She's pretty hazy in my memory. I don't think she was ever very pleasant to her foster-daughter though. From what I remember, she continually berated Mum for being friendly to people. Personally, I think she was jealous—angry at Mum because she wasn't able to make many friends herself. My foster-grandmother distrusted anyone who wasn't family and lived a fairly insular life.

Anyway, that's enough of my life story!

I understand what you're saying, Glorion, about not falling for you. Once I finish this email I plan to forget our bizarre Sunday. Trouble is, I keep getting reminded. I was playing computer games with Lena's son, Ben, who is our age and goes to another school. He's cool and good at Spatchawokki (but not as good as me—I beat him four times last night and I'd only just learnt the game the night before!) Anyway, what I was going to say was Ben wears a jacket with a hood like yours, only it's not light in colour, it's dark blue. It doesn't have sleeves, and it doesn't have the zip in the same place yours does, and the hood is just for decoration (it's sewn down so it won't go over his head). But apart from that (and a little medallion on his right pocket, which looks like an Australian dollar coin, and the actual size of the jacket) it's exactly like yours. It gets me in the heart, you know, Glorion, and I don't want to keep talking like this. I want my attitude towards you to be 'out of sight, out of mind'. So I'll just tell you this.

I wish I'd never met you.

I don't know whether I'll ever be strong enough to clear a heart-stopping image from my mind, a memory-snapshot of my school buddy framed in moonlight after he pushed the grate off a dungeon we ran through and stood elevated against the starry sky.

But I accept you're gone and that life moves on and, yeah, who knows, I might be visiting you in that Dream Sphere place when I sleep, although I doubt I'll have any recollection of it.

I wish I knew what you meant about being a deva. I've begun reading *Our True Ancient History*. The book isn't ours—it belongs to

Royston (one of the Friday Fortnight members). Since hearing you retell the story, I've been fascinated. Wouldn't it be weird if *you* were one of the people Lillibridge has mentioned? There's no mistaking one of your middle names is Pieter. It's all mega accessible on the internet: your name, your date and time of birth etc. You've got a Libran Rising Sign by the way (same as me) and the Moon and Venus in your horoscope are both in earth signs. Getting back to your middle-name and your insistence that there's such a thing as reincarnation, I'd love to know if you were an elf in a past life. (That's if elves ever existed, but you seem to think they did.)

Imagine if I was in the book also! I can guess who I would have been.

I would have been the rabbit. I have a real affinity with the character Fripso. From an early age, all I ever wanted to be was a bunny. Wore home-made cardboard bunny ears everywhere.

Thanks for the info about the buried crystals here. Haven't heard anything so far, but will, in the words of one of Burwood High's coolest and oldest science teachers, Mrs Johns: 'Keep an ear to the ground.' Do Lemurian crystals happen to be noisy? LOL! If yes, should I press my ear to the ground to listen out for them? If yes, do you think a rabbit's hearing would amplify their signals? Those cardboard ears stashed away in a cupboard might ultimately come in handy!

About the night we ran from SAPO. I sometimes get confused with dreams and reality, believing that a dream really happened or that an event in my recent life is repeated from a dream I had a long time ago. I haven't told anyone this, but it must have been the night of my birthday that I dreamt you and I were rising over treetops in an oval cane basket. Weird! When you were telling me about the silver boy and the golden girl, I had the feeling the two of us were transported somewhere magical by something multi-coloured and levitational, like a hot-air balloon. So that's probably the reason I dreamt we flew. When I was seven, I dreamt about a boy who told me, 'We'll have some years to wait, of course, before we get together, and then the world is ours to share.' Nine years later, I thought I'd met the dream guy. At school. This dream/reality thing sure has me spooked.

I'd better go. Just overheard Ben asking Lena where I am. I'm guessing he wants me to play against him again. Is this guy a masochist or what? Doesn't he know I can't be beaten?

Love and blessings, Your Royal Loftiness!
Izzie

XLIV

Content to listen to Eidred's musings, Pieter watched their sleeping daughter with pride.

'I'd thought my faerie godmother to be the lady who visited me once,' Eided said, 'who you later told me would have been Maleika, your own mother and Clan Watcher. I expect she was there in search of you, not to help me as I so selfishly assumed. 'Tis Orahney who is my godmother.'

'And yet godmothers, as a rule, are those who travel from other dimensions to predict a significant earthly arrival,' said Pieter. 'Faerie godmothers foretell the birth of a child whose fate affects the world momentously, thus the reference to godliness.'

'Oh, I see.' Eidred rested her head on Pieter's shoulder. 'I'd thought they were simply motherly people who granted wishes.'

Pieter gave thought to the mother Eidred had never known. 'As far as motherly goes, Orahney is certainly that. As Clan Watcher she was indeed the mother of many sprites.' In reference to Eidred's voice, nature and mannerisms he added, 'I often thought you could almost have been her daughter.'

Eidred laughed sleepily. 'Faeries can never be mothers of Gold's Kin. This is one of the reasons the Solen denies them their beauty-creation, to ensure the removal of their life-giving powers.' Eidred blinked, yawned, and smiled down at their sleeping infant. 'Many centuries earlier, the magic-robbing ceremony did not take place. According to the stories I've heard from the women at court, the solens of the times insisted the captured faeries' wings were removed to prevent them from escaping.

'Courtiers who dallied with the prisoners could not see them without the help of the palace's fey-detection cloaks. The faeries would inevitably tear at the cloaks to damage the power within them and were considered elusive creatures indeed.

'Plenty of the faerie prisoners, probably those whose Kindness Merits were plentiful enough, escaped with the use of magic. Harsher means of capture were then devised. 'Tis the reason heart-radiance theft emerged. It made the victims firstly solid and visible as mortals are, yet devoid of mortal qualities such as fertility.' Softly, Eidred said, 'I am falling.' She lowered herself drowsily to the ground, next to Lunara's basket. 'Falling asleep, beloved.'

With gentleness, Pieter helped his wife recline upon the cool palace lawn and then looked sadly upon his daughter. 'I intend to welcome you into the Dream Sphere, Beauty,' he told Eidred. 'And should I be the first to emerge from the slumbering spell we are now falling under, I shall awaken you with a kiss.' He did not admit to his fear of not returning.

When Pieter succumbed to the Dream Sphere's beckoning brightness, a bell-like distant voice filtered through to him. It emanated sharply from the place Rahwor's winged victim was melded to the obelisk, a voice that rose in a wail of grief.

'Storlem,' the voice cried. 'My love!'

Shattering the silence of a slumbering court was the heartbreaking echo of an autumn faerie's sobs.

To:.........Isobel Redding
From:......Rosetta Melki
Sent:.......18 May 2008
Subject:...*Eureka!*

Hello, Future Sports Journalist!

You and I must have laughed and cried for at least an hour during last night's phone call. I'm still in a state of amazement at how something as fortunate as this could have happened to us, Izzie!

It must have been torture for you being at school today, a great interruption to dreaming all your dreams. Still, your marks are consistently excellent, so botching one day is hardly a blip on the radar. You've set yourself up beautifully for Years Eleven and Twelve with all the hard work you've done. When you go to uni you'll have a little luxurious place all of your own, in whatever suburb you choose.

To think you were going to put that excellent mind of yours to waste and dodge uni! I know you were prepared to waitress full-time instead so that I wouldn't have to support you. I would never have neglected your education, although I must admit I wasn't looking forward to the struggle. And as for working part-time while you're studying, that's not necessary now. But if you decide to all the same, it will only be for the love of it and for gaining an understanding of the workforce.

Just think, Izzie. We can travel anywhere in the world during your school holidays. You can see Machu Picchu as you've always wanted to. And I can see Egypt and France, and we can tour the Scandinavian nations! How exciting is that? I swear I slept for little more than twenty seconds last night. I was too excited! And too busy! In my imagination I was decorating our imaginary Milsons Point harbourside apartment.

It didn't sink in on Monday when I saw the gorgeous three-storey that Bobby grew up in. I saw it as Bobby's house, and I felt like some kind of intruder. And then I reasoned it would never be sold.

It was a sensitive subject. The last thing I wanted to do was burden a bereaved man with property division details. And then darling Bobby brought it up last night, asking what I'd like to do about Daniela's estate. I told him, 'Something as beautiful as that should be kept in the family,' wanting to reassure him that I'd never fight to sell it, that I respect it's been the home of his childhood and that I share his idea of sentimental value outweighing dollar-signs. Izzie, did I tell you last night about the way he reacted to that? He turned around to me, shrugged one shoulder, lowered his lovely kind eyes and said, 'Oh. Sure. If that's how you feel, I guess.' And then he said, 'It's just that I'm fine with selling it. There are heaps of memories tied up in that place. Mum isn't a part of it anymore. Going there just makes me sad.'

I reassured Bobby that I'd follow his lead and go along with whatever he felt was wisest. So that's when he suggested we get the place valued and, as you know, the rest is history. We'll get a few more opinions from other valuers. Personally, I'm perfectly happy with the first evaluation, but, in the words of your (foster) grandfather, 'I no complain'!!

Izzie, next to my wedding day and the day you were born, I believe yesterday was the happiest day of my life.

The request I made of my guardian angels has finally been answered. I can now press ahead with my goal to help end global suffering!

It's 2.45 in the morning, and, you guessed it, I'm unable to sleep. Did you sleep okay last night or were you wide-awake like me, planning all the holidays we'll be going on?

Right now I can hear an owl hooting somewhere in the distance. At my bedside are two framed photographs of Daniela, one of them on the night she received an award for her third album. Rain is streaming down the windows, and tears (of the happy variety) are streaming down my face.

Joy is a difficult one to handle. I always thought I'd be much better at coping with gigantically proportioned happiness, but rather than swanning around Christchurch with a beatific smile on my dial, I'm plodding about with my head down. Every few hours I've been bursting into tears! This multi-millionaire mum of yours is a mess. A blubbering mess, but I'm sure it will pass once I grow accustomed to having 'Money, Money, Money' (to quote a favourite pop group of Daniela's and mine).

The more I hear about Daniela, the more gratitude I feel, and I'm enormously proud to have discovered that this very special person was my mother. She was, and *is,* such an angel. And she's looking after us, Izzie. Your grandmother is ensuring our security. She's making sure we are more secure than we've ever been in our lives.

Love and kisses to you, Flopsy,
Mum

To:...........Isobel Redding
From:........Sara Belfield
Sent:.........18 May 2008
Subject:.....*bummer*

Hi Izzie,

Pity your mum and my dad broke up. They couldn't have been going out for longer than a week I reckon. Did you know that had happened? I knew they'd kept in contact after you moved from Punchbowl, but I did *not* know they'd started dating!

I hope that isn't why your mum went to New Zealand—to get over my dad. If yes, let her know he's not that great. Now we'll never be step-sisters!

My mum's in Vanuatu. She's bringing me back some island jewellery. Can't wait to see what it's like.

Glad all those news crews stopped stalking you. You can now go back to leading a boring life!

Did you end up finding the bracelet Jandy gave you for your birthday? Like I said last week, go back to the cliffs at Brighton Beach. You probably dropped it there when we went on our boy search.

Better go. My stepdad wants to use the computer.

See you tomorrow (in case you didn't know: assembly is 8.30 from tomorrow onwards).

Hugs & Chocolate

Sara

To:..........Sara Belfield
From:........Isobel Redding
Sent:........18 May 2008
Subject:....Re—*bummer*

Hi Sara,

The trip wasn't about your dad. I don't think Mum and Grant were dating. Mum says they'd only met up for a Chinese lunch a week or so after they took us ice skating, so, unfortunately, I reckon the chance of us being step-sisters is one in a zillion.

Then again, they *are* friends, so there's the possibility I guess that their friendship might one day blossom into love (Wink!) Your dad's going to be collecting Mum from the airport when she gets back from NZ. Could this mean we actually will be step-sisters ?????

I remember her being sad to leave our flat in Punchbowl 'cos she liked having your dad for a neighbour, and we felt safe too, with Grant being a police officer etc.

Even though we hated living there, I'm glad we did. You might never have become my friend. When your dad introduced us last year, I was like, 'I'm in Year Nine,' and you were like, 'I'm in Year Eight. I have a science teacher at my school named Mrs Beeker,' and I was like, 'Hey, me too!' But then I realised you'd said Beeker and not Bleager. It was *soooo* funny how I got Mrs Beeker for the geology elective when I changed over to Burwood High.

Don't worry—I understand what you were saying before the lunch bell interrupted you, about how you're sure that if your mum had known that you already knew my mum and that my mum wasn't just some random stranger who answered her newspaper ad for a 'firm but amiable stand-in mother', she probably would have hired her to drive you and your sister to parties etc when she went to Vanuatu. Mum's not offended. Promise. She had to go to New Zealand in a rush, so she's glad she didn't get the position because that might have left your mum in the lurch.

About the bracelet. *Please* don't tell poor Jandy I lost it. Haven't had any luck finding it either. Once I noticed it missing Mum drove me across to Brighton-Le-Sands, and we walked up and down the beach, then up to the (boy-search) cliff, but it was nowhere.

We happened to pass a junkie with black hair, and Mum freaked out saying, 'It's him! It's him! He was here on the night of your birthday, and now he's here *again*.'

And I'm like, 'So?'

And she's saying (in this embarrassingly loud voice) 'The Punchbowl stalker!'

She couldn't have been more wrong. I've seen the guy. And you've actually heard about him — he hung around your dad's flats when we were living there (a goth your dad told us to avoid). For a start, he was much taller than the guy shuffling along the street—I remember him having to duck under the clothesline when he was running across to the footpath. The guy Mum and I walked past in Brighton wasn't even up to my shoulder, and Mum had to admit that she'd only ever seen the fake-fingernail dude when he was crouching, so had no idea of his height.

I also pointed out that the guy at the beach was much thinner and that his eyes were bright blue and roundish, definitely not green like the goth's. Artists tend to notice things like eye colour and orbital shape. As my art teacher would say: 'If you're naturally artistic, your visual sense is highly developed'!!

Ah well. I'd better get on with the *What's Going on in My Family* 'Private' Journaling Project. I know Mrs Gunning says she doesn't look at what we write, just at how much we've written, but I'm not so sure about that, Sarie. When you're out of Ninth Grade and have to do this, just make sure you don't scribble down anything you feel would cause major embarrassment to your folks!

See ya tomorrow.

Izzie

WHAT'S GOING ON IN MY FAMILY
By Izzie Redding—Year 10 English 3B—Mrs Gunning

My mother, Rosetta Melki, is currently away on a trip to Christchurch in New Zealand, and I'm staying at her friend's place in Bondi. She got a letter about a will she is to share with her biological brother, Bobby, who she'd never met.

Her mother and my true grandmother, a woman neither of us knew about, was a singer. Her name was Daniela Ryland, but she went by the stage-name of Danna Nolan and became an international success.

Mum's biological father, Miguel Demalza, an economist and Member of Parliament, was Minister for the Arts in New Zealand between 1971 and 1983.

My grandmother was 19, unmarried, still at school and singing in a trio ensemble on Friday nights at a Christchurch restaurant when she fell pregnant with their child. My grandfather, a boyfriend for almost a year, had already broken up with Daniela a month before she found out. By that time my grandfather was back with a previous girlfriend, and he'd made that new girl his fiancée pretty darn quick. He had zilch interest in his newly born daughter. He feared media coverage of her arrival would put an end to his rising political career, so he ever so politely warned Daniela that if she spoke to journalists about their past relationship he would deny the child was his.

Since Daniela had no husband and no means to support her child, her parents insisted she adopt the baby out. She named her baby, unofficially, Odetta Sophia. If Mum hadn't been adopted, her name would have been Odetta Sophia Ryland. Daniela passed onto the adoption agency a request that her baby keep the first and middle names she'd given her.

A Greek couple with a family adopted Mum. George Melki did not like 'Odetta' for a name at all. Mum has only just discovered this information. A bit over a week ago, Mum found a way of contacting a long-lost foster aunt. The lady, a sister of my late foster-grandmother, remembers what happened. She said the man who became Mum's new dad had the name on a notepad while Mum was asleep in her cradle, and he crossed out the 'd,' in Odetta, replaced it with an 's' and added an 'R' to the front. And then he said, 'Now we're talking.' George Melki had a passion for Egyptian archaeology, and The Rosetta Stone was one of his favourite topics of conversation.

Amazingly, Mum was always a huge fan of Danna Nolan's singing. I've had a close look at some of the CD covers at home and can sort of see the family resemblance, although there's none of that sad, shy dreaminess in my mum's face.

It's great knowing more about our heritage. Danna/Daniela was an indigenous New Zealander (like Mum's friend Eadie, who looks a lot like Mum). My politician grandfather, Miguel Demalza, who died ten years ago from a heart attack, was Chilean-born, which makes Mum an Aussie Latino Kiwi and makes me, I guess, much less Australian than I thought I was. (Wish I'd inherited the olive skin tone but I'm stuck with my Scottish father's pale, red-haired freckliness!) Finding out I've got South American genes has been a pleasant surprise, however. I have always been drawn to Peru (and South American countries in general) and I do seem to be okay at the odd bit of Spanish, whereas the opposite is true of Greek. Despite Mum's best efforts at teaching me, I'm just not a natural, so maybe a smidgen of my true grandfather's language (and culture) flows sneakily through my corpuscles!

19 May 2008

C/-Gascoyne Luxure Hotel
121 Hakeney Way
Alice Springs NT 4484
AUSTRALIA

Dear Rosetta,
Well, here it is. Keeping fingers 'n' toes crossed it'll land on your brother's doorstep before your stay in New Zealand ends.

You'll probably be disappointed when you unwrap the crystal—they're only small, kind of like jagged slices of something larger, and they look like they've crumbled apart over time.

We discovered their rather ordinary appearance is deceptive. Within them lies a powerhouse of soothing energy that we're taking time out to research. Already we've sent a small boxful across to a geology lab. Scientists there have agreed to test them.

Tell me what you feel when you place it in your palm. Some of us have noticed changes in the stone's actual temperature, others get a mildly giddy effect. I probably shouldn't tell you that—don't want you to be unduly influenced!

Loved catching up with you on the phone on Wednesday evening. I miss my Friday Fortnight gal. Like I was saying in that call, discovering those crystals last year was the most profound thing that's ever happened to me.

Dalesford led us to the site—said an angel in a dream had shown him a map. He'd apparently woken up that morning with an exact location memorised. He sat in the backseat and lorded it over us, which annoyed the driver something terrible (the driver being me)! He argued over where we should go to set up camp. Jim Murray and Jannali and I had other ideas, and Jannali spoke sharply to him about back-seat driving. 'Leave Craig alone,' she said, but old Dalesford was like a dog with a bone. Insisted we were being guided somewhere important to our futures. So we went where Dalesford wanted, and just after dusk, set up our camp and lit a cosy little fire.

And then it happened. Like I was saying to you on the phone, we spotted a silver glow to the left of the campfire. That was when the apparition appeared. She was a stunner, this apparition. Reminded me a bit of you. Not in looks so much. She looked tribal—dark skin and even darker hair. The way she held herself: *that* was what reminded me of you. Upright in a stately sort of way with her hair flowing down her back, and her voice was low-pitched and resonant. All I could think in my befuddled state was that she must have been a Dreamtime ancestor. As you know, I was soon to discover who she was, and *man* was I surprised. You'd think a ghost appearing at our campsite would have been surprising enough without all those other revelations that ensued.

So about that job with our new company or my 'secret project' as it's (prior to now) been known. If the guy you told me about Matthew? Or was it Michael? (You said you met him at a send-off when he left his finance role). Well if whoever he is happens to be interested in our start-up managerial role, tell him to give me a buzz. We're screening with preliminary phone interviews, so he'd need to have the right sort of legal/financial experience. If he ticks all the boxes, we'll fly him up here for a face-to-face.

By the way, Soozi and I broke up on Thursday. Nah, no need to send condolences my way. We both knew it was inevitable we'd drift apart.

Yep, I'm on the loose again, so if you happen to know anyone compatible, send her my way (preferably a brunette bombshell with a strong social conscience and passion for soulful music). Don't suggest Eadie. Lovely girl, but she doesn't fancy me. Even if she did, we'd drive each other insane, and I don't tend to go for gigglers.

Email soon, OK?

Warm hugs,

Craig

To:........Isobel Redding
From:......Rosetta Melki
Sent:......21 May 2008
Subject:...Craig's Crystals Discovery

Hi Sweetie,

Home in two days, can't wait to see you again.

Craig is having an amazing time up in Central Australia/Northern Territory. He posted me a tiny, silvery pink crystal. It arrived at Bobby and Tanya's this morning.

On the phone Wednesday night, he told me an incredible story about how he and a friend of his, who used to work in the mining industry, had a profound experience last year. They'd been invited by Conan and Jannali Dalesford to a campfire sing-along one night in a place considered sacred in Alice Springs.

A being appeared before them!

She was transparent like a ghost, a shining goddess shrouded in autumn tones. Conan Dalesford felt sure this apparition was Orahney, the faerie Lillibridge wrote about. She led the group to a clearing in the wilderness and told them to scrape the dirt back. It wasn't long before chunks of glassy rock became apparent, crystals embedded in the red earth. Jim Murray had noticed a silver glow around the site. The being then said, 'They have emerged through erosion from deep within the ground. The time has arrived. Humanity must be silvered.' And then she vanished!

They've since discovered these crystals are quite bizarre. I don't know whether I'm imagining it, but the one Craig sent me seems to have an inner luminance if it's held for a certain amount of time.

Craig and Jim (and Jim's mining mates) want to start excavation to retrieve what appears to be thousands upon thousands of them. The gems they've discovered lie quite close to the surface, and so mining them won't be too difficult, and we'll only carry out processes that are ecologically sound. They're determined not to harm or deplete the earth.

They've all banded together to create a company with Conan and Jannali Dalesford and others, and Craig believes they'll never have to work again once the profits roll in. So far they've found multitudes of them, Izzie! Soon they'll be going through all the red-tape with the government, to make their company official.

I told Craig I definitely want to look into this. I haven't committed to anything. Craig's schemes in the past, as you know, have tended to amount to nothing. I hope with all my heart that this venture turns out to be lucrative and not some crazy fantasy that leaves Craig sad and sorry. The vision they had of Orahney is certainly a significant omen, but between you and me, the stone he sent looks suspiciously like a chunk of mica (the pearlescent stuff that's sometimes found on rocks). Pinker though. Less flaky too – *and* less fragile.

Craig now needs to employ a good finance person who preferably, like him, has a background in law. Economics too, if at all possible. I immediately thought of Sara Belfield's stepfather. Have you ever met him, Izzie? You probably haven't—you only ever mix with Sara at school or at Grant's.

I met him a few weeks ago at his work send-off. He was Adam Harrow's workmate. (The strains of 'It's a Small World' are currently playing in my imagination!!)

Izzie, could you do me a favour? I know this man's looking at setting up his own firm. I've only met the guy once, but he mentioned to me that setting up his legal firm would take time. He's left the place where he was working alongside Adam, and it so happens that Craig wants someone who can work independently, but he needs someone fast. I'd like to give Sara's stepdad the benefit of this information if he's at a loose end work wise, because he appeared to be easygoing and honourable, and I feel he'd get along well with Craig if he took the offer up.

The attachment I've included with this email is a small note. Could you please print the note up, pop it in an envelope marked 'Mr Matthew Weissler' and hand it to Sara at school tomorrow?

Thanks, honey. Will phone you tomorrow afternoon. I would have phoned now, but we're about to go out to a swish restaurant and won't be back till late.

I hope you're making a list of all the best venues you and I will be dining at once I'm back!

I'm having such a fabulous time finding out about your uncle and aunt. We've been having fun with tarot and Rune-stone readings. Tanya's into all that stuff too. She meditates every day, and she's currently doing a course in crystal therapy. Naturally, she's eager to hear all she can about Craig's new company, and Bobby is interested in the Alice Springs crystals too, but from more of a financial perspective.

Love and kisses,
Mum

Chapter Six

Diondra tucked a strand of platinum hair behind a diamond-sparkly ear. 'Thanks for meeting up with me, Matt. I really hate those get-togethers. They serve the canapes too late and then you're expected to listen to hundreds of speeches.'

'No problem,' Matthew said. 'I was in the CBD anyway, so it seemed to suit us both okay.' A wasted trip. Crystal Consciousness did not have *Our True Ancient History.* Diondra's tennis 'do' had run over and she'd texted him to say she'd be an hour late. Why Diondra had insisted they meet in the city rather than some local haunt like the surf club cafe, Matthew couldn't fathom.

Crystal Consciousness hadn't delivered at all. He'd found neither the book nor Rosetta, who he'd stupidly referred to as 'Lucetta' before Grant corrected him the other week. When she'd turned up with Adam Harrow at the bar for his retirement send-off, Matthew hadn't immediately realised he'd seen her somewhere before. She'd looked different at night with her hair up. The first time he'd encountered Rosetta had in fact been on a detour to that shop.

He hadn't known the name of the shop back then. He and Harrow had been marching towards the parking station, discussing the Greenknowe takeover. Harrow had called his fiancée to let her know he was on his way home, and Matthew had unthinkingly wandered into Crystal Consciousness alongside him. The first item he'd seen in there was a cleverly designed poster of an enchantress of some sort. Her body was draped in autumn leaves, and her eyes held a mystique that intrigued him. She stood by a tree that had a window built into its trunk. It was familiar, that poster, and yet he couldn't remember having seen it previously.

He'd turned to ask a shop assistant about the poster's artist, and that was when he saw her. Eyes of light-brown, as compelling and as passionate as those of the enchantress. Long, lavish hair, unruffled demeanour, a confident desirability that couldn't be ignored.

He'd straightened his tie and stepped towards her, but Harrow was already there at the counter, false charm oozing from every pore, pointing out a picture of crows to Ms Voluptuous as an excuse to get chatting and verify her 'single' status, making a grand show of purchasing Dalesford's *Thoughts on Tomorrow's Tycoon War* before binning it once he was out of sight. Harrow's insincere posturing had worked. The girl turning up at the bar with him was a testament to that.

And then Matthew happened upon her again, at Grant Belfield's of all places. He'd gone there to collect Laura and Sara from a weekend at their dad's. That she'd ditched Harrow was hardly surprising. A smart girl like Rosetta wouldn't have taken long to wake up to Harrow's sleaziness. Grant was a much nicer bloke. Didn't seem to be Rosetta's type though.

The café Diondra had arranged to meet him at was closing. Matthew pointed out a bar across the road.

Diondra, tottering beside Matthew in heels that were red and dangerous said, 'I'd prefer a bar anyway,' and placed a chummy hand on his elbow.

'They rationed the plonk at your tennis get-together did they?'

Diondra sighed, smiled and said softly, 'Nuh-uh. I know my limits, Matthew.' They neared the King Street crossing. At the pedestrian lights, Diondra squealed. Matthew turned to find her leaning forward with her arms flailing. One of her towering heels had lodged in the paving. Matthew dashed across to steady her. She clasped his elbow again, this time for support, and smiled up at him. 'It's just that I like bars better. They're more intimate.'

An unusual description. Sticky-floored venues were always too dark and noisy. If you shared secrets that were—in Diondra's words—'intimate', you had to contend with the knowledge that you were sharing them with half of Sydney. Secrets weren't really secrets when yelled loud enough to compete with digitised sound-systems.

Diondra liked that the bar had a white-washed exterior and potted plants. Said the geraniums added vibrancy to its iron-barred balconies. Diondra made a beeline for the bar. He got her the boysenberry blush she requested and himself a light ale, then directed her to the courtyard so that whatever was troubling her could be confided quietly.

'But *I* want to go *here*,' Diondra said, putting on the same face Bernadette adopted when she 'really, really, really' wanted something. The table was bang-smack next to the dance floor. One centimetre further over and it would have been *on* the dance floor. Matthew placed Diondra's glass down as she settled into her seat. Groovers with their backs to him were striking poses. Sitting at eye-level to swivelling butts made Matthew uncomfortable. To avoid being mistaken for a perving desperado, he turned his chair further round to face Diondra.

The drumbeats quickened. Diondra took a hurried sip of her boysenberry blush, then promptly morphed into a hyperactive chair dancer. The awkwardness of her actions called up an image for Matthew of one of Jim Henson's fuzzy creations, complete with self-conscious grin. Considering they were there for a serious talk, head-flicking, shoulder-shrugging and finger-clicking didn't seem appropriate.

Had to be about money. Why else would Diondra set up a meeting? The Wallaces' lifestyle probably exceeded Dominic's salary. It wouldn't have been the first time Matthew had given financial advice over a drink. Short-term loans from his personal account too, if the circumstances warranted it.

He began with, 'So what's Dominic up to lately?'

Diondra halted her rhythmic shrugs. 'How should I know? I'm hardly the first person he tells when he's "up to" something.'

Matthew pretended to study the label on his beer bottle. He didn't quite know what to say to that. He'd never been comfortable with Dom's disrespect for Diondra, and the only man impressed by Dom's extramarital exploits throughout those one-sided blokey conversations was Dominic Wallace himself.

Diondra was yet to say why she wanted to meet up. Once discussion about the Wallaces' renovations and school holiday travel plans dwindled, Matthew took the reins of their conversation. Defaulting to his managerial side he leaned back in his chair, as he'd often done with anxious staff members, adopted a pleasant tone and said, 'Okay, Diondra. Shoot.'

Diondra folded her arms and looked down. Both sides of her bobbed hair swept forward and settled at either side of her mouth. Dressed in a style he admired: the smart urban career-woman look, somewhat deceptive considering Diondra hadn't worked since her early twenties when she'd modelled casually for Myer. Ornately chic. Exaggeratedly aware of the blatant masculine attention directed at her from across the bar.

His thoughts drifted to Rosetta again, an enthusiast who probably worked hard. Human Rights was her area, so why Crystal Consciousness? He didn't doubt Rosetta's capabilities, but juggling a legal career and a retail business wasn't something everyone could do. Might have been taking a break from law. He would have liked purchasing *Our True Ancient History* from a shop belonging to someone he knew.

'It's about Dette,' Diondra said.

'About Dette?' Matthew straightened. 'Why? Have you heard something? Is everything okay with her?'

'She's...' Diondra looked down again.

'She's what?'

'She's *not* in danger as far as I know, if that's what you're asking.' Diondra took a sip of her drink and pursed her lips. She made an elaborate gesture of readjusting the lace-edged neckline of her cream silk blouse and smoothed a hand over the central button of her tailored jacket. 'The Dette I grew up with was never the sophisticate you married.'

Surprised at the randomness of that statement, Matthew paused to take a swig of his beer. 'I never said she was.'

'But all this talk about being a *lady*. And all that pride surrounding her great-uncle mingling with royalty throughout his childhood. It's just bluff. She's trying to hide the fact that the Doultons weren't exactly...financial.'

Trying to make himself heard over the deejay's *doof-doof* monotony, Matthew said, 'I hardly think that's relevant to us. What the Doultons were worth isn't anyone's business.'

'But Matthew! It explains why Dette's so obsessed with spending! She sent Grant broke. And now...' Diondra lifted a shoulder and gestured to Matthew with a flick of her hand. She attempted an unnatural smile. 'Where do you think we first met, Dette and I?'

'Not so sure. At some beauty activity I think she said.'

'The Grooming and Deportment course that the school put on over the summer hols?'

'Right.'

'Wrong. She misled you, but I already knew Dette would never admit to the truth. Not even now. We did go to the course, and that's where we "officially" became friends. Truth is, neither Dette nor I wanted to admit that we actually first met in the school's second-hand clothing shop.' Diondra chewed her lip. 'At the time, we were both as miserable as each other, knowing that the people raising us were so badly off. They wanted us to have a posh education, and yet they couldn't afford new uniforms! How crazy is that?'

'You wouldn't have wanted to be me. I was sent to a public school.'

'That's not the point, Matt. You would have been liked wherever you went. Dette was rejected by her classmates. They called her a "try-hard" because she talked in boring cliches like an elderly toff and never wore the latest brands.'

'Kids can be cruel.'

'Dette was lucky to have me for a friend. I was more shrewd. I've always had a flair for getting included. I'm adaptable, Math-yoo. I can zone in on people's expectations and live up to them. So I helped Dette wise up. Eventually, we got to befriend some exclusives. The girls in that clique all had fabulously successful families. Once we got accepted amongst them, we got to surround ourselves with fascinating people, and...what can I say? The rest is history.'

'I appreciate you sharing all this, but is that all you had to tell me?' Trying to make light of Diondra's bland declaration, Matthew added, 'I was expecting something more scandalous.'

'I hate having to tell you this, but you won't be disappointed.'

Matthew shifted in his seat.

Diondra appeared to be enjoying his concern; her smile had become authentic. 'Dette was tough-minded. Always said she didn't care who she married, as long as the guy was rich. She thought having wealth would take away the shame of having been poor, but if you ask me, she's no happier. And she's just horrible to you, Matt. I know she is.'

'I wouldn't say that. Look, I realise you'd know by now that the two of us haven't been getting on, but I'm just as much to blame.' Trying to deflect the discomfort of Diondra's candidness, Matthew checked his watch. 'I'd better get moving.'

'Do *not* go!' Diondra sighed, turned away, and made a dramatic show of scowling at a guy who was trying to attract her attention with a gap-toothed grin. She turned back and watched Matthew steadily with round, doll-like eyes. 'I'm about to tell you something bad, Matthew, so please. Stick around. I wouldn't reveal any of it if I didn't respect you. But I just don't think it's fair.'

'You don't think what's fair?'

A drumbeat trebled an angry finale and simpered into silence. The deejay zipped across to the bar. The butt-swivellers sauntered off the dance floor.

'What *she's* doing to you.'

'But she's not doing anything.'

'You sure about that?'

'Well, I mean—'

'She's cheating on you.'

'Huh?'

'Your wife is sleeping with another man.'

Matthew took in a slow breath. A lie most likely. 'Diondra, what makes you say this?' He allowed the air to seep from his lungs. 'How can you know for sure?'

A fabrication. It had to be. Diondra was known for her acts of revenge. An undercurrent of competition ran continually between the two friends. Bernadette's regret at her own modelling career having comprised three photo-shoots for Furphy's Furniture was a major example of this, and both she and Diondra got mighty catty when they disagreed. Bernadette cheating? Not a chance! She was nothing if not loyal.

Diondra placed both hands upon his and watched him with an expression that didn't seem to match the situation. Playful, that's how she looked. Not serious, concerned, apologetic, upset. A practical joke? Not likely. Diondra was no kind of prankster. 'She's seeing an ex-colleague of yours.'

'Ex-colleague?'

Diondra nodded regally.

'I'm really sorry, but I find that hard to believe.'

'I've brought along proof.' Diondra picked up her handbag and unzipped it efficiently. Matthew was sceptical. What was she going to produce from the bag? 'Exhibit A' a pair of monogrammed men's underpants? Instead, she brought out her phone. Despite the absence of deejay music, Matthew hadn't heard it ringing. All he'd heard was the pounding of his pulse at Diondra's improbable revelation.

She passed him the phone. 'Press that button,' she instructed. 'I've saved a couple of her voice messages.'

Following the deeply humiliating process of hearing his heart-of-stone wife...Correction...*Ex*-wife...jabbering between high-pitched laughter about the 'sublime' body of the man Matthew wanted to smash apart with his fists, he gave a nod and excused himself. 'I have to go home,' he said. His voice had become a monotone growl. His brain had turned to molten rock.

Bernadette incriminating herself. Between hiccup-style giggles, she'd uttered a name that had made the bile rise in his throat.

Adam loves that sort of thing. Adam says I need to eat more. Adam loves sending roses.

Adam.

Adam Harrow.

Matthew's thoughts flicked back to the send-off. Rosetta standing alone...Bernadette and Harrow seated cosily on a two-seater...Harrow giving Bernadette the daiquiri meant for Rosetta.

Warding off vile images of that despicable bastard all over Bernadette, he said a sombre goodbye and made his way to the door.

Diondra click-clacked after him and looped her arm through his. 'I'm sorry I had to come with such bad news.' Her voice rang with satisfaction.

He was up with the truth now. Should have been relieved. Couldn't help thinking, though, what a sly act it was of Diondra's to replay private voice-mail. How would she feel if he'd replayed everything Dominic had said during those torturous golfing-green brags? Matthew couldn't do that to Diondra. It would hurt her to hear about Dominic's dripping-with-decadence frack shack.

Did she think she was doing him a favour? He'd never voiced any suspicions. Why did she feel she had to protect him from Bernadette? Matthew was quite capable of sorting it all out. The marriage was soon to be over anyway. He would rather not have known he was the target of Diondra's pity, that he was the fool in the middle, the ham in the sandwich—laughed about by the gutless creep who'd lured his wife away from him—totally unaware he'd been the object of trickery. Trickery! The bloody runes hadn't been wrong about that.

'If ever you want to go out in future, Matthew. You know what I mean, to...talk.'

Engulfed in a seething daze, blinking from the glare of streetlights that met his sight once they'd exited the dingy bar, Matthew turned to Diondra, only to become aware of a previously indistinguishable vibe. Enlarged pupils. A grip on his arm that had tightened. The frantic moth-wing flicker of brown-dusted eyelids. It struck him then. She was flirting. Giving him the eye in a tense and graspy lunge. His sympathy for Diondra in relation to Dominic's infidelities lessened a little. The trust in that marriage was markedly zilch. With a shock he realised his own marriage had disintegrated into something similar.

'Well?' Diondra said, and her smile was hopeful. 'Do you think we might see each other? For drinks again?'

'I don't think so, Diondra. As you may have noticed this evening, cheating wives don't do it for me.'

At home Matthew checked his account online and was hit with another slab of unwelcome truth. The credit card statement displayed twin purchases. Two of everything. Two airfares, two breakfasts, two dinners, two catamaran lunch cruises. Two. No kidding. The woman sure wasn't a Gemini for nothing.

The list continued. He logged out. He wasn't going to sweat over the remainder of Bernadette's double-dipping. The cousin's Vanuatu trip was supposedly a birthday present from the cousin's parents. As Matthew understood it, Bernadette had been shouting no-one.

He made a call to the hospital to ask Bernadette's grandmother a vital question. He'd been going to call her mid-week anyway, to tee up their visit on the weekend. Upon his request, Grandma Carmody amiably read aloud the phone number belonging to her granddaughter, Marguerite.

Pushing away the ghastly memory of black ringlets and curling talons, Dette gazed at Adam in the passenger seat beside her. She glanced out of the too-small window where, 30,000 feet below, a grey ocean as vast as the love she felt for him gleamed in crinkled dents, like aluminium foil.

'How long to go now?' Dette asked him.

Adam stared at his watch and twisted his mouth to the side. 'Another twenty to thirty minutes.'

'And then?'

'And then what?'

Dette pushed her hand into Adam's tanned one and ran her thumb across the golden hairs on the backs of his fingers. She offered him a trio of suggestions. 'Option A: we'll go out to dinner, Option B: we'll eat at your place and you can demonstrate your culinary skills, Option C: we'll skip dinner and allow our beautiful holiday to end with a bang.'

Adam cleared his throat and shifted in his seat. With downcast lids he said, 'Shouldn't you be getting home to your kids?'

To avoid the ageing effects of frowning, Dette jutted her lower lip. 'Of course I should, but I'm sure they'll survive an extra night without me. They're very independent, my girls, just like I was as a child.'

In answer to that, Adam went to sleep. He reclined his seat and pressed his head against it, nose tilted in the air, face dominated by the two black holes that were his nostrils, mouth an unflattering oval. Strands of saliva clung to the corners of his sun-chapped lips. For the first time since she'd met him, Dette looked upon Adam's appearance with disdain. Could it be possible she was falling out of love with him?

Not a chance. She was angry, that was all. Angry that he wasn't taking her seriously about wanting to be together in those last precious hours before she returned to mundanity and Matthew. Poor Adam. Dette felt sure if he knew how ridiculous he looked right now—snarling as he exhaled, wheezing as he sucked his breath in again—that he'd be highly embarrassed.

Not going to Adam's tonight would really spoil her plans. At the island's internet café that morning she'd contacted Matthew to say stormy weather had necessitated putting off her flight. Another fib of course, but her situation demanded a 'cruel to be kind' approach. She hadn't bothered to run the email through Spell Check. At times Matthew's need to spell everything correctly was enough to make her yell: 'Words are just words!' Back in the early nineties though, she was grateful he valued the way words looked. He'd made his partners agree to a new reception-area computer with grammar-edit software. They'd been ready to replace Dette at Garrison Weissler Brumby, and the man who had a crush on her, the boyishly attractive lawyer who got tongue-tied whenever she spoke to him, had saved her job.

Ten years later, after she and Grant had been married and divorced, she'd waltzed into his new finance workplace after having tracked him down, and he'd asked her out. Within months she had snagged Matthew. And he'd treated her like a princess.

Adam sinking into a doze so quickly struck Dette as odd. The tightly shut eyes and disruptive snoring did tend to look exaggerated. Could he be faking sleep?

She sighed. 'Fake' seemed to be something Adam was supremely at-home with. Dette had discovered on the holiday that her lover's eyes weren't green after all. Those lively, pale emerald show-stoppers were the result of tinted lenses that Adam wore to mask an unremarkable blue. Purely cosmetic were these lenses; they had no actual sight-focusing function. Adam couldn't bear to be without them, because they made him 'so much more interesting'.

His preference for artificiality didn't stop there. Contrary to Matthew, who favoured the natural look on women, Adam only liked faces that were heavily made-up, and so Dette had felt obliged to forego her nightly cleansing ritual. Tina at Luscious would have a seizure if she knew the damage Dette had inflicted on her generally well-treated complexion.

Trying to shut out the wheeze and sigh of Adam's theatrical snooze, Dette slipped on Adam's iPod. Doctor Cyanide roared at her rudely. 'Gimme!' he screamed. 'More. More. *Moooo-wah! Moo-moomoomoo-moomomomoomoo...*' Thoroughly disgusted, Dette yanked off the earphones and folded her arms. Why had Adam resorted to grumpiness on their very last day together? Perhaps he was still sulking over the cancelled karaoke night. He'd wanted to sing 'Gimme' for her—God knows why!—and had even packed props for his Doctor Cyanide act. But if Honeymooner Haven didn't adhere to their program, then how could that have been Dette's fault?

Feeling heavy all of a sudden, she drifted off, only to descend into a dream about the event two days earlier that continued to haunt her. Rattling the locked bedroom door of the holiday cabin and calling out to Adam. Rushing outside to the cabin's garden in the hope of appealing to Adam through the window. A stranger in their room and no sign of Adam. Tangled black hair snaking down a cloaked back...black witches' talons...glassy, kohl-edged eyes watching her with icy amusement...

She awoke with a jolt, her mind murking with worry. Perhaps Adam was still angry at the accusations she'd made the other night. His apathy when he'd found her unconscious had been weighing on Dette's mind. And she hadn't liked the unfair remark he'd made about Matthew. Despite all the annoyances of her marriage, Dette could not agree that her husband was an arrogant creep. Nothing false about Matthew. The green of *his* eyes was authentic.

When Adam whined about going out for another stroll into the village for a bite to eat, Dette's stoic resolve to talk no more about the intruder all but combusted into flames. 'I *cannot* believe you ran from me,' she'd shrieked. 'You found me lying outside this cabin, unconscious, when that maniac kicked our window apart. You didn't even stay to see if I was all right!'

Adam's eyes had blazed with impatience. 'For the hundredth time, Dette, I was running to get help. You needed medical attention.'

'I'd fainted, Adam. I didn't need First Aid. I was recovered by the time the front-office man got there.' Sitting in the garden. Dazed and terrified. Shuddering at the memory of the intruder's glittering eyes. 'You couldn't cope with the situation. You panicked when you saw I'd blacked out, and you fled. I could have been killed by that...that—'

'No-one was there when I found you, Dette.'

'No. Just a blond man running away from the scene, according to another guest. I feel as if you doubt me. I feel as if you think I'm making it all up.'

'Well, it did sound a bit surreal. A girly looking guy in make-up leaping from our window then never being seen again? What are you on, Dette? LSD?'

'I am a wife and mother, Adam Harrow. I do *not* do drugs.'

To avoid further argument, Adam had flicked open his finance paper.

That had been yesterday evening. Today, as she gazed out of the plane's porthole at water, water, water...and even more nauseatingly boring *water*, Dette worried that the accusations she'd flung at Adam for not having hung around to protect her would sabotage the little talk they had to have. If only Adam could bring up the subject of living together! If only it wasn't all up to her! She wanted to tell him she'd redecorate his home to reflect the style of her own Georgian-inspired showpiece; that she'd treat him so divinely he'd feel utterly miserable when she wasn't around. Like Matthew, Adam would value her pampering, but it would be so much better than it had ever been with Matthew. Adam was her god, her idol, a rock she'd been able to depend on during her stormily uneventful days with Mr Nice.

The plane touched down at Sydney Airport, and Adam woke. Without uttering a word to Dette, he ambled through the airport ahead of her, marching through the glitzy blur of luggage checkouts, souvenir shops and fashion stores, then tumbled into a cab outside the foyer.

Infuriated he hadn't waited for her, Dette opened the cab door, darted in beside him and said, 'Hmmmph!' while the driver, still at the boot of the car, juggled their excess baggage in a huffy-puffy effort to make it all fit.

'Cabarita Heights,' Adam said once the driver climbed in.

This had surprised Dette. 'But I'm not going home!'

Adam didn't respond.

Dette snuggled against Adam's tensed shoulder. 'I don't want to let you go *yet*,' she cooed. 'I want to spend more time with you.'

'Oh?'

'Of course I do. You're not trying to get rid of me, are you, Adam?' She nudged him with her elbow and forced herself to giggle.

Adam drew in a deep breath and moved away from her. 'No I'm not,' he said. 'I'm not *trying* to get rid of you, Dette. I *am* getting rid of you.'

XLV

Eidred looked down upon her sleeping self as she rose upwards within a beam of silver. Was this ray of soft light she was travelling along the same substance from which silver cords were made? These etheric bonds, which streamed from sprites' hearts and connected them with The Dream Sphere, divorced them from their powers of beauty-creation when severed.

'No severing has taken place for me,' Eidred reminded herself. 'I have not passed over. I am only slumbering.'

She was now by a lake of deep blue. Its glassy smoothness was oddly familiar, and yet she couldn't recall why. There came the sound of music. Low and haunting. The soft, sweet whistle from a pipe made of reed. The piper was none other than her prince, emerging from a forest of pine trees.

It had all happened before, when she had first ever laid eyes on Pieter, or Adahmos as he was now known, when he, not quite a man, had thought her to be the autumn faerie in this lakeside world, just like Maleika had when she'd visited the palace.

Soon after first encountering her beloved-to-be, Eidred was drawn back to her earthly body. She'd seen impressions of her glimmering chamber and had ached to return to it. Instead she'd been transported lower, into the Nightmare Realms. The elf had tried in vain to prevent this from happening. Would she be returned to the Nightmare Realms again?

Adahmos drew to a stop when he saw her. Delightedly he said, 'So there you are, my Eidred!'

Eidred's first word to him was their daughter's devic name. 'Lunara...' she said.

'Our daughter is safe and well,' Adahmos assured. 'Angels are looking after her in the infants' realm. You look uncertain, Beauty. Do you not remember your former travels here?'

'Adahmos, whatever do you mean? I have only been to this place once before.'

'Ah,' said her prince, 'this is probably true. Except for the time I believed you to be another, I have not encountered you here by the lake.' He beamed and placed a kiss upon her cheek. 'You are confused still, Beauty. You are yet to regain your Dream Sphere memory. Soon though, you will. Soon you will remember the life you lead here when inhabiting your soul self, just like I have had to each time I visit.'

'How surprising!'

'So it might appear as a shock until you regain your fuller senses. Senses in the Dream Sphere are unlimited. In our world below we can only hear with our ears, see with our eyes. Touch and taste is segmented too.'

'Adahmos, I don't understand.'

Eidred's husband laughed. 'You don't need to understand. It just is!'

'When I was last here by this lake, you believed I was Orahney.'

'Indeed I did. And I see why. Your auric colours are strongly visible in the Dream Sphere and they greatly resemble hers. Orahney has already provided a solution to this puzzle.'

'It was the crystal under my pillow when I was young. The fragment from her wand.'

'Orahney's beauty-creation signature was taken on by your impressionable infant heart. Apart from your physical colouring, you are startlingly similar.'

'I thought I only went to the Nightmare Realms when slumbering.'

'Mostly you did. Simply by habit.' Adahmos gazed at the glimmering water. 'Being silvered by the crystal armed you with capabilities. You often tried to remain in the Dream Sphere but would allow yourself to be drawn downward. Eventually I taught you how to remain here. Do you not remember any of this?'

A memory flitted back to Eidred, a memory of her husband and someone named Alcor advising she had to avoid fearful thoughts. Fright and other destructive feelings would send her immediately to an inferior slumber world. She told this to Adahmos, and he agreed.

'You are gradually remembering where you go in your sleep. Now we shall travel to our Dream Master's realm.'

'Alcor ...' said Eidred vaguely. 'Yes, we must now see Alcor.'

Adahmos took hold of her hand. 'Everything here,' he said, 'is achieved with a wish. Wish yourself to the Devic Great Hall.'

Eidred did as instructed. For a moment, she and her beloved were encased in a multitude of singing stars, fragrant as spring blossom.

Taste of palest blue...Sound of peace...

The fluffy downiness of sunset entwined in a rosebud...

She blinked at the sight that met her, a hallway with a transparent ceiling of sea-spray and a bearded fellow who must have been Alcor, regarding them kindly. Alcor led them across to an archway made of pearls and told them, 'Your autumn faerie friend is here.' Two cherubs adorned in roses guarded these gates.

Adahmos turned to the Dream Master, frowning in confusion. 'Alcor,' he said, 'if Orahney is behind there, she has ended her existence below.'

In a voice as calm as the sea on a windless day, Alcor said, 'This Clan Watcher died of a broken heart.'

Eidred thought of the guard, in eagle form, who Rahwor had turned to stone. With sadness she remembered Orahney's tortured wails.

'Ah well,' said Adahmos, all too cheerfully, Eidred thought. 'You are evidently aware, Alcor, that Eidred and I are to be here for one-hundred season-cycles. It is as though we are passed away too. We can spend a great deal of time with Orahney.'

'You are not here for as long as you think, Pieter,' said Alcor. 'Orahney will tell you more.' He nodded to the rose-clad cherubs. They drew open the luminous gates. Beyond them a rainbow cloud floated invitingly. Adahmos bounded into the blur of colour. Eidred, hesitating, stood back.

'Off you go, dear lady,' Alcor said to her.

'Alcor, sir,' said Eidred. 'I trust this means my husband and I won't risk death by entering that part of the Dream Sphere.'

'You trust correctly,' said Alcor. 'Your dream self will return to your slumbering self in the Grudellan Palace grounds. You and Pieter are simply visiting someone who is here until her next incarnation.'

For a sickening moment, Dette stared at Adam, aware her eyes were blinking uncontrollably. In a toneless voice she said, 'Please don't joke. You're making me nervous.'

Their cab pulled out of the rank and lurched onto the road.

'I wasn't joking, Dette. Didn't you get it? I'm getting rid of you.'

She stared at him, disbelieving. Tears flooded her vision, turning the image of his uncaring face into a wobbly blob, a funhouse-mirror reflection that taunted her with its parody. 'I don't understand! You love me! You *told* me you loved me! You...you even hinted at us living together.'

'I did not.'

'You did so! You said, "I could sleep with you, Dette Weissler, every night, for the rest of my life." You said it Thursday. Don't you remember that?'

Adam snorted. 'Did you happen to be horizontal at the time? Driver, change of plan. Can you drop me off first? Vaucluse. Chanteaux Parade.'

'No problem.'

To Dette, the driver's voice sounded faint. Too faint. Everything though—the traffic outside the cab whizzing along beside them, the rumble of the engine—*everything* was drowned out by the drumming of her terrified heart.

This couldn't be happening. It wasn't how things were meant to go. What had she done to anger him? Whatever it was, she needed to patch it up, and she needed to patch it up fast. Matthew's actions equalled a man getting tired of a relationship, but Adam found her irresistable. What had got into him?

'Dette, thanks for the great time. Flings are fun, hey? Truth is, like you, I have someone.'

Barely able to sputter the words, Dette said, 'You...you...haven't, you haven't. You...' Shock prevented her uttering anything more.

'I'm engaged, Dette. To a woman who's beautiful. And witty too.'

A greyness settled into Dette's heart. Her mind went into defence mode. Those carefully mulled-over objectives shrivelled rapidly into one searing desire: to remove herself from the double-crossing bastard who had, only seconds ago, shattered her self-esteem and smashed apart her happiness. She increased her voice to a shout. 'Stop the cab!'

Adam attempted to calm her. Without emotion he said, 'Come on, Dette, don't be unreasonable. Did I ever throw tantrums over you being married? To Weissler of all people?'

'So this is revenge! You're getting back at me!'

'Now that's delusional, Dette, don't you think? Keep going, driver. Vaucluse.' He drew close, lens-tinted eyes glittering greenly. 'I thought I told you I couldn't give a hundred percent. In the whole scheme of things, Dette R Weissler, you're actually of no importance to me.'

'Stop the car now!'

A confused voice from behind the wheel filtered through to the back. 'Do I stop?'

'Whaddya think I just said?' Dette glowered at the back of the driver's head.

They drove on in silence until the cab driver found a safe spot to park.

'Get *out*,' Dette screamed. She slammed her fists down hard against Adam's biceps, screeching hysterically, clawing at his jacket, slapping at his face. 'Get out! Get out! *Get out!*'

Ducking and cringing, Dette's golden-skinned deserter exited the cab. Dette spun round to the window to make sure he was gone. She jumped. He was peering at her smirkingly through the open car window. In a rasping whisper he said, 'Don't forget to thank that idiot of a husband of yours for treating me to Vanuatu.'

The exasperated driver groaned. 'So is it Cabarita Heights now?'

'Of course it is,' Dette said snappishly. But she couldn't go home. Not yet. Today was Thursday. Matthew wasn't expecting her until tomorrow. That final night was supposed to be spent at Adam's. 'Hang on.' She reached into her handbag for her phone. 'Forget about Cabarita Heights. Get me across to Punchbowl.'

Grant. She needed to see Grant. After that horrifying ordeal, Dette needed some loving. Kindness. Comfort. Assurance that she was both pretty and amusing from a man who had never really fallen out of love with her despite the seven-year span of their separation. She wasn't in love with her ex like she was in love with Adam...Correction...Like she *had been in love* with Adam, but Adam was a fake, a grimy illusion she'd been clueless enough to trust. Grant was someone she'd always been able to talk to. When Matthew was too busy celebrating or commiserating with co-workers, when Adam refused to answer her calls, when the world seemed to crumble around her crazily, Grant had always been there to listen.

Fingers shaking, Dette pulled the phone from her bag's inner pocket and texted Matthew with the words:

Calling in to couzin's once I get back towmorro to see her new furnashings. Home arund 3.30 p.m.

Guilt washed over her. How could she have favoured a two-timing low-life like Adam over a man who had only ever wanted to rescue her and make her feel safe? Everyone made mistakes. She'd be extra nice to Matthew once she got home.

She placed the phone back in her bag, annoyed that the cab driver hadn't started the motor. 'Can we get going, please?'

'So it's Punchbowl now,' said the driver. 'Are you sure about that?'

'Yes, driver.' Any minute now she would break into a torrent of endless sobs. 'Of course I'm sure! But *can* we get going? Soon would be good.'

'Bit of a comedown from Cabarita Heights,' the driver mumbled, and Dette noted the sarcasm.

'Shut up and do your job!'

The driver snorted. 'And begin driving again while your ex-boyfriend's still at the open boot?'

'Fine with me,' Dette flung back. 'More than fine. Aren't you supposed to be out there supervising him?' Quivering with hurt and fury, she wrenched open the door and marched around to the rear of the cab. Adam was undoing his suitcase to pack away the finance paper in his hand. 'What's the *fracking* hold up?' she shrieked. 'Forget about your precious little paper, Adam. Get out of my life. Now!'

Adam turned to her, his face devoid of emotion. Anger, amusement, scorn...anything would have been better than that automaton stare. He turned back to the boot and continued to unzip his case. Had he even heard her? The case flipped open. He tossed the paper into it, zipped it up, hauled it from the boot and walked away.

Dette stumbled backwards. Her heart contracted, as though gripped by a vicious hand. 'Oh God,' she squealed. 'Oh God!'

She couldn't have seen that. She couldn't.

But she had. She had seen everything in those past few seconds.

Everything she needed to know.

When Adam had opened that case, he'd cruelly and carelessly given himself away.

Settled at the top of his clothing had been a chilling heap of blackness. Coat, curls, claws. Splayed across Adam's case like a disembodied monster. A macabre token of that predatory chase.

An identity.

A perpetrator's disguise.

Dette staggered back to the cab. Grant's warnings about a stalker at his flats...her instructions to the girls to stay well away from the 'Goth guy' Sara's friend Izzie had seen by the clothesline...Grant's urgent voice telling her over the phone that the man had been found in an outdoor laundry, his barely audible words spurred by the concern that their daughters might hear.

Dette's skin prickled. The girls had been in Punchbowl when Izzie's mother discovered the intruder. *A lizard*, Grant had said gravely. 'She said he was threatening to eat a lizard.'

Adam Harrow did not deserve to exist. In Dette's ideal world, the scumbag was already dead.

She'd heard him tell someone in a phone call earlier that he'd be working a half-day tomorrow: that he'd be at home after two in the afternoon.

Grant. She was soon to see Grant, soon to stay there overnight.

And the next day...once Grant left for work...Dette would steal across to Vaucluse.

She could only hope that the leather pouch in Grant's wardrobe was still in the same place. She'd seen it two or three years back, after one of the many times Matthew had got narky at her for spending too big. She'd needed somewhere to sulk, and the comfort of Grant's arms had been the obvious solution. Grant's target-practice gun had been inside the holster, strung up on a coat-hanger beside the uniform he'd changed into the following morning.

But before she returned to Cabarita Heights, she would make Adam pay. He would need to be shown he could never go near her, or her daughters, again. Her last say. A crucial act of defence that she, as a mother, was forced to make.

She would make him pay for creeping around Grant's flats, and for terrorising her on the holiday.

She would not relax until she made Adam pay.

Chapter Seven

XLVI

Behind the gates within the Dream Sphere, Eidred discovered more cherubs, plump-cheeked and smiling. They directed her and her husband to a grove of autumn trees.

Orahney was sitting in the shade of an oak, bronze light playing on her hair. She rose, swept across and enfolded them in a hug. 'My dears,' she said. 'There is so much I must tell you.'

'Are you all right, Orahney?' said Adahmos.

The faerie was quick to reassure him. 'In the Dream Sphere, dear friend, I am always all right. In my next incarnations, though, I suspect I will have to carry the memory of heartache.' She turned to the oak and waved her hand across it. Within the tree's trunk appeared a window. 'Alcor and I have undone the time loop that resulted from your involuntary time-travel,' she said. 'It seemed that you would live two lives because of the Backwards-Winding. We have placed a seal on the life you lived before the Backwards-Winding took place, to prevent all cyclic repetition. You may now live a full life with Eidred when you awaken, and after that life is over, you may incarnate again in the world below, if you so choose.'

'Dear Orahney,' Adahmos said. 'I cannot thank you enough.'

'There is one condition though.'

Unable to contain her curiosity, Eidred cried, 'And what condition is that?'

'That the two of you remove yourselves from Norwegia. You must go to another land.'

Feeling as though her heart had dragged to a stop, Eidred said, 'Not Ehypte, surely!'

'You will go where the presence of Gold's Kin is naught,' said a mysterious Orahney. She gestured to the window in the tree. There before them was a visual account of the time-loop alteration. The faerie and Alcor were hovering above Norwegia, uttering incantations. A spiral appeared in the earthly sky, a spiral the colour of the lake Eidred had arrived at earlier.

'All in the palace will get a great shock when this is seen upon waking,' Eidred remarked.

'It will not be visible to them,' said Orahney. 'Although it will be possible to view one day. A few season-cycles before The Silvering comes about, the earth's devic frequency will strengthen. Many will see it above your land.'

'And when will that occur?' said Eidred. 'How old will my prince and I be when The Silvering descends?'

Orahney looked down wistfully. 'Not in your lifetime, Eidred,' she said. 'One day though. One day, many millenniums into the future, it will happen.'

'Then we shall make sure we incarnate at that time,' said Adahmos, and he gripped Eidred's hand warmly. 'If we are not living in Norwegia in our next lives, we shall journey there, just to see this beauty-creation symbol Orahney and Alcor have conjured.'

'Although it will not be known as Norwegia in that future time,' Orahney said. 'It will be known as "Norway". The blue spiral over Norway will be a puzzling phenomenon, although I daresay those who don't want Earth's people to believe in magic will trivialise it.'

'Will this happen in the same millennium as the Sonic Unity Gathering?' Adahmos wanted to know. 'There is a woman named Det-ah-wise-la who will help to return the world to its former harmony.'

'Ah yes,' said Orahney, smiling now. 'Yes, it is certainly the same millennium and divided by only a small number of season-cycles. I believe I, of all people, will have a part to play in this interesting future. Alcor is yet to tell me of all the lives I am to lead on the planet below.'

Eidred asked, 'Do you know, Orahney, what your next life will be?'

'I shall be a forest elf next time. This, as I understand it, is to be my destiny.'

Within the tree-window appeared the image of a crystalling. Eidred leaned forward to see. Within one of the Grudellan temples was a crib, with twelve bewitchers gathered round. At one end of the room stood the Solen and his chamberlain, four pterodactyls and an eagle-winged Crystal Keeper. A woman in a servant's cowl hovered beside the crib. 'My nursery maid,' Eidred exclaimed. 'This crystalling ceremony is mine!'

'Indeed it is.'

Eidred watched in fascination as Rahwor materialised from the ether, masked in an aged and feminine face, and clad in a hooded bewitcher's cloak. The scene played out just as her nursery maid had once told her. Rahwor snatched up the wand of one of the spell casters and ordained that Eidred die. He hurled the wand down, then vanished in a flash of smoke.

The twelfth former faerie, meek, rounded, and smaller than the others, took two steps forward. She held her fractured wand aloft and announced her blessing. 'The princess will not die. She will sleep. All of gold will sleep for one hundred years.' As the Solen turned to leave the domed ceremony hall, the benevolent bewitcher stooped to collect the broken half of the wand's crystal and tucked it hurriedly under the crib's pillow. It appeared that no-one except the nursery maid had noticed.

'Do you know who this twelfth faerie might be?' Orahney asked Adahmos.

Adahmos stepped closer to the tree window, paused for a moment, then gave a shout. 'This is no former faerie. This is an elf. A Brumlynd. My Clan Watcher Maleika, disguised as a bewitcher.'

Eidred clasped her hands together. 'Another faerie godmother!'

Through the tree-trunk window, the scene replayed again, but when due to announce the antidote to Rawhor's spell, the elf woman faded to nothing. Not even her voice could be heard.

'I have been puzzling over this future scenario ever since I arrived here,' Orahney told them. 'It seems to me that Maleika undoing most of the spell is only a possibility. It is fortune rather than fate. I believe I must find a way to send a message to her.' She turned to Eidred's husband. 'And I believe this is something you must assist with upon waking. You will be leaving here shortly. Neither of you are under the spell of a century-long slumber.'

'We heard Maleika's decree a moment ago though,' Eidred said. 'Maleika has ensured that all will sleep.'

In confusion, she turned to Adahmos. He was frowning, deep in thought. At last he fell into laughter. 'I understand now,' he said. 'Maleika said all of *gold* will sleep. You are not golden, Eidred. The crystal under your pillow silvered you long ago.'

'Precisely,' said Orahney. 'Both of you were expecting to sleep, and so you did.'

'And the fright from Rahwor's threats would have wearied us,' said Eidred, 'along with the shock of seeing Fripso in danger.'

'Wearying us too was the lateness of the masked ball,' Adahmos said. He placed a comforting arm around Eidred, and she nestled against his shoulder. 'We were expected to remain there well past dawn. 'Twas a night of endless rituals.'

'Very tiring those palace dances,' agreed Orahney. 'Especially for us, Pieter, with our devic nocturnal natures. Now listen closely, my dears. Freedom is soon to be yours, but there are three tasks you must carry out upon returning to your earthly lives.'

⊰⊱⊰⊱⊰⊱

Matthew re-read Bernadette's text from the day before. Her flight had been cancelled. She was remaining in Vanuatu another night.

He checked the internet for Thursday's flight arrival times. No cancellations. None.

'Matt!' Marguerite on the other end of the line sounded surprised.

'You enjoyed the holiday?'

'Uh, yes...I did!'

'So who got the window seat on the flight back?'

Marguerite, after a lengthy pause, mumbled, 'Bernie did.'

'Now, that can't be possible, Marguerite. Bernadette's flight's been delayed. Do you want to tell me the real story?'

A shocked hesitation. And then the sound of a gasp and a sob. 'Oh, Matt, I feel so bad! I'm sick of her doing stuff like this!'

'Doing what?'

'Using people. Getting people to cover for her. Paying them off.'

'She *paid* you?'

Silence.

'Did she pay you, Marguerite?'

'I've felt so guilty about it.' *Sniff!* 'I'll give you the five-hundred back. I'll get it across to you tomorrow. I'll...I'll send you a postal order so that you can—'

'The money's not an issue. Just tell me what you were covering for.'

'She...' *Sniff!* '...wouldn't say.*' *Sniff-Sniff!*

Matthew asked again, and Marguerite maintained she'd told him all she knew. She had no idea what 'Bernie' was 'up to.' All she knew of her cousin's trip was that Bernadette had an unnamed travelling companion.

He had a fair idea where Bernadette might be. He'd soon be putting a stop to her thinking she could get away with making an idiot of him.

Dinner was a Spanish omelette and broccoli in nutmeg sauce; Rhoda was now privy to his recent aversion to meat. He regretted once he stacked his plate in the dishwasher that he'd been too lost in thought to enjoy the flavoursome combinations.

He checked his watch. He'd be collecting the girls from their gymnastics class in half an hour.

The home phone rang. He answered it in the study.

'Is she back yet, Math-yoo?'

'Nope. Did you know something about that, Diondra?'

'Hmm, not really.' The words were said lazily, stretched into a slow sigh. 'Although nothing would surprise me about a bimbo like her.'

'I thought the two of you were buddies for life.' He'd said this almost, but not quite, in defence of Bernadette.

An answer was not forthcoming.

Impatient with the lack of response, Matthew pushed a hand through his hair. He needed to get Diondra off the phone in case Bernadette dared to call. If Bernadette hadn't been chronic at hanging up when phones went through to voicemail, this wouldn't have been a problem.

Diondra lurched back into the conversation. 'Who'd be friends with a liar like her?'

Increasing his grip on the phone, Matthew stared glumly at the pro-nup on his desk.

'I want to get this straight with you, Matt. I've never cheated on Dominic and I never plan to.' Diondra's voice had taken on an injured tone. 'I think you were unfair in assuming I was just like Dette.'

He thought back to them leaving the bar. Her suggestion of meeting up alone, his comment about cheating wives. Although Matthew knew he hadn't misread the situation, he made an attempt to smooth things over. 'Sorry about that. My mind was elsewhere.'

'Dominic and I are breaking up also.'

'Sorry to hear it.' Hardly a shock. He'd wondered how she'd put up with him throughout the years.

'And, Matthew...'

'Yes, Diondra?'

'I've got something really, really *really* important I have to tell you.'

Matthew drew in an apprehensive breath. Could there actually be more about Bernadette? Wishing he hadn't answered the phone, he said, 'And what's that?'

'I'm sorry about what I said tonight in the bar.' Instead of bar, Diondra had said *baaaaaaaa*. Severely plastered. Must have continued drinking the minute she'd got home. 'I realise it was a really bad time to...you know...' Her voice descended into a choked sob.

'Diondra?...Diondra...are you okay?'

'No, I'm not okay. I'm really upset.'

The admission made Matthew feel like a bit of a bastard. This was the second time in the space of an hour he'd caused a woman to cry.

Diondra hiccupped, apologised for hiccupping and continued slurrily. 'I've accidentally let my feelings show. But Matthew, it's been torture for me, it really has.'

'Look, don't worry about that.' He hardly thought it terrible of her to indicate how she felt about Bernadette's behaviour.

'But I *do* worry, Matthew. I worry all the time!' She was wailing now. Loudly. Matthew pulled the phone away from his ear.

'It's not my fault that I've adored you all these years.'

Matthew pressed the phone back to his ear. 'Didn't quite catch that.' Either he'd heard incorrectly or the alcohol had jumbled her words. Diondra's flirting with him in the bar earlier was little more than a whim born of boredom, and he'd extinguished it promptly with a bland retort.

'You heard me, Matthew. I love you.'

'We love everyone when we're drunk, Diondra.'

'You mean to say you didn't know?'

Ah no. She was serious. 'I...um...' Matthew tried to find the right words. 'Well it is a surprise.'

'Just like you, Matt, to not realise how attractive you are.' Her voice was cracking. She'd become weepy again. 'The only reason I'm drinking is because I'm down about you misunderstanding me.' Diondra went on to tell him that she thought he was amazing, that she'd always thought he was amazing, ever since he'd been introduced to her six years earlier, as her friend's new man. 'Oh, Matthew! This is *sooo* embarrassing.'

Just in time Matthew stopped himself from agreeing.

'Do you think, like, once *you've* broken up and *I've* broken up...' Diondra had taken on the same hopeful tone he'd noticed in the bar. 'Do you think you'd like to learn more about who I am?'

A friend of his ex-wife? An ex of Dominic Wallace? Never in a million years.

As kindly as he could, Matthew told Diondra he wanted to be on his own. He appreciated her honesty, he said, but would never regard her in the same way because of the 'friendship factor'.

Diondra had taken it well he thought. Up until he added he was sorry. 'It's your loss,' she snapped. She burst into another bout of hysterical sobs, then hung up sharply.

Matthew slumped into his seat and groaned. Why did he always manage to bungle that sort of situation?

That evening the notion of Bernadette and her gutless gigolo laughing about how they'd fooled him dominated his anguished thoughts. Harrow. Long before any evidence showed up, Matthew knew the bastard was slippery. Always knew he lacked severely in the dealing-with-people department, a conscience for a start, not to mention an ability to uphold the truth. Lila Donevski discovered this all too late. A year or so ago Lila confronted Harrow. Matthew had been standing next to the Xerox, discussing an update with a couple of other traders. They'd overheard Harrow's phone conversation, his setting himself up with a date that evening.

Lila's normally placid voice was shrill with shock. 'But Adam,' she'd said, and she'd said this pleadingly. 'What about us? You were taking me to see *Invasion of the Star People!* What's happening? We were going to the Blue Mountains on Saturday!' Her volume had risen with each word. Heads in the neighbouring cubicles swivelled. Pairs of curious eyes zeroed in on the pair.

'Not anymore, my friend.' Harrow had said it in a weird, serpentine rasp. To shut Lila out, he shouted to a staff member that he'd succeeded in getting Greenknowe 'by the balls'. The tough-guy boisterousness was a tormenting contrast to Lila's quiet bewilderment.

According to Celia, the two had been dating for the past few months. Celia was worried about Lila. In a matter of weeks she'd gone from assertive and vivacious to timidly jumpy. 'I get the impression he's not treating her well,' Celia had confided.

Lila had hurried out of the office. Matthew found her in the tea room, shuddering violently. 'I made a scene,' she mumbled. 'And I feel hot and cold and sad. Must be 'cos I'm sick. I was throwing up earlier. I don't want to go back in just yet. Don't want to face them.'

'Lila,' he'd said gently. 'Take the rest of the afternoon off.'

'But I've got all those deposits to do.'

'Celia's quite capable of taking over.'

'I'm sorry, Matthew. I've let my relationship rule me. I realise it's unprofessional. I'm—'

'No apologies. Go home and take it easy.'

As Lila got up to go, Matthew had added, 'If it's any consolation, I've been to *Invasion of the Star People* with the kids. It's not worth seeing.'

She'd nodded shiveringly. Attempted a smile as she clutched at her handbag in readiness to leave, but her chin wobbled. He'd wanted to add that Harrow wasn't worth seeing either. Not exactly appropriate for a boss to make this type of comment.

Nothing would prevent him from saying that now. He would gladly crucify the creep's reputation. Would, without hesitation, show him up for all the pathetic masks he cowered behind.

Getting a restorative amount of sleep turned out to be wishful thinking. After a night of glaring at the ceiling, roaming the neighbourhood and enduring the wide-awake ranters on pre-dawn TV, he phoned Celia at his former workplace and asked to speak to Lila. Celia told him Lila was suffering from pre-natal morning sickness and wasn't due at work until the afternoon, but she'd tell her to call Matthew as soon as she was in.

When he phoned again after midday, Lila was in a meeting. The third time he phoned she'd gone to arvo tea. He asked Celia to email her again.

By now it was 3 p.m. He was by this time wrestling an agonising gamut of emotions. Aside from his outrage was an overwhelming sense of disappointment in who Bernadette in reality was.

A lying, stealing, conniving user. Not only had she seen their marriage as a bottomless-pit gift certificate. She'd regarded his devotion as a convenience; had twisted to her advantage his pathetic belief in her loyalty. It wasn't as though he'd even expected all that much of her. Somehow he'd managed to tolerate her self-absorption. Decent human being, he'd thought, was a given. He'd been wrong.

Five-thirty in the afternoon. Still not home. She'd been due back two hours earlier.

The phone rang. Celia on the other line said, 'Lila's back, Matt.'

'Excellent. And Celia, can you tell me if Whatzizface is in the office?'

His former secretary's lovable hearty laugh rang out. 'The two of you were *such* wonderful friends! He went home early. All tanned and vain today. First day back from annual leave.'

'He's been on a holiday?'

'Yep. One of the French-speaking islands.'

Matthew's hand ached. He unclenched his fist and stepped away from the bookshelf he'd slammed it down on. Any mention of Harrow brought on a seething compulsion to fight, but fighting with inoffensive timber seemed pretty damned pointless.

'Very bourgeois today too. Sprinkling bits of bad Francais through all his conversations. Okay, Matt, I'll put you through to Lila now. Oops! Sorry darl, she's just picked up another line. Care to wait?'

'No probs.'

Piano music rang irritatingly through the earpiece. Flipping the trills onto speaker, he took up his mobile and texted the words, *Aware of your betrayal & want a divorce.*

'Lila Donevski speaking.'

'Lila!'

'Matthew! Hi! Sorry I haven't phoned you back until now. How are you enjoying retirement?'

'It's brilliant. Better than I could have expected.'

A text bounced back to him.

Feign.

He assumed she'd stumbled with the predictive text. Instead of 'fine' it had thrown out a word describing trickery. If she'd been more language-savvy she might have done that deliberately to quote her motto of deception. When it came to the art of feigning commitment, Bernadette was an unsung genius.

'Listen, Lila, I've got something to tell you.'

Another text beeped. This one said, *Will collect my stuff and the girls towmorro.* No inkling of an objection, not even a mild declaration of remorse. Just an efficient finished-with-you-anyway reply.

'Okay Matthew, I'm all ears. What have you got to tell me?'

'Lila, I've found out through friends that Harrow's up to his old tricks again. To make a long story short, I want to go and tell him what I think. Would you by any chance have his address?'

Matthew turned the key in the ignition. Impatience escalating, he punched in the destination. One-four-one Chanteaux Parade, Vaucluse. Harrow's address. His ex-wife's hideaway. No intricate directions necessary. Just follow the road to depravity.

The phone started up as he pulled out of the driveway.

'Yeah,' he said. Whoever it was had better be quick.

'Matthew it's me, Celia.'

'Celia, I'm in the car. In a hurry at the moment. I'll call you when I'm home.'

'This is urgent. You're on your way to Adam Harrow's I expect.'

Great. Lila had told Celia the reason for his call. Urgent did not sound good though. He pulled over to the side of the street. 'What's happening?'

'Matthew, I'm really sorry, but Lila told me you were angry with Adam and paying him a visit. Who's the current victim?'

'Look, Celia, you know I never got into office gossip. This is all pretty personal if you must know.'

'You've got me wrong. I'm *not* quizzing you out of idle curiosity. I'm concerned. Really concerned!'

'Sorry, Celia. We'll have to talk later.'

'Don't you *dare* fob me off!' Using the same words she'd used on her kids, Celia added, 'You will listen to me, and you will listen to me *now.*'

Matthew leaned back in his seat. 'Okay, Celia. Shoot.'

'I've gone into the bathrooms to call you privately. No-one's in here of course, but I'll have to be quick. There are things Lila's told me in confidence about Adam, which I won't reveal, but what I will say is that the man can't be trusted.'

Big revelation! The creep who'd been sleeping with Bernadette could *not* be trusted! Did Celia have any more of these obvious statements?

'Matthew, is this latest woman he's dating anyone I know?'

'Good question, but I'll pass.'

'You're going to his home. He'd have to have done something really bad for you to do that. Answer me this, Matt. Is someone we know in trouble?'

Matthew remained silent.

Celia's reply was exasperated. 'You *know* I'll keep your confidence.' She was right about that. Matthew had never known a more loyal secretary. 'For God's sake, Matthew! It's not like it'd be the first time you've ever confided in me. I've gone to your wedding! You've gone to both my kids' twenty-firsts! We've been through a bucketload of smiles and tears together.' True to form she added, 'The tears, of course, being exclusively yours.' In less tensing circumstances, Matthew would have grinned. Celia Owens was the weepiest person he'd ever known. Working alongside her for eleven years had turned him into a veteran comforter. In Celia's better days, once she'd got over the heartbreak of divorce and remarried, he'd been pleased to note that the tears she'd thereafter shed were happy ones. 'And what's more,' Celia said, 'you sound stressed. Can't you tell me what's happening?'

Admitting an enemy had hoodwinked his wife was humiliating beyond belief, but Celia might have suspected this had happened; could even have valuable information on where Harrow went after having worked his half-day.

He thumped his fists down on the steering wheel. And then he relented. 'It's Bernadette,' he said. 'I'm pretty sure she's there with him.'

'Oh my God,' Celia said. 'My God!' She was almost as freaked as Matthew had been when he'd found Bernadette out. 'Matt darling, I'm scared for your wife.'

'What is it?' His fingers tightened around the ignition key. 'What's going on?'

'Matthew, I'll let you go. You've got to get over there.'

'That's the plan.'

'You've got to get there fast. I've reason to believe he's dangerous.'

'A creep for sure, but...Expand on dangerous for me, will you?'

'Let me put it this way.' Celia's tone was quick and low. 'There's a code amongst us girls when we're working late. If he's leaving at the same time any of us are leaving, we go back into the office and wait until he's gone. No remorse. No conscience.'

Bernadette in danger. Harrow a threat to her safety.

'None of us get into an elevator with him if we're alone,' Celia was saying. 'He...he's...I won't say much, but Lila and one of our juniors here experienced violence. Jarrod Turner's pushing for Adam's dismissal. Dette shouldn't be anywhere near Adam Harrow. I'm serious, Matthew. The man is twisted.'

On the homeward-bound flight, Rosetta reclined in her business-class seat, smiling rapturously. Clouds outside the porthole were pinkly yellow in the afternoon light, a whirly conglomerate of party-meringue pastels.

Jubilance in its purest form had rarely left her during her stay with Bobby and Tanya. She hadn't realised how much she'd missed belonging to a family. Her three foster siblings, the people responsible for bullying her throughout her childhood, had been strangers for a long time. Age hadn't mellowed the Melkis. Attempts at reconnecting with them were always met with a chilly sort of indifference.

For the first time in years, Rosetta felt safe. Secure. Part of an exclusive club that bestowed her with the role of sister to a man she admired as a person. Apart from her daughter, the jewel of her heart, she mostly attributed the word 'family' to her longstanding friends, the Friday Fortnighters. They had never let her down. Once she'd finished high school and fled the prickly nest that rarely felt like home, friendship had made her feel more welcome in the world. So had motherhood, the phenomenal transformer well-known for its realigning of a woman's priorities. Bringing up Izzie had illustrated that the gift and receipt of love hadn't eluded her as it had in her youth.

Knowing Izzie would be comfortably off for the rest of her life was a joy. Rosetta now wanted to ensure Izzie would continue with her studies and that she'd find a sense of purpose through career rather than the shallow aimlessness a cushy lifestyle might encourage. Izzie wasn't drifter material though. The teen had rarely shrunk from challenges. Winning an animal rights award for zealous door-to-door collections was pretty impressive, and appearing on the evening news for having struck up a friendship with a Swedish prince was something Rosetta might one day have a chuckle about with Izzie's future children.

Beyond the plane's wing, clouds had cleared to reveal an expanse of turquoise. Water, water...and more inspirational water. The impact of the shock was yet to fade, but Rosetta was growing accustomed to the idea of wealth. She'd now ceased to shake her head and whisper to herself, 'It happened to *me*. Of all the people there are in the world, this incredible luck chose me!' When she wasn't marvelling at her astounding good fortune, she was thanking her guardian angels. Someone had to be responsible for granting her philanthropy wish, and any of the celestial beings rumoured to watch kindly over humankind could well have been Lady Luck.

One of those angels might have been Molly Carr. Hadn't Molly hinted in the dream that Rosetta needed to track down her heritage? Hadn't she told Rosetta that her name didn't sound quite right? The old name would still be retained. People who already knew her couldn't be expected to change it.

Few would have believed the story of Molly Carr. Thank goodness for the Friday Fortnighters! Lena, Eadie, Royston, Darren, Craig...They'd all assured Rosetta she wasn't crazy when she'd confided in them about that weirdly real dream and disappearing rabbit. One minute she was dozing on the verandah while waiting on a new tarot client, the next she was hastening across to Izzie's netball club, after waking to find that the wind had slammed and locked the front door.

She'd retrieved the house-key from Izzie's bag, accepted a lift home from well-meaning stranger Molly Carr and offered her the tarot reading meant for the client. That was when Molly had taken over Rosetta's role as tarot reader. Insisted the man in her future was the man Rosetta had nicknamed 'the GEG', a.k.a. the Green Eyed Guy. Pity Molly hadn't told her the man in her future was temporary. It would be difficult now to view any GEG without a certain amount of doubt. Adam Harrow had prejudiced her against green-eyed guys for life. If auras happened to exist, Rosetta's was from this moment onwards a GEG-free zone.

A voice, richly baritone, returned Rosetta to the present. 'Can I get you a tea, ma'am? Or a coffee?'

Wait a minute, she imagined herself saying. *Haven't I put a ban on you guys?*

A handsome thirties-ish *green-eyed* man was grinning at her from the other side of his tea trolley.

'Good afternoon, this is your captain speaking.' The inflexion was smoothly relaxed and Australian. 'We trust you've enjoyed your flight so far on this bright winter's day. It's a cool sixteen degrees Celsius in Sydney. We'll be landing in another ten minutes.'

Rosetta's thoughts returned to that mystifying, realer-than-real dream about the eccentric fortune teller. When Molly Carrr had scrambled into that dilapidated car, said goodbye to Rosetta and knocked over both wheelie bins on her exit from the driveway, Rosetta had woken – *again* it seemed, and yet the fact transpired that she'd never woken in the first instance. No locked front door, no walk to the netball courts, no Molly Carr. No rabbit. That had been the only odd part of her dream. Molly's grey-splodged white rabbit, who Molly called 'Curry'. Stood on its hind legs in the backseat, face half out of the car's open window, ears flapping backwards in the breeze.

Curry appearing in real life the following week had been more than a little disturbing. A rabbit she'd dreamt of lolloping through the garden! She'd said to her book group, 'The rabbit just vanished!' Told them how she'd tried to prevent Curry from leaping in front of an oncoming vehicle, a Jag of shining red, and how Curry had faded to nothing. Ghosts had been Eadie's explanation. Prophetic Molly Carr and her car-dodging bunny. Benevolent spirits able to visit dreams. Spooky. And too mind-boggling to fathom.

Rosetta reached for her notepad and scanned the schedule she'd mapped out in Christchurch. Top of the list was checking out those crystals. Were they as amazing as Craig made them sound? They'd so far inspired, Craig had said, sudden flashes of enlightenment, and each epiphany had been different, although mostly surrounded a comforting feeling of harmony, a strange new sense of goodwill towards everyone else in the world. In his last email Craig told her that crystal purchasers were also reporting complete reversals of physical ailments and that Conan Dalesford believed anyone who wore them close to their hearts was promptly enveloped in a sense of peace.

She took a satin cosmetics purse from her carry-on bag and re-trieved the capsule-sized sliver of rock that Craig had sent express to Bobby's address. Not mica as previously feared. Craig had wanted to know if Rosetta could sense anything calming or enlivening when holding the crystal. She'd reported back to him the bubbly sensation she'd felt upon pressing it to her heart but added that this feeling was pretty much more of the same. Since meeting her adorable mystery brother and then hearing of Daniela's startling inclusion of her when the will was read, she'd radiated delight. That and the humbling grati-tude for a mother's far-sighted generosity towards a daughter she'd never known had fluctuated of course. Guilt over having never located Daniela was a constant throughout the New Zealand trip. 'So I'm a difficult subject,' she'd told Craig via Skype. 'Today, at least. A week or so earlier might have been a fairer test. I was angry with myself. Coiled up tensely with a bad case of red rage and blue sorrow.'

'And yet you might have tested the same,' Craig had said. 'I was talking to one of the Aboriginal elders, about it.'

'Jim Murray, do you mean?'

'Yeah Jim: the retired geologist I told you about the other day. He explained their various effects. Seems to think the crystals work most dramatically on those whose hearts aren't fully open.'

'I wonder if it's got something to do with chakras...the heart chakra maybe? I've been learning about them in Tanya's book on eastern religions. Invisible energy vortexes around the human body.'

'You couldn't be more right about that. Conan Dalesford and I believe the crystals work on repairing damage to that energy centre. And heart-chakra damage applies to most of us, or at least anyone who's met with difficulty when either giving or receiving love.'

Rosetta promised Craig she'd make arrangements for a trip to Alice Springs the minute she returned to Australia.

Matthew Weissler would have received her note by now via Izzie and his step-daughter Sara. Craig had said he so far hadn't heard from him.

Like Rosetta, Matthew might have felt wary of Craig's start-up company. He might also have felt wary of Rosetta. Someone he hardly knew approaching him about business! Everyone needed to be alert to scams.

Craig had suggested she mention in her letter that the legal/financial advisor he planned to appoint was likely to profit hugely. Aware of Craig's propensity to overestimate future success, she'd steered away from this, along with any claims about the crystals' strange properties. Cause for regret, this deliberate evasiveness, now that her inbox lacked replies.

She placed the crystal back in its holder and shrugged off her idea of Matthew expressing interest in Craig's company. It wasn't as if she'd ever see him again. She'd had this same thought after his work send-off. She'd been wrong. She had happened upon him at Grant's.

He'd looked different in the daytime. Eyes lighter in colour, an interesting green. Not green in the bright, limey way Adam's were; more of a blue-green, similar to how the ocean looked right now beneath the passenger jet, in its less sunny patches.

She and Grant had been watching DVDs in his Punchbowl flat. Grant's daughter Sara was in the kitchen talking to friends on her phone, and Laura was out on the porch steps reading aloud to her dolls.

A little earlier they'd returned from a lunch with the kids at Grant's local Chinese restaurant. That had been the second time she'd met up with her former neighbour since the Burwood move. The week before, they'd taken Izzie and Sara ice skating. By the time they were nestled in front of the TV on that dismally gusty Sunday afternoon, watching one of Grant's favourite teenage-boy type of movies, Rosetta was eager to get home.

Despite robust efforts at proposing a dinner date, Grant had been sensitive to Rosetta's attempts at changing the subject. During another of the movie's monotonous bin-lid fights, Grant said, 'You're a gorgeous girl, Rosetta, and heaps of fun, but I think we're better as friends.'

'I agree.' She gave him a cheery peck on the cheek.

She liked Grant. He was affable and kind-hearted, a meat-and-potatoes man. It wasn't Grant's fault that his sense of humour had begun to grate on her. His anecdotes and one-liners were hilarious the first time, kind of funny the second, but aggravating by the time they trundled into Round Three.

Grant thanked her for being so good-natured about 'his decision' to just be friends and urged her to stay until the end of the movie. Feeling she needed to live up to that good-naturedness, Rosetta made Grant another tea, then settled into Grant's least comfortable armchair, gritting her teeth through the movie-teens' predictable scenarios that made Grant *hee-haw* with red-faced mirth.

At the sound of a car slowing to a stop below, Grant said, 'That'll be Matt to pick up the kids.'

She heard footsteps on the stairs and the warm, modulated sound of Matthew's voice saying to Laura on the porch, 'And who's this particular doll? Would it happen to be Laura Lou?'

Feeling suddenly self-conscious, Rosetta tucked a wayward bra-strap back under the neckline of her top, swallowed hard and smoothed her hair.

Grant rose as the door swung open. Rosetta rose too.

Grant's little girl flew in, pale brown hair fluttering out in wind-messed tangles, followed by Matthew.

He was taller than she remembered. Weekend stubble suited him. He stared at Rosetta in confusion, evidently trying to remember where he'd seen her before. When Grant began to introduce her, Matthew's words had been, 'Yes, Lucetta and I have already met.'

What happened next was imprinted firmly on Rosetta's memory. Grant telling Matthew he'd got her name wrong...Matthew apologising profusely.

In words that tripped over themselves, Matthew said he'd noticed a BMW on the street with its interior light on: was the car Rosetta's?

'Yes,' she told him. 'Yes, the car's mine. Thanks for letting me know.' Not *I'm minding it for a friend...*or...*It's on loan for the next week*. She'd lied and said the car was hers!

Half-expecting Grant to correct the statement since he'd already spot-lit Matthew over a name gaff, she excused herself and dashed out to Craig's car.

She unlocked the midnight-blue sports and switched off the interior light, all the while thinking about Matthew's attractiveness; about how he'd looked in his casual khaki shirt and jeans. The shirt was well-fitted and emphasised his swimmer's shoulders.

Aware the memory of that day at Grant's had made her uncomfortably warm, Rosetta slid the porthole screen across, closed her eyes and recalled how she and Grant had chatted with Matthew while Laura and Sara packed from a weekend spent at their dad's. She'd joked and laughed with them about nothing in particular, and then Matthew and his step-kids were gone.

Big-noting. No other word for it. She'd always wondered why people exaggerated their status, but on that day at Grant's, she had done the same. With Matthew. Again! When Matthew said previously at the bar, 'You're a lawyer,' she hadn't rushed to explain that she was, in reality, a law student deferring her studies because of inadequate finances. She'd instead changed the subject, then replied when pressed that she specialised in human rights. And now she'd inferred Craig's luxury car belonged to her!

What would Baba have said if he'd known she'd meddled with the truth? Probably no more than 'Rosetta-Rosetta!' But the bowed head and sorrowful brown eyes would have been enough to make her feel like she had at age seven, when she'd played dress-up in Mama's heirloom wedding gown and bumped into Stavros and his glass of red cordial.

Rosetta left Grant's soon after Matthew, and she'd taken Grant up on his offer of a lift home from the airport in ten days' time. Throughout those ten days, she'd hardly given Grant a second thought. Matthew, on the other hand, had been thought about quite a lot. She didn't have a crush on Matthew—he was *married*—and only on her mind because he exemplified the sort of man she hoped to meet. After that day at Grant's, she'd whispered a mostly non-believing prayer to the otherworldly beings Molly Carr suggested were helping her invisibly. *I want a guy like Matthew who isn't Matthew* she'd confided to them. *But he has to be footloose and fancy-free, and less intimidatingly good-looking.*

Shortly after her plane touched down in Sydney, Rosetta leaned back in the passenger seat of Grant's Holden. Once they were cruising down the shrub-lined freeway, she asked, 'When are you back on duty, Grant?'

'In another hour-and-a-half.' Grant was busy munching on a roast beef roll. He held the half-eaten roll out to Rosetta and asked if she wanted a bite. She swiftly declined. 'I'm not looking forward to working tonight, Rosetta, I can tell you. Got hardly any sleep.'

'Ooh, so you had a hot date last night,' Rosetta teased, partly to reassure him she was no longer interested. Grant didn't answer.

Maybe he did have a hot date, she thought. That was a bit intrusive of me.

Aloud, she said, 'It's really good of you to give me a lift home. I could have caught a cab.' And couldn't she! Now that money was no object, she could have hired a stretch limousine and still not felt the pinch of poverty.

'No problem, Rosetta. Like I said a couple of weeks back when we had our little chat: you're a top girl. It's the least I can do, and I know your money situation isn't great at present. Don't waste your dough on cabs.'

Rosetta didn't add to that. It wouldn't be right to flaunt her new-found wealth. Telling someone who wasn't affluent that she'd inherited big would make her feel guilty, and she wasn't out to make anyone envious. Sharing the information with her close friends was fine: she'd be working on making their lives better materially as soon as she could. As far as money was concerned, her good fortune was theirs as well.

They drove on in amiable silence. 'Besides,' Grant said. His voice lowered. He laughed, embarrassed. 'Bernie came over last night and...er...it looks like we've sorted a few things out.'

'To do with your kids?'

Grant hesitated. 'To do with us. It looks like we might be getting back together.'

Rosetta gulped. 'Really?' Could Dette seriously want to get back with Grant? Despite being married to Matthew? Surely the only reason Dette had flirted with Adam Harrow at the bar in full view of her husband was to make him jealous. Could encouraging Grant be yet another attempt at that?

'So I've got *you* to thank, Rosetta, for agreeing you and I weren't suited, and for helping me see the light.'

'Glad to be of service,' Rosetta droned.

'Excuse me, Rosetta. That's my phone.'

Through the car's speaker a deep voice blared, 'Grant, where are you?'

'I'll be there in an hour-and-a-half, Brian. I'm on the 7 p.m. to 3 shift.'

'Nah man. I need you here now. It's to do with your ex-wife.'

'With Bernie? What th—'

Rosetta turned to look at Grant. His forehead had crumpled in concern. What was going on with Dette?

'One-four-one Chanteaux Parade, Vaucluse. Get here fast. She's in a bad way, and she's been asking for you.'

What could have happened?

Grant's tone became strained. 'Who's got her there? What have they done to her?'

'Listen mate, she's not hurt...'

Rosetta breathed out a thankful sigh.

'...But she's confused. Seems as though she's shot someone, Grant.'

Rosetta stifled a gasp. Had she heard correctly? Had Dette Weissler actually *shot* someone?

Grant stepped on the accelerator. The force of the car grew stronger. 'Oh God! Not Bernie, man! Tell me it's not Bernie!'

The reply was: 'I'm sorry Grant.'

Grant's voice rose into a roar. 'Give me the address again,' he shouted. 'I'll be there as soon as I can.'

Chapter Eight

XLVII

aving woken before Eidred, Pieter was now no longer by the thorn thicket. Already he had sipped the Remembrance Essence, which his wife had prepared from Wondalobs water and stored in their chamber. Armed with the knowledge gained in his Dream Sphere visit, he hastened to Orahney's empty pyramid home as she'd advised, to recover the wand within. It was settled next to a chair etched with oak leaves.

He exited her home, clunking shut the arched wooden door, and ran to the body of Rahwor. In the palace grounds where the sorcerer lay, it appeared there might have been three dead men rather than one. The eagle-winged guards responsible for carrying expired Rahwor to the Grudellan mausoleum, had sunk rapidly into their hundred-year slumber, arms flopped out in front of them, brown wings crumpled unevenly against the flat, moss-like grass.

'You must free the eagle turned to stone,' Orahney had told him. Storlem, locked in his eagle form, was in danger of remaining a statue forever, perched upon an obelisk, a sordid reminder of Rahwor's vicious sorcery. Orahney had provided Pieter with a solution. *Free Rahwor into the Dream Sphere, then all of Rahwor's spells will lose their hold.*

And so, Pieter pressed the crystal of Orahney's wand against the dead sorcerer's ankle. A soft, silver light appeared and surrounded Rahwor in a soothing glow. 'Good luck, dear soul,' he said. 'You are now silvered.' Pieter knew that Rahwor's soul self, now unable to be drawn into the Nightmare Realm in death, would soar to the inviting luminance of the Dream Sphere. There, Rahwor's personally appointed Dream Master, a guide who worked as Alcor did, would show him all the havoc he had wreaked in others' lives through his magic and would grant him the chance to expiate. If this were to occur, Orahney's lover Storlem, forced to face eternity with the feeble heart and mind of a Gold's Kin eagle, would be granted the return to his silvered self. All things going well, Storlem's soul, trapped between heaven and earth, would soon fly free to the Dream Sphere.

Rosetta pushed the car door open and clambered out. Within minutes of a colleague's phone call to Grant about Dette, they'd sped to Chanteaux Parade, a street of overpoweringly large homes, and Grant had raced towards a police car parked on a front lawn.

Outside the property—a white jumble of Gothic spires with a central water feature—a constable stood by his car, talking into a two-way.

The police officer directed Grant to an open double door. Grant ran in. Rosetta followed him. She followed him into an entrance with a circular skylight and black marble flooring, then into a vast and dimly musty room at the end of the imposing foyer, an expanse of turn-of-the-century grandeur, with the kind of wall tapestries and fireplaces found in English country estates.

The sound of sobbing rose up from behind one of the leather chesterfields. Grant remained in the doorway, glancing from left to right, unsure where to move next. Rosetta rushed towards the panicked sighs.

Beside one of the armchairs sat a crumbling Dette, looking like a doll left out in the rain: mascara streaked wetly across her cheeks; hair twisted into tufts; trembling thin arms hugging trembling thin knees.

On the floor, a small distance away from Dette, lay a gun. Lying beneath a gilded glass table was a hypodermic syringe.

Grant was beside Dette now, having sunk to his knees. 'Bernie, it's me.'

As though emerging from another world, Dette lifted her eyes to take in her ex-husband.

Grant's voice was soft and urgent. 'Now, tell me from the start what happened. Why are you here?'

Dette's answer was a shout. 'I killed him!' Her breath had turned into small wheezing gasps. She'd plunged into a quivery state of shock; was rocking to and fro in confusion.

'With that gun?' Grant turned and studied the revolver.

Dette didn't answer.

'Bernadette, is this my gun?'

'Yes!' Dette rounded on Grant. She stared at him with unseeing eyes.

A shuffling sound and the rumble of male voices filtered from the staircase. Two paramedics carrying a stretcher halted briefly on the landing. Grant leapt to his feet and left to approach them while poor, frail Dette continued to weep. In other circumstances, Rosetta would have comforted her. Knowledge of what had just taken place cautioned her against this. Right now Dette appeared as harmless as a little girl caught stealing from a lolly jar, and yet the voice on Grant's phone had referred to her as the assassin.

The ambulance men made their way across the sitting room. Rosetta looked away from the lifeless victim. It wouldn't and couldn't be right to stare.

Grant asked the men questions in a lowered voice. Unable to decipher their words, Rosetta took a step towards the stretcher.

'I see,' said Grant. 'I see.'

The paramedics steered the stretcher around one of the mahogany tables. The body was only partially covered by a sheet. Despite her determination to remain discreet, Rosetta edged closer and looked upon the dead man.

The sight that met her made her step back. On the stretcher was a creature as ghoulish as the supernatural villains of Victorian horror novels, the type that had to be warded off with crucifixes. Death would have made the face white, but the lips were scarlet, and hair fell across the shoulders in dark, ratty ringlets.

Grant's colleague entered the room. The two discussed the detective's finds. 'There's a fiancée,' the colleague said. 'Away apparently. Staying at her mother's.'

Rosetta gripped Grant's shoulder. She looked once more at the body, and her grip tightened. She knew who this was. Grant ceased his talk and turned to her distractedly. 'The laundry man,' she said in a gasp. 'The laundry man, Grant! The prowler.'

'Jeezus! What's he doing hanging around my Bernie?' Grant's voice rose. 'Bernie, what did he do to you?'

'Nothing, nothing, nothing,' Dette muttered, still hugging her knees, glazed eyes a flood of despair.

'Okay, I've got the story straight now,' Grant said. 'You're not a murderer, Bernadette. You didn't shoot him at all. The ambos found no bullet wounds, and that gun of mine's never loaded when it's at home.'

'I know I didn't shoot him,' Dette screeched. 'I *said* I *killed* him!' She rested her forehead against her knees and wailed until her shoulders shook.

'Bernie, you're in shock. Other than that, are you all right? Tell me he didn't take you here against your will.'

Dette shook her head. 'He didn't. I came here by myself. I just wanted to scare Adam. Just wanted to make him understand how I felt when he upset me. Just...But I never meant to hurt him.'

Another Adam! Why would Dette intrude on someone as creepy as this? Had she been stalked by him? Taken the law into her own hands? Rosetta's heart went out to her. Dette must have been truly scared to do something as dangerous as this, harassed to a point where she'd suffered a lapse of judgement.

Grant was on the floor beside Dette again, clasping her in his arms.

Perhaps tea, Rosetta thought.

She would do that. She'd find the kitchen and make Dette a tea. Strong and with extra sugar, to calm Dette's jangled nerves. She approached Grant and cup-and-saucered her hands in question. He gave a small half-smile and shook his head no. It was then that she noticed the police tape. Three doorways exited the far end of the main room, and all were cordoned off.

Knowing the two needed time to discuss all Dette had been through, Rosetta made her way out to the garden. She neared the foyer. Dette's voice seemed to follow her. 'He died of a heart attack. I think that's what it was. I can't be sure.'

'Why do you think that?' Grant murmured.

A series of whimpers. 'Adam's hands went to his chest. I held your gun at him...and he clutched at his chest and fell. I checked his pulse, but it was gone.' Her voice descended into a moan.

Rosetta wandered through the foyer and stumbled onto the soft lawn. Afternoon had melted into evening in the short time they'd been within the house. Still dazed from all she'd encountered, she pulled her jacket firmly around her and wove across to a sundial that stood by a small fountain. She leaned against it to rest her trembling legs. Darkness had invaded the sky. A sharp wind sprang up. It whipped at her hair. Slapped strands against her face. She pulled the strands away absently, twisting them into a loose knot at the nape of her neck.

The ambulance men on the other side of the lawn were discussing the situation.

'Overdose apparently.'

'Smack?'

'Yup. Okay details, please, Sam. Name?'

'Adam Harrow.'

'Age?'

'Thirty-three.'

The words wrapped themselves around Rosetta's heart in icy spirals. Couldn't be!

A name she despised had crept back to haunt her because of its commonality. The Adam she'd dated was also thirty-three...but...Her thoughts returned to the sight of the dead man. Nothing like Adam. And why would Adam wear a disguise? The jaw had been strong and square like Adam's, and the lips full, but that didn't mean...or did it? Same age, matching first and last names. Dette's husband's workmate.

It had to be him.

Oh God. *Adam Harrow* dead! And he wasn't who he appeared to be. Rosetta would never have guessed Adam to be a voyeur. The ghostly creature on the stretcher, the man who had leered at her in the outdoor laundry.

He must have known of her at least a year before he'd slipped into Crystal Consciousness and asked her out. The man she'd famously called her 'gorgeous GEG'—the Green Eyed Guy—tall, smiling and golden, was nothing like this man, an intruder who taunted her with the threat of devouring a poor fragile skink, his clawing black talons a source of recurring nightmares.

This was too much. Glorion, the Prince of Perelda told Izzie the man was confusing. What might Adam have done if she'd continued to see him? What was he capable of? He'd sat beside Dette the evening of Matthew's send-off, on the bar's purple couches, a not-so-nice scenario for Rosetta since Adam had been her date. He'd chatted to everyone but her, and he'd lavished Dette with attention. If it hadn't been for Matthew keeping her company, Rosetta would have upped and left, and yet Adam Harrow continued to lure her in. Adam must have latched onto Dette back then and made her his next target. Horrible. Too horrible, and too absurd.

A Jag pulled up. The driver stilled the motor and stepped out. 'Rosetta!'

He'd said her name in surprise. His voice had an odd effect on her, making her feel as though she were suddenly home. Someone familiar was here, someone to help make sense of all that had happened. Matthew's poor wife was a mess. Adam was dead.

'What's the cop car and ambulance doing here?'

Rosetta closed her eyes and groaned inwardly. He didn't know. How was she going to tell him? In a voice robbed of feeling, she found herself saying, 'Adam Harrow passed away. He died of an overdose.'

Matthew's eyes widened in disbelief. 'Where's Bernadette? Is she...'

Rosetta was quick to reassure him. 'Bernadette's fine. She's in a state of shock of course. She's blaming herself for his death, but everything's okay with her.'

Matthew folded forward. The action was only slight, barely perceptible, but Rosetta sensed the pain. She wished she could reach out and give him a sisterly hug.

Grant and Dette emerged from Adam's house, Dette clinging timidly to Grant's elbow.

'Matt!' Grant said, drawing near. 'Do you know the resident of this house?'

'Workmate,' said Matthew without much emotion.

'I'm sorry to tell you this,' Grant said, 'but he died of an overdose this afternoon. My colleague investigated the premises. Found the medicine cabinet and bedroom drawers full of the stuff. The man was a definite junkie. And a cross-dresser it seems.'

'You're kidding.'

'He was wearing a wig and fake nails when they found him. Bernie was—'

'Don't tell him, don't tell him, don't tell him.' Dette, propped against Grant with her mouth near Grant's ear, had uttered the command shakily, too lost in shock to realise her stage whisper was more than audible to Matthew and Rosetta.

Echoing, inadvertently, the words Rosetta chose before, Grant mumbled, 'Bernie blames herself for his death,' and added tactfully, 'but she's really done nothing incriminating.'

Looking as stunned as Rosetta felt, Matthew nodded.

'Anyway, Matthew, I can get her across to the doctor after she's been to the station for questioning unless you'd prefer...' Grant cleared his throat. 'How did you hear about this? Or were you on your way to meet up with her anyway?'

Matthew strode across to Grant and said something to him in a low voice, something that sounded like: *We're horsing.* Cavorting? Rosetta couldn't discern it.

'I see!' Grant frowned. Strangely, as Matthew turned away, Rosetta detected the flash of a grin on Grant's face. Given the morose circumstances, Grant's transient beam looked entirely out of place. Grant gave Dette's back a couple of enthusiastic pats. She nestled against him weepily. 'I'll accompany you down to the station with Brian to make a statement, Bernie,' he told her. 'We'll get you to the doc for a tranquiliser and then you can stay at mine.'

'Okay.' Dette's voice was faint. 'Okay.'

It seemed odd that Grant should suggest Dette stay at his place. Wouldn't he deliver her home? Rosetta subtly observed Matthew, wondering why he wasn't making an effort to console his wife. He hadn't attempted to hold her, and there'd been no exchange of words.

He was talking to Dette now, although rather flatly. 'Don't worry about a thing, Bernadette. The girls are fine. Rhoda's looking after them at home.' He stared at the ground. 'I think it's best you go with Grant, don't you?'

Dette lifted her chin. A look that was almost defiant crossed her face. 'Yes,' she said.

'We'd better get going.' Grant nodded to a colleague taking the last of the details from the paramedics. He turned to Rosetta then and looked at her as though seeing her there for the first time. 'Oh yeah,' he said vaguely. 'Listen, Matt, could you get Rosetta home? I was giving her a lift from the airport when Brian called me about Bernie.'

'Not a problem.'

'Thanks, mate. And Rosetta...' He shook his head. 'I'm really sorry to have dragged you into all of this.'

'Please, Grant, it's no-one's fault. I just feel bad that I wasn't of more help.' She went back to Grant's car to collect her bags. Mulling over how she could have been more useful than she felt she'd been, she promptly remembered the crystal. She went to the front seat, snatched up the cosmetics purse in her overnight bag, then hesitated. The mention of crystal healing might only increase Dette's distress. She turned to see Matthew beside the car.

'Are those cases on the back seat yours, Rosetta?'

She affirmed to Matthew that they were. He opened the car door and lifted them out.

It was worth a try. No need to give an explanation. Craig had said that even two seconds of exposure to the healing energy of these Alice Springs gems was all anyone needed, to feel soothed and at peace. She returned to the huddled-together ex-spouses, retrieved the crystal from its enclosure and handed it to Dette. 'This will help calm you.'

'Surely it's not a tranquiliser.' Dette was astounded. 'I couldn't possibly gulp *that* down!'

Grant laughed, tightening his hold on Dette, and gave her shoulder an indulgent shake. 'It's just a stone, darlin',' he said.

This small gesture of Grant's caused Rosetta to realise just how much Grant adored Dette Weissler. Was it possible Dette might feel the same about her ex? Rosetta doubted it. Dette would have been playing games.

'You're in shock, sweetie,' she told Dette. 'Everything feels surreal when we're in shock. Just hold this.'

Dette stretched out her elegant fingers, plum-coloured nails gleaming morbidly in the fading light, and plucked the crystal from Rosetta's palm. She enclosed both hands around the small gem and hugged it to her heart as though cradling an injured sparrow. Within seconds the tension twisting Dette's features eased smoothly away. 'I think I'm feeling a little bit better.'

'Are you sure?' Grant was puzzled. Rosetta knew Grant's opinion on her belief in metaphysical concepts. Powerful frequencies that scientists hadn't researched would have been labelled 'whacky' in the logic-seeking side of Grant's internal filing system.

'Thank you.' Dette's eyes had cleared. She gave the crystal back to Rosetta. 'Sorry, what was your name again?'

Surprised someone in shock would make the effort to reach out with this small show of thoughtfulness, Rosetta quickly re-introduced herself, then crossed to the ambulance. The door of the van hadn't closed. She might well get the chance to carry out her intentions.

He was dead, yet she felt compelled to do this. The crystal might assist him in moving on. It was common knowledge amongst psychics that the souls of deceased addicts got trapped on the earth plane. Helping Adam's spirit locate the other side's celestial luminance was imperative.

She stepped up into the ambulance. Ignoring the shouts of 'Hey' and 'You can't do that, I'm sorry,' from the surprised paramedics, she stumbled towards the sheet-covered corpse. The stretcher was at least a metre away. Rosetta hesitated. She didn't want to intrude. The crystal grew warmer, encouraging her to persevere.

She closed her eyes briefly and drew in a breath. In one sweeping move she leaned forward, stretched out her arm and skimmed the pink glowing shard across the top of Adam's foot. Feeling she had better say something ceremonial, something that would indicate to Adam she wished him well, Rosetta whispered words from *Our True Ancient History*, the words Pieter had uttered to the deceased Rawhor. 'Good luck, dear soul.'

One of the paramedics rose to usher her from the wagon. She stepped out and crossed the lawn towards the street.

Grant and Dette were getting into Grant's car.

Matthew was standing near the passenger side of his own car, a vehicle of shining red, his face still noticeably blank.

'My bags,' Rosetta said vaguely.

'Packed.' Matthew opened her door for her. 'All ready? Okay, Rosetta, let's get you home.'

XLVIII

Remembering Orahney telling him he had a number of Kindness Merits at his disposal, Pieter dashed towards the eagle statue. He willed himself to peer with his etheric eyes beyond the stone of the eagle, beneath the stilled creature's frozen exterior.

He saw a mountain top, the soul of a bird circling it. Was this not the same mundane world he encountered when Alcor presented him with the choice of three doors? Pieter's recent dose of Remembrance Essence allowed him to lucidly recall this Dream Sphere visit, an encounter he'd innocently denied when the bird had visited the Brumlynd camp in dream-self form.

He pondered the eagle's past words.

Fearsome bird below, clad in pointed cap. Does it not see this is my dwelling? Neither me nor mine. Inferior.

Some try to encroach on me but are yet to win, for I ingeniously defend my territory. I leave them with little doubt as to who owns what.

'Why did I not recognise the eagle's soul-thoughts to be borne of gold?' Pieter asked himself now. He remembered peering into the future of this uninspired creature and did so again. He firstly saw as he had before, a spinning wheel and then a cauldron. If warmth were mastered, the eagle would become a moth; if light learnt, a blossom on a tree; growth understood, a tree himself. In accomplishing the silent wisdom of a towering pine, the evolving creature would become warm-blooded in the incarnation that followed: a sparrow in search of humility. Humility gained, a kingfisher over yonder, in the mysterious Land of Mu.

Pieter heard a faint conversation, although he heard it with his etheric ears. Apart from softening Rawhor's fiery spell on Storlem in flight, his magic hadn't been used for an entire season-cycle, and so exercising it again felt surprisingly foreign.

'And so, Rahwor,' boomed a resonant voice that brimmed with warmth, 'You wish to enter the Dream Sphere. Are you prepared to relinquish the darkness you wielded with sorcery in the life you led on Earth?'

Rahwor's reply was, 'Most certainly, Alcor.' Alcor was to be Rahwor's Dream Master! 'I gratefully accept the honour of your invitation. Truly thankful, I am, to have been silvered by the elfin prince, Adahmos.'

Overjoyed at the sorcerer's decision to reverse malicious deeds and hopeful of now freeing Storlem, Pieter turned his attention to the guard in his eagle form: stone wings expanded in that moment of landing; eyes, once golden-green and direct, now dulled in their unmoving greyness.

Reminding himself that Storlem would soon be free of his stone body, Pieter wondered what would happen to the statue left behind. *Trapped in stony ignorance*, the eagle had said when he'd visited the campfire in Elysium Glades. *My spell caster is Rahwor.* Pieter's remorse at having not believed Storlem was easing now that he knew how to put things right.

In a flash, Pieter saw a vision of Maleika standing by a silver-gold ocean belonging to the Oracle. The Oracle's ocean quivered vividly with feeling, was shadowed yet bright, and chimed—with silken subtleness—the ploddingly quick chords of depth and majesty. It said:

> Three flights of stairs
> The lost one's room
> Is sanctioned off in lofty gloom

Pieter turned over this advice in his mind. He had just returned from the one-roomed pyramid in which Orahney, as a bewitcher turned soothsayer, had spent the last of her days. Her room, however, was in no way raised from the ground.

Remembering the trapdoor, and the descent he and Eidred made to meet Orahney's rescued dragon friend Sluken, Pieter smiled. From the cavern below there were most certainly three flights of stairs leading to Orahney's dwelling quarter.

> Revisit where the eagle's flown
> Its earthly shell
> Is set in stone

Still in a state of intuitive seeing, Pieter now observed an event during the century of his birth, his mother Maleika arriving at the

Grudellan Palace in search of him. Maleika paused at the statue and noted it to be a landmark but was too distracted to hear, etherically, the eagle's vainglorious thoughts:

My feathers are fashioned from gold. My creator was a sculptor. Carved me from a stone block. Added jewels for eyes and breathed the fire of life into me.

Pieter peered further into the future and saw the eagle, upon its stone perch, struck by future lightning. Beak, wing and claw broke away from the statue as it toppled to the ground.

The groundsman summoned the court's blacksmith. The blacksmith crafted clever replacements. As commanded by the Solen, he sculpted and gilded the eagle's wings, added emeralds to characterise the eagle's eyes and restored this magnificent symbol of a body king's wrath to its lofty obelisk pedestal.

Again the eagle's words returned to Pieter. *My creator was a sculptor.*

The eagle had identified a palace blacksmith as a sculptor, and his very own creator. In the eagle's eyes, this humble embellisher was godly.

Pieter, standing alone in the darkness, was shaken from his timeframe glimpses.

A crash rang out from the stars.

A wriggling streak of sizzling pink charged thunderously down to the earth.

In a high-pitched hum, which softened as it neared, the illumined zigzag undulated towards the statue. Pieter watched in wonder. The heaven-sent light settled on the stone eagle's outline, immersed it in a glow rosier than the sweetest clouds of dusk and then leapt from its target to Pieter, clipping his ear with a far from unpleasant whirr before retreating whence it had come.

Pieter was suddenly drowsy. At the other side of the palace grounds his wife and child lay dozing in the moonlight. 'Am I being sent into a century of sleep, like every royal in the palace?' he whispered. Was the startling pink light a belated spell to keep him and his little family from escaping the Grudellan Palace?

Robbed of the opportunity to wonder this any longer, Pieter was briskly returned to the Dream Sphere.

On the way to Rosetta's place, Matthew tried to get his head around all that had happened in the past half-hour.

He'd left home with itching fists, way too tempted to knock down a threat named Harrow. He'd wanted, also, to confront Bernadette for betraying him. And then there'd been Celia's call that left him fighting off images of Bernadette battered and unconscious. He was met instead with a desperate little heap of helplessness suctioned onto Grant like a squid attached to the walls of an aquarium. This and the knowledge that Harrow was dead.

Harrow dead! Ashamed to recall now, the reality was he'd been relieved to hear it. If he'd got to Harrow earlier, the death might have been a homicide he'd regret for the rest of his life. That was where Monopoly and real-life differed. Dodging jail wasn't as easy as paying two-hundred dollars, unless you had crooked cronies in the judiciary, although he knew he really didn't have it in him to harm anyone.

Grant had been pleased, too pleased it seemed, to get Bernadette back to his place. It was more than likely this ex-wife of Matthew's—*ex* being the only attractive syllable in that title—was on with her former husband as well. Matthew was past caring. Whether she'd been cheating on him with one or one-hundred was irrelevant. She was not who he'd thought her to be.

A junkie. It explained a lot, Matthew realised. More than a few workmates considered Harrow to be devoid of a conscience. Drugs did that to people, ate away at their divisions between right and wrong. He supposed he should feel pity for the poor sod, but at this stage he felt nothing. He was numb. Drained of anger, certainly, unanswered questions swimming through his brain.

Who had Harrow been really? A cross-dresser, Grant had said. Could that be right? The thought was almost laughable. It felt good in a vicious sort of way that the man Matthew's wife had gone after was, of all things, an undercover woman. Bernadette must have been mortified when she'd caught him in a dress.

Resisting the urge to laugh, Matthew swiftly eyed his passenger whose large, creamy lids were lowered in contemplation. He hardly wanted Rosetta to think him some kind of ghoul, gloating over how a dead man's gender identity would have horrified his wife. Ex-wife. Matthew exhaled forcefully. She was his ex-wife now. No confrontation. Bernadette's tragic fragility had instantly dissipated his need for atonement.

When he'd seen the flashing lights, he'd thought the worst since ambulance plus police equalled crime and injury. He'd immediately worried that Bernadette had been attacked; had blamed himself for not getting there earlier to protect her. Her emergence from Harrow's house unharmed and Rosetta's assurance that Bernadette was fine had liberated him from his sense of dread.

There wouldn't have been much of a future for him, for Harrow. Unless the poor joker had checked himself into rehab, life would have descended into a nightmare. Was it wrong to believe someone was better off dead? There had to be a type of heaven—Matthew was sure of this—and it would have to be a darned sight better than this crazy charade called living. A world of bliss awaiting those who passed on made sense in a way. Somehow, it made sense.

Matthew took another sidelong look at his passenger. Yep. Still beautiful, even in these circumstances.

He cleared his throat. 'So it was Burwood, you said, Rosetta?'

Rosetta told him that yes, it was.

This was extremely awkward. Rosetta had been dating Harrow. He had no idea if she knew of Harrow's involvement with Dette. But now Rosetta was Grant's girl, and yet Grant had left her with Matthew in favour of looking after Matthew's wife. Shouldn't it have been the other way round? Matthew again stifled a laugh. He and Grant were chauffeuring the wrong girls. He didn't know why he felt like laughing after such a harrowing ordeal, *Harrow* being the operative word. Must have been the shock, but the sense of freedom after conveying to Bernadette his wish for divorce was weirdly intoxicating.

She was no longer his responsibility. He wasn't required to patch her up with reassurance anymore, as he'd frequently done with each triviality that traumatised her. Now that she'd been affected by a real drama, not having to take her home and endure the resulting tantrums was like a refreshing breeze during a forty-degree scorcher. She was Grant's responsibility this evening. Grant was a good bloke. She'd be perfectly safe with Grant.

But smack of all things! Bernadette, thankfully, wasn't into that stuff, but could anyone be sure about anything when it came to

Bernadette and her secrets? Mathew had thought she meant it when she not so long ago said she embraced loyalty in partnerships the way he did. Could Bernadette have dabbled in drugs? Was that, amongst other things, her attraction to Harrow? The thought struck him like a slap.

Breaking the silence, he said to Rosetta, 'It was heroin was it?'

'Appeared to be, yeah. I overheard the police officer saying he'd found filing cabinet drawers full of syringes.'

Matthew whistled out a sigh. 'Unbelievable.' Images of Bernadette sharing syringes with Harrow flew at him like wasps. 'Bernadette didn't...I'm assuming Bernadette wasn't...'

'No, she wasn't.'

She'd sensed what he was going to say.

Rosetta went on. 'There was no talk of Dette using the heroin. The ambos would have checked her pupils. She looked shaken up, probably because...well, she was shocked. Adam was your workmate. The three of you were friends.'

Matthew's sarcastic laugh sounded more like a groan. He didn't want to explain what was going on in his head. He did *not* want to admit that his wife had been sleeping with Rosetta's ex. Apart from making Matthew look like the guy women ran from, talk of Adam's escapades would, without a doubt, upset Rosetta. He had to keep quiet about the catastrophe called Harrow and Bernadette. Two times two-timers, 'two Geminis', as Rosetta had said at the bar with the fancy lampshades. Double bloody trouble.

When he'd arrived at the white monstrosity that Adam Harrow would have called home, he'd felt, from deep in his chest, a frenetic sort of somberness that seemed to weigh down the air. All around had been strangers. Flashes of red and blue emergency lights piercing the dim calm of descending nightfall with their artificial brightness, hushed murmurings, the smell of fresh-cut lawn and the hoot of an owl had all accosted his senses. He'd looked wildly around him only to see a sun-dial before a fountain, and it gave him chills.

Then he'd turned and seen Rosetta. It was like she'd been the only thing real in that topsy-turvy scene. Even when Bernadette had emerged, even when he'd mentioned in confidence to Grant the divorce, the only reality was Rosetta. She'd earthed him with her presence.

He clutched at something practical and responsible to say. 'Ashdowne Avenue?'

'Ashbury.'

He mouthed the word 'Ashbury' a couple of times as he stared ahead at the road's white lines. Aware his silence might be considered oafish, he murmured a few things about the weather and about the autumn having ended, in staccato remarks that didn't invite much of a reply.

Rosetta glanced sideways at him and smiled, and his heart sped up. 'I realise it's a tough time for you at the moment, Matthew.'

Uh-oh. He didn't want to talk about it. Where were excuses when you needed them?

'And I realise you'd rather be alone with your thoughts.'

She realised this?

'So don't feel you have to make polite conversation. You'd be stressed out.'

Aha! Was she having a go at him? Bernadette often spoke in opposites when annoyed. 'I'm sorry, Rosetta. I realise I'm not the best company at the moment.'

'Don't be!' Abrupt, husky laugh. Was that a scathing laugh? 'Matthew, your workmate has *died*.'

He had too! This was true.

'This must be *terrible* for you.'

It was.

Her voice became quieter. 'Get some rest when you get home, hey?'

Briefly, he turned to look at her. She was concerned. Not for herself but for him.

Taking his thoughts from himself to the person who had pointed out that he had every right to be quiet, he said, 'It's not just me who's had a loss. Adam Harrow was...' What should he say? Your boyfriend? Your fair-weather pal? Your deserter?

'No he wasn't.' There she was, intuiting Matthew's answers again. 'He was a fake. When I was seeing him he propositioned one of my friends. It's a long story. I shouldn't really...I mean...Talking about someone who's just died probably isn't appropriate.'

Bingo! Not appropriate! A *great* excuse for not talking anymore about Adam Harrow. And for not going into details about who had been entertaining who. Matthew did have a question concerning it all. Was she or wasn't she still with Grant? He threw out a prompt. 'Grant's a good bloke though.'

'Oh, no, I'm not with Grant.'

Played well, Weissler!

'But you're right. He is a good man.'

'Uh-huh.' Matthew smiled. The girl knew her own mind and also, to some extent, knew his. She was nobody's fool.

Unable to clear the smile from his face, he became aware of who the fool was now. He was getting over a wife's betrayal and coming to terms with a man dying tragically. It was ludicrous. He'd only encountered Rosetta twice before, but the fact remained that he felt unaccountably happy.

He couldn't think of anything less glamorous than driving away from the scene of a fatality on a late-autumn evening, and yet he felt as though it were summer; that he was fifteen again, with the sun on his shoulders and passion in his veins.

And somehow, it made sense.

Matthew and his passenger travelled towards Burwood in sombre silence. Rosetta, Matthew learned, had returned from New Zealand. Grant had been giving her a lift from the airport when he'd got the call about Harrow.

Rain tumbled down. Diamond-tinted droplets framed the windscreen. Beyond the windscreen-wipers the road was a river of black, daubed with coloured reflections. Passing the Norfolk pines on New South Head Road, Matthew tried to think of something non-controversial to say. He commented that he'd often seen an eagle circling these trees at sundown.

'It would have well and truly done its circling by now,' Rosetta said. 'I can't believe it's six-thirty already.'

'You've had a big day,' Matthew said, not daring to add that she could do without the drama that Grant had hauled her into. Any topic surrounding what they'd just endured had to be avoided. Their exchange about pine-circling eagles—fascinatingly majestic creatures—had reminded him of the sculpture from Charlie. Strangely, the retirement-gift recollection summoned up the unpleasant rushing sensation of travelling backwards.

Matthew forced himself to keep his eyes on the darkened road. Afraid that he might lose consciousness, he blinked and shook his head.

And then he saw it. In a three-second flash of light.

There he was, as a toddler, gazing up at the jacaranda tree at the eagle above when the eagle spoke to him. 'Dinner at Joe's,' it said. *Dinner at Joe's.*

The vision left him disoriented. His car was veering towards the kerb. He grasped at the steering wheel and yanked it back to the lane he'd been in, blocking the van behind him as he did so. Predictably, a loud honk sounded, a blare so exaggeratedly drawn-out, Matthew wondered whether the driver's horn had a ten-kilo dumbbell bearing down on it. Would they have to put up with this noisy reminder of his driving error all the way to Burwood?

Thankfully, the toot came to an end. Matthew gave the angry driver a wave of apology, but the guy in the van raised a fist at him. The driver had every right to be annoyed.

Once comfortably restored to the right lane, Matthew turned to his passenger to check she was okay.

'Woo, that was lucky,' she said. Her long dark hair had fallen forward and curtained most of her face. She lifted her head then threw it back, brushing aside the smooth tresses dramatically. 'That could have been the end of us!'

'Yeah! Gee, I'm sorry about that.' These visions had better not bug him again. The results could be disastrous. Next he'd be dropping things! The butter-fingers nerdiness had never entirely left him, not even in his maturity.

Dinner at Joe's? What was meant by dinner at Joe's? Why would an eagle tell a two-year-old something as irrelevant as that? And why was he remembering this now? The first time he'd remembered it, on discovering the eagle statue in Charlie's office, the memory had played out like a silent movie. Today its volume had been turned up full blast.

The driver he'd inconvenienced caught up and was winding down his window, the expression on his face far from civil. 'Arrogant yuppie bastard,' he yelled. 'You don't *own* the road, you moron!'

Intent on outdoing the grump, Matthew sped up, and to cover his crumbling pride, laughed in a way he hoped was nonchalant. 'Bit of an overreaction,' he commented. He checked the rear-vision mirror. No danger of further abuse. The van had shrunk indignantly into the distance.

Rosetta was giggling, probably at the randomness of Matthew's road sense. He wanted to shoot that bloody eagle. If the eagle had been real, rather than a resident of his memory, he would have definitely given it a go.

Rosetta's laughter subsided. She said, 'I think it's hilarious how some of us react to innocent mistakes.'

She was laughing at the other guy, not at him. If it had been Bernadette in the passenger seat, the predominant words would have been 'shouldn't have.' You *shouldn't have* lost your grip on the steering wheel. You *shouldn't have* sped up. You *shouldn't have* made a spectacle of us.

Rosetta's home was a modest interwar single storey, complete with bricked-in verandah and old-fashioned garden. She was living there, she said, temporarily, while she looked at purchasing a new home.

When Matthew retrieved her cases from his boot, he arrived at the uncomfortable realisation that after saying goodbye, he might never see her again. While he now knew her address, he also knew she was moving soon. Good thing he knew where Crystal Consciousness was.

Prolonging the conversation in an attempt to shelve the goodbye a few moments more, he told her as he followed her up the verandah steps with her cases, 'I went to your shop the other day to look for a book, but you weren't...I mean *the book* wasn't there. Are you still on leave or are you back there tomorrow?'

'I'm not going back,' said Rosetta, smiling. 'I've left.'

Aargh! He didn't have any point of contact now. Not even her place of work.

'I didn't realise you worked for someone there,' he told her. 'For some reason I thought you owned it.'

She pulled her hair away from her face. Twisted it unselfconsciously into a low ponytail. 'It's funny you should say that. Lately I've been contemplating contacting Caroline to make an offer.'

'You should. It'd be a good little investment, that shop. Prime position.'

'What book were you looking for, Matthew?'

'It's called *Our True Ancient History.* You wouldn't know of it I guess?' He lowered her cases onto the verandah floorboards.

'But I do! I do!' Rosetta's vibrant eyes were wide and shining. 'It's an amazing book. We study it even! In fact...' She turned towards the door. '...My daughter's probably left Royston's copy in the sitting room. That's if she hasn't already returned it to him, or packed it away for the move.' She unlocked the door, telling Matthew that someone called Lena was looking after her daughter and that Lena had said she'd drop the girl home at eight-thirty, after they'd watched *Here and Afar* together. 'Listen, Matthew, I won't invite you in, because there's nowhere to sit. We're moving out next week, and I've given most of our furniture to the women's and children's shelter. Have a seat on the verandah here while I dash in and try to find it.'

Matthew sank into a cane chair. His stomach rumbled, reminding him dinner was due. He could do with a pasta. An Amaretti's pasta. He'd stop by on the way back, but first he'd better check this was okay with Rhoda. He took his phone from his pocket, dialled home and asked the housekeeper if she'd mind staying an hour-and-a-half longer with the girls at double the money.

'That's quite all right with me, Matthew,' she chirped. 'But I'm already being paid double the amount. Your wife proposed that before she left.' This was news to Matthew.

Rosetta returned, holding a dark blue book. Its tarnished silver lettering suggested it might have been bound in the 1920s. She sat beside him, pointing out a poem at the beginning of the chapters and chattering enthusiastically about a place called Elysium Glades. 'You're welcome to borrow it,' she said. The fragrance she wore evoked tropical flowers, which, for the second time since he'd been in her company that evening, prompted Matthew to recall the summers of his youth.

A small yellow and black hatch pulled up in Ashbury Avenue. Matthew drew back when a wiry sort of guy with no hair and shortish whiskers exited the car and rocketed towards the verandah.

Rosetta shouted, 'Royston!'

Who was this? Another boyfriend? She'd been Adam's girl, then Grant's girl. Was she this Royston bloke's girl now? Matthew rose to face the gate crasher.

Royston screeched delightedly and ran to Rosetta with his heels flicked out. Matthew breathed out a grateful sigh.

A plethora of squawks and kisses followed. Rosetta introduced Matthew to her friend. The friend's high regard for Rosetta was obvious since he spoke to her in a cascade of affectionate superlatives. A whirlwind of disjointed gabble ensued, then Royston was off.

To a party he said. Before Matthew knew it, Royston had apologetically snatched up the book he was holding, the book Rosetta said Matthew could borrow, and sped off with merry abandon in his bumble bee vehicle.

'I'm really, *really*, sorry about that,' said Rosetta. She looked crushed.

'No, that's fine. He'd promised the book to someone else.'

'Yeah. Someone at the party apparently. What a bummer he was giving them the book tonight.'

Now Matthew had no means of follow-up. He'd reached a dead end and couldn't think of another excuse to see Rosetta again without sounding like he was chatting her up. Highly inappropriate since he was still technically married, and Rosetta was more than likely already involved with someone new. He and Rosetta would part ways, some supremely lucky guy would get to claim her heart, and Matthew would get on with making a life for himself as a single.

They said their goodbyes, and Matthew watched the long-haired siren wander to her door. It was time to cut his losses and go. He was looking forward to eating at Amaretti's. A basket of garlic bread, a plate of Napolitana. Joe Romano was an awesome cook. He'd have dinner at...And then the vision came to him again. A circling eagle. A tree with purple flowers. The eagle's command.

Rosetta wrenched the door open. When Rosetta stepped languidly inside, Matthew found himself shouting, 'Dinner at Joe's.'

Rosetta stepped back out and spun round to look at him, the dark arches of her eyebrows raised in inquiry.

'Um..Just wondering if you're hungry. I'm off for dinner at Joe's. You're welcome to join me if you feel like a quick meal out.'

Rosetta looked down and laughed. Then she shrugged.

'Unless there was something you needed to do instead,' he added.

'The only thing I needed to do was drive down to the supermarket and get something quick and easy for dinner.'

Rosetta's blue BMW, the one that had its light left on at Grant's block of flats the other week, wasn't anywhere in sight. 'Where *is* your car?' he asked. 'Can't see it in the driveway.' What if the car wasn't hers but a live-in boyfriend's? What if the boyfriend was a hefty, madly jealous ex-boxer, about to return any second?

Rosetta pursed her lips. 'That's right. It's not. My car is...' she looked uncertain. 'With Craig. A friend of mine. I've lent it to him. Ah, well. I probably need the exercise.'

'I'm happy to drive you to the supermarket if you'd rather not walk.'

Rosetta shrugged again and her face lit up with that thousand kilowatt smile. Could she be amenable to the idea of dinner?

'Otherwise save yourself the trouble. Join me for a casual bite to eat at my local Italian place. Joe's a brilliant cook. He specialises in Sicilian gourmet.'

'Ooh, Sicilian sounds tempting.' Rosetta looked away. 'I...I wonder what stage your wife's at now.'

'Yeah, poor Bernadette.' He kicked away a pebble beneath his foot. She was probably at the police station now, giving her statement. 'I'd phone her, but I don't think it'd be right considering the circumstances.'

'Why wouldn't it be right?' Rosetta was looking at him intently now. She could most certainly be excused for thinking he'd got his priorities wrong.

He drew in a deep breath and said, 'Bernadette and I have separated. We're divorcing.'

'Oh good.'

Matthew's mouth dropped open. Had Rosetta really meant to say that?

Rosetta hesitated. Slapped the palm of her hand against her forehead. 'No, that's not it! I didn't mean to say *Oh good,* I meant to say *Oh God.* Aaaaargh! Those two little words... Good and God.' Short, loud laugh. 'So easy to mix up.'

'I mix them up all the time, myself.'

Rosetta's eyes were lowered and she was shaking her head, glossy hair swishing from side to side.

In a further attempt to rescue her from her awkwardness, Matthew added, 'And it *is* good actually. I should have broken up with Bernadette years ago.' He checked his watch. 'I don't think she'd appreciate me phoning her tonight. She's been through enough. I'm planning on phoning Grant instead, in an hour or so, to check how things are going.'

Rosetta nodded and sighed. He wished she hadn't had to witness that sordid scenario at Vaucluse.

He changed the subject back to eating out. 'So, what do you say, Rosetta? Will it be dinner at Joe's?'

Matthew was back on the road, cruising towards a drive-in bottle shop the GPS was directing him to, elated at having convinced Rosetta that going to the restaurant with him was a good idea.

She'd wanted to stay home and freshen up while he went to track down a chilled sparkling red to accompany their meal.

At five to seven he was back in Ashbury Avenue, heading towards the verandah steps of Rosetta's old-world charm house. The door with its array of stained glass windows opened soon after he rang the bell. The flyscreen door she stood behind veiled her in a misty elusiveness. She half-opened the screen door and shrugged. 'I hope this isn't too much for where we're going. Everything else from the trip needed laundering.'

Hip-skimming skirt, elaborate red blouse, sparkling earrings. Eyes even more exotic now that she'd made them up. Stunning.

'No, it's fine,' said Matthew. An understatement. He could do better than that. 'You actually look very nice.' Another understatement.

He flourished the bottle of premium wine.

Rosetta was suitably impressed. 'And good news!' She held up a book, a replica of the one the bumble-bee driver seized. 'Royston dropped it back to me and said you're welcome to borrow it. Brenda, his friend at the party, had already got herself a copy.'

'That's decent of him.' Matthew passed the bottle from one hand to another and helped her hold open the screen door by pressing an elbow against it. He reached out his other arm, awkwardly, to collect the book Rosetta held out to him, and strove to increase his grip on the frost-slippery wine. When he clasped the book, his eyes made a swift connection with hers.

The bottle slipped from his hold.

A *clank*, a *clatter* and a *tinkle* jolted him back to earth.

Matthew tried not to groan. He didn't want to look down. He wasn't in the mood to witness the disaster zone at his feet.

'I'll get the dustpan and broom,' Rosetta said pleasantly and disappeared down the hallway.

Matthew glared at the havoc he'd created. Shards of glass, swimming in a claret-coloured puddle, littered Rosetta's verandah.

He gritted his teeth. In frustration he turned, reached up, and punched at the air. His knuckles clinked against something spherical...the verandah's dangling light globe. It swung angrily towards him. He sprang out of its way and stepped forward again to steady it. He could only be grateful he hadn't caused that to shatter too. No question about it. The butter-fingers nerd was back.

Chapter Nine

XLIX

Stunned at having been zapped into drowsiness by enchanted lightning, Pieter found himself standing before Alcor in the Dream Sphere.

'Do not concern yourself, Pieter,' Alcor said. 'It is only a short visit. The breaking of the stone-eagle spell was so very powerful that it rendered you unconscious. Would you like to see the future you have enabled for Storlem?'

'Of course, master.'

'You no longer need to refer to me as your master. You have grown greatly in Kindness Merits, Pieter, through this service to one trapped in darkness and the brave journey you made to meet your beloved. I am a brother. We are equals in our masteries.'

'All right then, brother,' said Pieter, amazed he had earned this honourable title. 'Please reveal to me the future of the eagle-winged guard.'

Alcor waved his hand.

Through a mist of palest emerald, Pieter encountered a vision of Storlem entering the Dream Sphere's pearl-encrusted gates of the afterlife and saw Storlem search in vain for the woman he loved. A cherub told him Orahney was preparing for her next life as an elf woman and needed to be released from her previous life's heart-connections. Storlem nodded sadly. The cherub suggested he plan a return to the earth in a further lifetime of Orahney's, for in this one she was betrothed to another.

Orahney was to be a water sprite, the cherub said, after her life as an Elysium Glades elf. There appeared to be no-one as yet who would play the role of her beloved. Perhaps Storlem would accompany her there?

Yes, agreed Storlem. What and who was he to be?

The cherub handed Storlem a scroll. 'Instructions from Alcor,' the cherub explained. 'You are to sing very powerfully in this future life of yours.'

Pieter watched Storlem unfurl this sacred text and nod with satisfaction. 'Mortal again,' he said. 'I shall be employed within a sort of temple.'

The vision of Storlem faded.

Remembering his observation of the spinning wheel and the cauldron, the moth and the blossom and the tree, the sparrow and the kingfisher, Pieter said to his Dream Master, 'His forthcoming existences are free of entrapment.'

Alcor agreed. 'The future, as you see, is not set in stone. And what will follow this temple life of his, Pieter? Where do you suppose Storlem will go next?'

'You had better tell me, brother,' Pieter said.

Once more, Alcor gave a magical wave of his hand.

Before Pieter appeared the interior of a cottage where a man was seated at a candlelit table, a man with a feather in his hand. He was writing upon a page with the feather. A woman with dark hair and eyes was watching him from a doorway. The woman's aura held the same hues as Orahney's: crimson, gold, amber, orange.

Pieter was then transported into that same domed construction in which the Sonic Unity Gathering was held, hovering invisibly above a man whose eyes of green displayed a sparkling eagerness. The man was seated amongst many others, and he was holding the hand of Orahney. The faerie, in contrast to the woman she was in the life before, was possessing of smoother hair—although dark again in colour—and a broader mouth. She radiated not only autumn colours but pearlescent overtones as well, direct from the cosmos.

'And now,' said a disconnected voice. 'We introduce King Nikolaus.'

The image faded.

'This Sonic Unity Gathering that Storlem is to attend one day,' said Pieter to Alcor. 'It is somewhat important is it not?'

'The Sonic Unity Gathering is enormously important, Pieter,' said Alcor. 'It heralds a new history for the world below. This congregation of world leaders is a celebration. They are there to honour The Silvering.'

'Thank God it wasn't loaded,' Rosetta heard Matthew say into his phone.

They were strolling along a tree-lined street towards Matthew's favourite Italian restaurant while the last of autumn's leaves flitted down from the branches of towering elms. From what Rosetta could make of the conversation, Dette had at this stage given her statement. Judging by Matthew's responses, Grant was filling him in on Dette's plan to threaten Adam.

Matthew continued with, 'Unbelievable. I realise she knew it wasn't loaded, but what if...? Hm. Dumb decision.'

It had been a bizarre evening. Rosetta could never have guessed that a lift from the airport with Grant would result in a panicked detour to the home of Adam Harrow. Images of the event rolled back to her in flashes. A distraught Dette Weissler sobbing beside a handgun. Emergency crew discussing Adam's tragic overdose. Adam's lifeless and unrecognisable form.

And now the married guy was divorcing his wife and wanting to eat a meal with Rosetta. His intent was innocent of course. He needed someone to talk to. He needed a friend. Probably needed someone to talk him back into his marriage.

During their chat on the verandah earlier, Matthew had mentioned the topic her Friday Fortnight group centred on; the book that had her puzzling over past lives and lexigrams in names; the book that had inspired her, decades ago, to write a flowery rhyme about Pan, the god of nature, freeing an eagle that had turned to stone.

She'd offered to lend him *Our True Ancient History*; had found it on the window ledge once she'd dashed inside. She caught a glimpse of herself in the hallway mirror and the image that greeted her triggered a frown of despair. Her head looked as though she'd dipped it in diesel oil. The lanolin conditioner bought in the land of sheep farming was a purchase spurred by her tourists' curiosity but it hadn't delivered its promised results. Her hair was the opposite of 'sleek and manageable'. Wondering whether she could risk tidying up the lankness without keeping her guest waiting, she breathed out a sigh at the sound of Matthew speaking on his phone to someone named Rhoda. Then she ripped a newly bought spray from her packing case, tore away its crisp plastic wrapping and blasted her scalp with it.

The hairspray was an explosion of tropical florals. Its saccharine reek, similar to the frangipani in suntan oil, would suggest to Matthew she'd run in from the verandah to lather herself in perfume, that she'd wanted to smell sweet in his presence! Thoroughly peeved with the manufacturer, she doubled over and shook her head energetically, hoping to lessen the tropically fragrant evidence. It wasn't until she placed the spray on her dressing table that she noticed the words on the can. *Rainforest Room Deodoriser.* It had been next to the hair products at the souvenir shop, the colours on its label identical.

Trying not to dwell on her disastrous observation skills, she'd snatched up the book and hurried back to Matthew. He'd commented of course. How could anyone *not* notice such a horribly heady scent? Said she 'smelt like summer'. It could have been worse, she supposed. He could have compared her to a fumigated kitchen, or turned away from her, gasping for air.

That was just before he invited her to his favourite local restaurant. His trip to the bottle shop had allowed her enough time to shower, throw on the new 'going-out' clothes she'd bought in Christchurch and re-do her make-up. He'd driven her to the picturesque street they were now in, where windows of elegant houses gleamed through the darkness in shades of amber.

Further along the footpath, they came to a stop outside a small iron gate. Matthew ended his call to Grant. 'Thankfully Dette hasn't been charged.' He breathed out a sigh, clinked the gate open and gestured to a flight of stone steps. 'After you.'

Rosetta virtually skipped up the lamp-lit steps of the restaurant's garden. She'd expected Amaretti's to be little more than the cramped fluorescent-lit kitchen she'd been to with Adam the night he'd fled the retirement dinner.

Matthew's 'casual bite to eat' reference was hardly a description she'd use for the upstairs terrace. Exquisite lacework and a pale coral glow behind the windows suggested refined dining. Inside, the black and white chequered tablecloths were graced with cut flowers. Dainty silver vases glimmered in the candlelight. Unsure whether she should have worn something dressier, Rosetta scanned the seated patrons. Would she be greeted by a tuxedoed dining-room attendant?

A dark-haired man dressed informally in a T-shirt, jeans and apron, stepped towards them with his arms outstretched. 'Matthew! Where were you last week?'

'Had to meet up with a friend. Missed out, I'm afraid, Joe.'

'No wonder you look so hungry!' Joe turned to Rosetta and beamed. 'And who is this?' he asked. 'Is this your lovely wife?'

'Er...'

Rosetta understood Matthew's hesitation. Once he said no, he'd have to explain his wife's absence and introduce someone unfamiliar who he'd delivered home less than an hour ago. And they were nothing more than acquaintances—He hadn't even answered the note she'd got Izzie to forward to him. If it hadn't been for that crisis between their exes, they wouldn't even be there.

Leaning forward, Rosetta accepted the hand Joe offered. She would say she was a family friend: Matthew's stepdaughter was a pal of Izzie's, and Rosetta had known the girl and her younger sister for at least a year.

Matthew beat her to it. Lightly, he said, 'Rosetta's a friend of the family.'

Adding to that, Rosetta told Joe she'd just got back from the airport and admitted she was hungry as a horse.

'Okay, *bella*, we'll make sure we remedy that.' Joe gestured for her to follow as he moved towards the far end of the restaurant. 'This way please, *bella*. Any friend of Matt and his family is a friend of ours.' Joe led them through an archway with sculpted roses, then into an elaborate hallway and indicated with a wave of his hand a row of tables-for-two lining the wall. 'Anywhere here is fine.' He turned and rushed towards the kitchen. 'I'll get someone to seat you.'

Friend of the family, in reality, was no great exaggeration. Rosetta had now happened upon Dette often enough to consider her a friend, not necessarily a good one, but that was a minor detail. She knew she was far from being a friend to Dette tonight. Hearing a waiter say, 'Is this your lovely wife,' to Dette's husband and thinking how magical the reply would sound if answered in the affirmative, wasn't something a true friend would do.

Then again, Matthew wasn't Dette's anymore. He'd sounded adamant about wanting a divorce, but people often made rash decisions in the heat of the moment. More than likely he'd decide to give his marriage another go. And he should, too.

Matthew stepped ahead to the nearest table. Rosetta's gaze skimmed over his broad and tapering back. Definitely a swimmer. He paused, turned, then asked which seat she'd like. The view from where she stood encompassed the darkened hallway that opened out to a courtyard with paper lanterns in a variety of pinks, violets and vibrant greens, but she indicated the chair facing the foyer, an area of interesting activity where new diners whirled in, and bill-payers threw tips into a waterless fish bowl.

Matthew stepped forward to pull out her chair, just as a waiter rushed across to do the same. The next few seconds were awkwardly slapstick. The two grappled stumblingly, then Matthew circled the waiter like a bristling-feathered hawk before halting and stepping aside.

The waiter gestured for Rosetta to sit down. Matthew slunk into the seat facing the courtyard, and the waiter handed them each a menu.

'For a moment I thought there might be a scuffle,' Rosetta told Matthew with a wink.

'Yeah!' Matthew raised his eyebrows. 'I was almost ready to deck him. Until I realised he wasn't trying to confiscate your chair.'

'You graciously let him win. Gave the chair up, but not without a struggle.'

Matthew lowered his voice to a growl. 'I would have done it better than him. That guy was a total amateur.' He opened his menu. 'Do you like pasta, Rosetta? The pasta's made on the premises and their sauces are out of this world.'

'My favourite is Napolitana.'

'Great! I'd planned to order that too.'

'You don't mind it being mostly tomato?'

'Not at all.' Matthew looked away, as though weighing up whether he should expand on this. 'I've got out of the way of eating meat these days.'

'You're a vegetarian? Me too!'

'Is that a fact? Are you really?'

'Ever since the age of seventeen.'

'I've only cut out meat recently. Something to do with a bloke comparing a lamb to a puppy. What got *you* into giving it up?'

Rosetta told him about her animal activist days, launching into a summary of her passion for promoting the protection of all living things. Whenever she looked at Matthew to check for signs of restlessness, she was pleased to find his expression brightly alert. Whenever uncertainty caused her to hesitate, he encouragingly urged her to continue. The glimmers of kindness in his eyes made her feel as though whatever she said would be understood. Talking to a man as attentive as this was a danger. She didn't want to feel *too* comfortable with someone else's husband.

With the drama of the tragedy earlier that evening, she'd been released for a while from her annoying fascination with Matthew. Right now she was mostly concerned for Dette, and the trauma Dette would be experiencing. But when Matthew had driven her home, they'd conversed a little, and she'd silently told Molly Carr's otherworldly beings, whoever they were, that she hoped they'd already arranged a man with qualities echoing Matthew's, to star in her not-so-distant future.

She wound up her monologue on the benefits of vegetarianism and asked Matthew where he'd heard about *Our True Ancient History*. It wasn't an easy book to get hold of usually. In the past year she'd noticed a resurgence in its popularity when celebrity psychics—household names—and social commentators such as Conan Dalesford had quoted from the book, saying Lillibridge's ideals highlighted the present economy's pitfalls. Some were even saying a worldwide financial crash was imminent towards the end of 2008. Many had talked about possible systems that might ultimately echo the

Currency of Kindness. This sort of news was like gold dust to Rosetta. She'd included much of it in the 'articles' section of her Friday Fortnight site. She wouldn't admit to the website tonight. She didn't want to appear too fanatical.

Matthew leaned forward, resting his forearms on the table. He was wearing a black shirt with the sleeves rolled up. The shirt with its open collar looked brilliant on him. Not many men, Rosetta thought, looked as good in black as Matthew did, but then, how many men had looks as good as Matthew's?

'It's bizarre,' Matthew said, 'how I heard about the book. I was at a poetry night. It was...' He looked down. 'It was on a friend's recommendation. Hey, I just thought of something. Rosetta isn't a common name. There was...Better tell you this in sequence. I'm all over the shop.' He drew in a breath and smiled charmingly. 'I happened to meet an author by the name of Conan Dalesford. You might know of his writing, Rosetta, having worked at Crystal Consciousness. Have you heard of *Thoughts on Tomorrow's Tycoon War*?'

'Have I ever! I arranged a launch for that author because I loved his philosophies.'

'You arranged that?'

'Sure did. Are you saying you went to it?' Maybe Matthew had attended the launch after she'd left.

'No. I saw it advertised on the Crystal Consciousness bookmark. I didn't get the book from there. It's second-hand.'

'Ha! I wonder who bought it from us initially. Craig was the one who first told me about Conan Dalesford's books. Craig lived in Alice Springs when he was younger, and they struck up a friendship. I thought Conan's observations on the greed-lack cycle were great. Really insightful.'

'I'm with you there. I found most of Dalesford's ideas to be pretty thought-provoking.'

The author had apparently suggested Matthew practice talking publicly. Matthew initially thought Conan had intuited a longheld whim of getting into politics. 'I've always wanted to help make a difference to society,' he told her. 'And although I'm all for fairness, I've since decided I'm not cut out for that sort of life.'

Reminded of the father she'd never known, a New Zealand member of parliament, Rosetta commented on the number of politicians with backgrounds in law. Matthew indicated interest in Rosetta being both a lawyer and a retail assistant at Crystal Consciousness, saying he remembered her mentioning her 'legal eagle' occupation at the bar. Was she an ex-lawyer?

She hedged around the subject artfully, avoiding untruths but skirting around the facts. She'd have told him if they'd known each other better, but they didn't, and there wouldn't be any further contact once they'd eaten their meal and said their goodbyes. If he thought she'd already got that degree and had achieved a career in law, did it really matter? It was true in another reality, a reality known as The Future. Daniela's legacy had freed her up to study full-time. She was well on her way to becoming a legal crusader for human rights.

The waiter arrived and poured them each a glass from the second bottle of red Matthew bought. The first was in pieces at the bottom of Rosetta's recycling bin. She still felt guilty about that. When she'd opened the screen door to hand him Royston's book, Matthew had caught her gaze and held it, and the air had turned into a swirling caress. A *clank*, a *clatter* and a *tinkle* had jolted her back to earth, the result of having dreamily foisted the book on poor Matthew when he'd already had his hands full.

Lilting melodies sprang up at the other side of the restaurant. A rather compact older gentleman with dark curling hair was playing the accordion. 'Looks familiar,' she said, mostly to herself.

Matthew regarded her wryly. 'Former boyfriend?'

'Hm. Possibly.' When Matthew registered surprise, she laughed and shook her head. Recognition dawning she said, 'Ah! I know who it is. And you do too, Matthew.'

'I do?' Matthew turned to look again at the musician.

'He was at the bar the night of your retirement drinks.'

'Hey, yeah! The Russian acrobat. Well spotted. You obviously have a stalker.'

'Or not.' Rosetta pressed her thumb against the table's edge and took in a shaky breath. Matthew's lighthearted remark had unsettled her. She reminded herself she no longer had anything to fear. A metaphoric mask had fallen away. From this day forward, she and Izzie were safe.

'Or not,' Matthew agreed. 'Definitely not. A fan more like it. One who means you no harm.'

The waiter took their orders. Matthew insisted Rosetta get an entrée as well. This took very little persuading since she'd already pored over each mouth-watering menu description and had prior to that reminded herself she no longer lacked funds.

Her weight was still an issue of course. She'd begin that diet tomorrow.

An aroma of roasted garlic pervaded Amaretti's, mingling warmly with the daphne on the tables.

Rosetta, listening to Matthew while she munched on an especially delicious Vermicelli Napolitana, found herself marvelling over how a voice could sound both commanding and soothing at the same time.

Matthew told her Conan Dalesford had suggested he do the odd spot of public speaking in preparation for a future that only Conan could see. He'd thought a poetry club would be a good place to start. The club Matthew had visited sounded the same as the one she went to with Darren. 'And then I hear, from the corridor, a woman reading a poem that reminds me a bit of these...' He looked away. '...These dreams I've had, to do with an elf and an autumn tree. And the woman then says to the host that she'd dreamt about an elf and—'

Serendipity!

'That would have been—'

'Funnily enough, your name, *Rosetta*, isn't common I don't think, and yet...' Matthew elaborated.

Synchronicity! Matthew had been introduced to her poem before he'd been introduced to her! Immediately Rosetta felt self-conscious about the attempt in her youth at describing both a dream and Lillibridge's world. But Matthew had taken the poem seriously enough to remember it. The poem had reminded him of a dream of his own.

'That's when I first heard about the book, when this poet named Rosetta happened to mention it at the community centre.'

Freaky! He'd dreamt about a world from a book he'd never even read! The elf he described did sound a lot like Pieter of the Brumlynds.

Matthew studied her, green eyes narrowing slightly. 'She even looked a bit like you. Her hair was sleek like yours is.' He then coughed and said, 'The woman who left early, that is. That mightn't have been the poet at all.' Matthew shifted in his seat, concerned, perhaps, that he'd assumed too much.

Rosetta collapsed into laughter. 'That was me!'

'Whoa!' Matthew leaned back in his chair.

'I was the one who wrote "The Piper!"'

'You're kidding.'

'And I recited it a few weeks back. Poets' Garret.'

Matthew clicked his fingers. 'That was the name of the group, yeah.'

'I can't believe the poem actually had some meaning in it for someone!'

'Y'know, the minute I started telling you, the penny dropped. I'm surprised I haven't associated you with that night until now.'

'Well, you only found out my name the other week at Grant's. That's ages since the poetry club meeting.'

Matthew grimaced at the table. His eyebrows rose in a single flick. 'Yeah, look I'm really sorry about getting your name wrong.' He shook his head and said in an incredulous whisper, 'Lucetta!'

Rosetta leaned forward to reassure him. In a low voice she said, 'Matthew, the drums that night were deafening. I think you did well to hear anything at all.' She listed all the accidental titles she'd been given over the years: Rosa, Marcetta, Rosita, and on one occasion even Bruschetta, and then mentioned the time a three-year-old boy had confused her name with a breed of dog his uncle owned and referred to her as 'Red Setter'.

Still watching her with those arresting eyes of his, he said, 'Your hair. Is it a different colour now?'

'Not sure.' Rosetta tried to remember when she'd been to the poetry night. Had Darren made her hair darker before or after that? 'There may have been some of the burgundy still in it.'

'Aha!' Matthew tapped the base of his wineglass. 'I sat in the row behind you.'

'I had no idea you were so perceptive. That's pretty cool.'

Matthew lifted the wineglass to his lips. 'Attractiveness affects me in that way.'

Had he been referring to her? Surely someone as charismatic as Matthew would only deem willowy model types like Dette, and ectomorphs in general, to be within his 'attractiveness' frame of reference.

Intent on appearing less stunned than she felt at Matthew's first impressions, Rosetta switched to another topic, repeatedly tripping over her words and pausing in all the wrong spots.

Matthew listened seriously. His appreciative glance swept over her as she talked, prompting the desire for all barriers to melt away; for Matthew's marital status to change to footloose bachelor, for the restaurant to be replaced with somewhere more intimate: the beach at midnight, perhaps, or a softly lit bedroom.

'I left the poetry night in a bit of a hurry,' she told him. 'I'd got a call from Adam, and it was the first time he'd phoned me. Second time he'd asked me out. I was so...' She hesitated, wondering how she would have reacted at the time if she'd known the true Adam. What would she have done if someone had told her the neat-haired blond Adonis was the same person whose gruesome presence had compelled her to move house? That he'd caused her to fear for her daughter's safety?

Matthew was watching her intently. 'You were so...?'

'...So enamoured with poor Adam that I couldn't think sensibly once I'd talked to him. I paced up and down in a little memorial garden near the car park, too over the moon to go back inside, but I did wait for the poetry meeting to finish because Darren was still in there. Darren is Royston's new partner.'

'And Royston is the guy who turned up at your place earlier?'

'That was Royston, yes. In my mind back then Adam was Perfection Plus.'

And now Adam was gone. She plucked a dessert spoon from the table. Its sheen responded to the candlelight in a pulsing sparkle. Heroin would have twisted Adam, would have whittled away at his mind and made him do stupid stuff like peering into windows, and even into clothes dryers! Had she actually been terrified of that person once? Now she felt nothing but pity. Two petals floated from the daphne arrangement and settled in the palm of her hand. She curled her fingers around them and sighed.

She told Matthew she'd been just as surprised as he was to learn of the drug addiction and confided the relief she'd felt at breaking up with Adam before getting too interested. In response, Matthew confided he'd found out Dette had been cheating on him with Adam. Since Royston's talk with her the night of Izzie's birthday she'd believed there was nothing Adam could do to surprise her. Conversely, this revelation of Matthew's was startling. Matthew had been two-timed by Dette and she, Rosetta, had been two-timed by Adam. She told Matthew she was sorry to hear such bad news and told herself his wish for divorce was justified.

'I should be the one saying sorry,' Matthew said, 'for revealing the details about someone you went out with.' He twisted his wedding ring grimly. 'You and I. We've both been conned. I needed to take more notice when you mentioned the penchant Geminis have for two of everything.'

'Did I say that?'

'Something to that effect. At the bar. Something about the planet Venus.'

'That's right. I did too. But Gemini isn't always like that. People with Venus in Gemini have more of a tendency to two-time because they're easily bored.'

'Is that right?'

'Yeah! And they love all sorts of interaction. They might choose to channel that amazing double-tasking energy into, say, running a couple of businesses, or juggling two careers. Craig, the guy I told you about in my note, the lawyer with the start-up mining company, has heaps of planets in Gemini, including Venus, and he's the most loyal person you could wish to meet.'

Matthew said nothing.

Rosetta's face blazed. He wasn't acknowledging her mention of the note she'd got Izzie to give Sara about Craig's startup. Probably felt embarrassed for her.

A number of seconds passed before Matthew replied. 'As a friend, though, or as someone you'd fancy going out with?'

'Craig? As a friend, I guess, although funnily enough, I *have* been out with him. That's a while ago now. Way back in the distant past.'

'Who finished it?'

'Me, but it wasn't because he couldn't be trusted. He's the opposite of fickle. More on the clingy side if anything: he'd tell you that himself. Cancerian Rising Sign.'

'I've got a Cancerian Rising Sign.'

'Have you? Wow.'

'At least, that's what my astrologer sister-in-law says.'

'You don't strike me as clingy at all.'

Matthew leaned forward, smiling. He caught her eye, raised an eyebrow, and in a low voice, said, 'Then what *do* I strike you as?'

Hot! was the first thought that sprang to mind. 'Cancerians are good with money,' Rosetta said, 'so it makes sense you've worked for an investment bank. And Cancerians can have a strong awareness of other people's feelings, which would have helped in your work as a supervisor.'

'A supervisor?'

'Adam told me you were a supervisor in the bank's call centre...with a staff of eight.' *In charge of eight people*, Adam had said. *And they all hate him.*

Matthew leaned back in his chair and chuckled quietly. 'I was nothing of the sort.'

'He made that up?'

'I was a trading manager like he was. In charge of thirty-five.'

'Thirty-five what? Thirty-five people, do you mean?' Realising how goofy the question sounded, Rosetta bit her lip. What else would he have been in charge of? Thirty-five indoor plants?

Regarding her calmly, Matthew gave a nod. 'I used to wish I could warn each new girlfriend of Harrow's that he was a bit of a...well, look, I'm not meaning to be disrespectful about the guy, but I think you'd agree he was never very honourable.'

Rosetta shook a stray strand of hair away from her line of vision. 'I wouldn't have put anything past him.'

Adam had complained about Dette flirting with him, and yet he would have already been entrenched in an affair with her. Rosetta had overlooked the flirty body language between the two once Matthew said Dette was his wife. She'd missed the flashing warning light; was all too ready to believe Adam's claim that Dette's advances were an unwanted surprise; had told herself Angus was to blame for that suspicious self-protectiveness of hers. His leaving her for someone else had put a long-term dint in her ability to trust.

'I always knew deep down I wasn't the only one he was seeing, or planning on seeing, so I hesitated to launch into any kind of relationship with him,' Rosetta told Matthew. 'I was never his girlfriend, but I think one of his objectives was to trick me into thinking I was.'

'I think you're right.' Matthew was studying the table, lost in thought. He lifted his eyes to stare at her. 'I'm glad you weren't fooled by the charm.'

The connection, although momentary, was intense. Matthew's spark-inducing eye contact had caused Rosetta to forget her next words.

Matthew gestured to the vase of flowers on their table. 'What did you say this flower was called?'

'Daphne.'

'It smells sensational. Reminds me of my grandfather's orchard during the spring.'

The sharp, clean fragrance of the purple and white florets had evoked for Matthew the memory of citrus blossom. His mother's parents were English, he said, and he'd visited them often because he'd lived in the United Kingdom up till the age of seventeen. His descriptions of biting into dewy plums and of helping his granddad build a chicken coop, of breaking apart the hot bread his grandmother used to make, made Rosetta feel as though she were there. His recollection of fighting through curtains of cobwebs on the apple trees he climbed with his brother, caused an involuntary shudder. 'Ugh!' Rosetta said. 'Spiders!'

The topics she discussed with Matthew throughout the meal, mostly to the strains of the Cossack dancer's accordion, were mundane at best, but somehow took on a passionate new vibrancy that wasn't entirely due to the wine, the candle flames or the sentimental music.

Matthew was amazed to learn Sara was buddies with Izzie, a sure sign he hadn't received the note Rosetta wrote him in New Zealand. 'Those crystals sound incredible,' he said once she told him the contents of her letter and some of Craig's claims. 'But crystals are pretty powerful anyway, aren't they? Dalesford has a brilliant one.'

'Powerful isn't a term I'd use to describe any I've ever owned or sold at Crystal Consciousness. Their energy seems to me to be soft. Kind of subtle. But who knows what's out there now?'

'I'll ask Sara where she might have stowed that note of yours, and I'll give Craig a call. Not necessarily to commit to anything, but I'd be curious to learn more. Thanks for thinking of me, Rosetta. I appreciate that.'

Just enough time for the final course before Matthew's house-keeper Rhoda was due to knock off. 'She's minding the girls,' he said. 'I don't want to be out longer than mentioned. She'd be keen to get home by now.'

Matthew ordered for Rosetta both the summer pudding and the gelato trio she'd been vacillating over, assuring her with a wink that he wanted to treat her to them.

'I'll end up as big as a hippopotamus,' she told him.

'I doubt your accuracy there.'

'You're right. Probably bigger. A pregnant hippopotamus. One that's expecting triplets.'

The accordionist waltzed up to their table when Matthew was handing the dessert menu back to Joe.

'This is Chippy,' Joe told them. 'Chippy or Zippy, something like that. Doesn't speak English, only Italian. Tends to be non-committal about his name. He and his twin Carla-Ann usually sing a duet of a Friday, but he's here by himself tonight.'

'Amazing,' Rosetta said, impressed at the man's versatility. Cossack dancer, acrobat, accordionist and now singer! 'Joe, could you tell Zippy—or Chippy—that I love the music he's playing?'

Joe happily translated.

The accordionist gabbled a reply and whirled around to her with a smile like sunshine. He embarked on an evocative vintage tune, which he sang along to in a resonantly pleasing timbre.

Delighted at the impromptu performance, Rosetta tapped her foot in time to the music. Matthew, she noticed, was trying to appear more comfortable than he felt. The accordionist noticed this too. He stopped crooning his song and halted the music. Diners at the other side of the room, intrigued by the sudden silence, turned to observe them. Unfazed by the interruption to an ambience he'd been instrumental in creating, the musician produced a pale pink camellia from the buttonhole of his jacket. 'Take it,' he said to Matthew. 'It will give you some-ting to look at. You makin' me nervous frownin' like that.'

Matthew handed the camellia to Rosetta, twirling it with a medieval flourish. She pretended to place it behind one of her ears, saying with mock seriousness, 'Which side indicates I'm available?'

Joe appeared, holding a rectangular plate aloft. 'Your dessert duo, *bella*,' he said. 'I've given you a small spoon to help it last longer.' He hurried away, saying over his shoulder, 'And there's a spoon for Matt too, in case you chicken out halfway through.'

'Super-generous serves,' Rosetta said. 'Matthew, you're going to have to help me with this.'

'Aargh, if you insist.' Matthew seized up the extra spoon and sliced through a corner of hazelnut gelato.

Rosetta jutted her lower lip and tried not to smile. 'Ooh, I had my eye on that, and now you've gone and vandalised it.'

She finished up her meal, and Matthew paid and tipped and chatted a little more with Joe. His way of guiding her to the door felt gently affectionate, but then, he was caring enough to treat any one of his friends with that sort of courtesy. Rosetta mentioned, as he walked alongside her towards his car, that the clock would move slowly while she waited for Lena to drop Izzie home. 'So I'll be sitting on a packing carton with nothing to look at but the walls.'

Matthew suggested he take her to Lena's in Bondi. 'Then you can watch the remainder of *Here and Afar* with them.'

Matthew's radio was tuned to a Golden Oldies Hour, the Chordettes in sublime harmony, trilling a song about dreams and the perfect man. The moon was full and golden against its nest of midnight-blue sky, turning the sand of Bondi Beach into dust the Sandman might strew. Its gilded-coin luminance reminded Rosetta of a comment Matthew made during their entrée, about the golden boys of the New York stock exchange. Rosetta asked what he'd meant when alluding to 'bulls and bears.'

'It's to do with market trends,' Matthew said. 'Strange term, I know. An upward trend is a bull market and a downward trend is a bear market.' He told her of a visit to Germany and his subsequent tour of Frankfurt's financial centre. Outside the exchange were statues depicting the two symbolic beasts eyeing each other warily.

Rosetta told Matthew as they glided along, that she was looking forward to seeing her daughter again. 'It's been two whole weeks!'

'Awesome,' Matthew said. 'Grant asked me to tell his girls their mother's been delayed in Vanuatu. I think the best thing to do is to protect them from all this as much as possible.'

'I agree. You're wise in doing that. Dette might choose to tell them after all, but that's up to Dette.'

They'd parked outside Lena's Edwardian stone cottage. Rosetta glimpsed shadows moving behind the maroon curtains, the same curtains she'd talked Lena into snapping up at the mall. It was time to say goodbye, and she wished it wasn't. The evening of lively conversation had lulled her into a zone she was reluctant to leave.

Matthew was drumming his fingers on the steering wheel. He took a deep breath, sighed and said, 'So when do you expect you'll be moving?'

'Within the next week or so. I'd like to buy an apartment on the lower North Shore.'

'Like Milson's Point, for example? I've got one there.'

'That'd be brilliant.' Milsons Point. Gorgeous harbour views, close to transport, a suburb that radiated a classical sort of affluence.

'I'll give you...' Matthew stretched back—reclining in his seat—and patted his shirt pockets, quite appealingly, Rosetta thought...and...*there* was that midnight beach again, making a nuisance of itself in her imagination. And the softly lit boudoir.

'No, I don't have his card on me.' He pushed a hand through his hair. 'Don't even have my own. Give me your card anyway, Rosetta, and I'll call you with the name of an estate agent I've found to be helpful.'

The only card she had was the one advertising her tarot-reading business. So far, she'd managed to steer Matthew away from the absolute truth, the fact that for most of her adult life she'd been far from successful. Increasing printers' costs had meant she'd resorted to her own amateurish handiwork. She didn't want him to see the purple paper squares with their squiggly gold-texta handwriting. She didn't want him to write her off as a New Age drifter. 'Er...Must have left the cards in my other bag,' she lied. 'I don't think I've got a pen on me either.' She scrabbled frantically through her handbag.

'I'll need your number, though, to return that book.' This sounded more like a question, delivered with a sidelong glance and lifted eyebrows.

Feeling dazed and panicked at the same time, Rosetta said quickly, 'My email address is on the attachment Izzie gave to Sara.' She bit her lip. The opportunity to see Matthew again depended heavily on whether Sara still had the note.

'No problem.' Matthew thumped his hands down on the steering wheel. 'Sara might still have your email attachment then. I seem to re-member her saying there was something in her locker for me. I thought it must have been a school newsletter.'

Without adding more, he turned and studied Lena's house. Rosetta didn't add any more either. Instead she observed the rare silence hovering between them and realised this was her cue to go. About to say goodbye, she stopped when Matthew said, 'Is your daughter happy with Burwood High, Rosetta?'

'Loves it.'

'Sara too. We were put off at first by the suburb the school's in, but all her friends were enrolled there and we didn't want to stand in the way of her going where she wanted to go, even if it did happen to be Burwood.'

In defence of where she lived, Rosetta said, 'Burwood's not such a bad place.' Quickly she added, 'But I wouldn't want to live there for any great length of time.' Now that wasn't a lie. Or was it? Could eighteen months be considered a great length of time?

Wait, she thought. I *love* Burwood! Why am I pandering to Matthew's dislike of it? What—

Her thoughts were interrupted with the sound of a groan. 'Sorry!' Mathew's hand flew to the back of his neck. 'Forgot that's where you've been living.' He shook his head and mumbled, 'Burwood', then added, 'I guess I'm prejudiced against it. When I lived in England I read about a spate of car thefts there. Whole neighbourhoods, and so I've probably always associated the suburb with burglaries. And yet it's really very nice. Good...er...streets. Yours especially.'

Rosetta remarked that burglars and Burwood both had the word 'bur' in them, a by-product of her newfound fascination with lexigrams. 'So you might have kept on connecting the two because of how they sounded. Actually, forget I said that. It's too way out.'

'Not way out at all. I think it's *bur*-illiant. In fairness to Burwood, though, the break-ins happened decades ago. Back in the early '80s.' He hesitated. 'I got lost in Burwood on my way back from dinner with Conan Dalesford. It turned out to be funny. A woman had planted herself in the middle of the road. Waved me down to play some weird sort of game of Charades.'

'Really?'

'Yeah! She waved me down wildly, then proceeded with an impersonation of some sort.' Matthew fell into laughter.

Rosetta laughed too. 'Who did this "wild" woman impersonate?'

Matthew tried to stop laughing but couldn't.

Seeing and hearing this made Rosetta giggle too. Someone finding something funny was always a laugh in itself. 'Matthew, don't keep me in suspense. What was she doing?'

'Ah, she was crazy,' Matthew managed to say. 'She...Ha-ha! She was hunched over, zigzagging everywhere and snatching at the road.'

'How bizarre.'

'Then, while she was still doubled over, she stuck her arm in the air. Like kids do when they're being elephants.'

'Hilarious!'

'Then she did this hopping kind of thing. I was sitting there in my car thinking: Frog? Kangaroo? Rabbit? She was obviously off her face.'

'Plenty of them are.'

'Not that I could see the face—'

'...The face she was off.'

'It was hidden by this mane of hair, and then...'

They chuckled together companionably.

Behind the chortles was a slight feeling of guilt. Rosetta wouldn't normally snigger at someone disturbed, but Matthew's mirth was addictive, and she couldn't deny it was fun to laugh with him.

'...And then, just as I started wondering whether she was impersonating a rabbit, she drew to her full height, yelled "Wasn't a rabbit" and marched off!'

Wasn't a rabbit.

Rosetta's laughter halted abruptly.

Rosetta froze into horrified silence. *Wasn't a rabbit.* This couldn't be happening.

Matthew was now reiterating what he considered to be the funnier parts of that awful scenario.

Rosetta's face burned with humiliation. A night she'd rather not remember had leapt back to haunt her. How could she explain she'd been tricked by an apparition? Saying nothing at all seemed the safer option. There was no way of convincing Matthew she'd stopped his car to protect an otherworldly bunny. No tangible proof. Rabbits weren't supposed to vanish into thin air. A hat-wielding magician might disagree but...

He was still laughing.

A heaviness descended on Rosetta's heart. The idea of Matthew thinking she looked ridiculous made her sick with self-loathing. Of all people, why did the driver she stopped that night have to be Matthew?

Pride kicked in. She could take no more. What right did the man beside her have, anyway, to talk about anyone this condescendingly?

He didn't realise it was her, but so what? Matthew, oblivious to her pain, was now making the flippant assumption that 'the poor girl' should have been 'locked up.'

Locked up. Rosetta's spine prickled. If she were a cat, she would have been arching her back at that fingernails-down-a-blackboard remark. Her volunteer work at the refuge involved keeping people who were troubled *out* of institutions, not conveniently removing them from the rest of the world. How *dare* he? She could stay silent no longer.

For the second time that evening, she uttered the words, 'That was me.'

Matthew stared, the shock on his face whitely evident. At last he said, 'I didn't really mean that about the—'

'Yes you did.' How could she explain this? She might as well leave it. Let him think she'd been high on something. For someone as unfamiliar with drugs as she was, allowing this was especially painful, but other options were far from forthcoming.

Molly and the rabbit had brought her to this. They had brought her to knowing she could never face Matthew Weissler ever again.

'It was a lovely meal, Matthew. Thanks for that.' Rosetta got out of the car. A cherry Jaguar. Of course. The one that nearly ran over 'Curry'. In a toneless voice she said, 'Let Sara give the book to Izzie when you've finished it.' She closed the car door, then made her way across the nature-strip, towards the winding garden path scattered with leaves from the liquidambar that Lena's husband Andrew had planted years ago.

Matthew opened his car door and called out to her. By then she'd already marched up to the porch. Pretending she hadn't heard him, she rattled the bell.

She was overwrought. The day had been one that she wanted to forget. She'd endured the death of a man she'd previously adored.

And now a man she'd really liked was perceiving her as irresponsible. And crazed! He'd used words like 'clumsy' and likened her to an elephant. A frog. A kangaroo. A rabbit. Being associated with an elephant was the worst, although frog wasn't much better. She hadn't appreciated the way he'd commented over dinner on her enjoying her food, inferring, she supposed, that she needed to watch her weight. How rude of him!

The hum of a motor quivered through the stillness. He would be gone in another moment. Disappointment at the way their evening had ended settled dully into her stomach.

She sighed, dabbed her eyes with her wrist and brightened at the sound of Lena's voice calling theatrically, 'Wonder who that is?' as if she didn't know. Must have peered through her new curtains, alerted by the clippity-clop of Rosetta's chic new heels.

Tomorrow was a new day. She was about to see her daughter again and her good friend Lena. This was something to be happy about. She had to get used to the fact that she was now a moneyed heiress and that the trip she'd just returned from had overflowed with rewarding surprises.

Beyond the door, the corridor floorboards squeaked with quickened footsteps. Blurry people-shapes appeared behind the porthole window's bubble glass. Rosetta ran her fingers over the window's bumpy coldness, her mind elsewhere.

Never. She would never again have dinner with anyone capable of angering her in the way Matthew Weissler had.

She would get to meet plenty of men in her expanded new world. Interest groups. Travelling. Singles nights. Men who weren't capable of that kind of cruelty.

Chapter Ten

'Cash or card?'

Rosetta eyed the pile of claret-coloured velvet on the counter and warded off a wave of guilt at the frivolity of her purchase. She hadn't bought an after-five dress in seven years, but it wasn't as though it were designer priced. 'Card,' she said.

Eadie had popped in earlier, before meeting up with a date, had helped her choose it and advised that the curve-enhancing V-necked number gave Rosetta the look of a 'slightly wicked enchantress.' She'd meant it as a compliment.

Life was exciting now that she could purchase treats for Izzie and the Fortnighters, and the odd indulgence for herself. In the past, buying groceries while attempting to make the remaining funds stretch to other living expenses was almost as difficult as solving a Rubik's Cube with the colours torn off.

Fifteen years now since the bank had sold up a property because of mortgage payments she could no longer afford. Fifteen years since she and Izzie had been propelled into their Gypsy life. A tenancy would end with yet another *For Sale* sign echoing the one that sent them into the unpredictable rental market in the first place, and they would experience that recurring feeling of having trespassed, of becoming a pesky interruption to someone else's financial gain.

Rosetta had finished her late-night clothes shopping in the swish end of the CBD. On the two-minute train ride home to North Sydney Station, rich swirls of sunset reddened the sky. She couldn't wait to show Izzie the daring new purchase she'd planned to wear for her performance at the finals of the Bondi Diggers singing comp.

Izzie, thinking up places she'd like to visit, had told Rosetta she'd like to see Wollongong because she'd never been there. Such a small ask! A lifetime of frugality had taught Izzie not to expect much for herself. Most girls of Izzie's age would have chosen somewhere romantic or action-packed like Milan or New York. Rosetta had told her, 'Sweetie, we can do better than a place two hours south of Sydney. But if that's where you want to go when school holidays arrive, then that's where we'll go. First. Then we have to agree on our overseas destinations.'

The trip would be good for Izzie. Would get her mind off Glorion. First love, while still very tender, had nothing with which to compare itself.

Rosetta exited the station and wandered down the hilly stretch towards the white serviced apartments in Lavender Bay where she and Izzie were living until the estate agent helped find them their ideal home. She moved through the sliding doors, waved to Brett, the concierge, then stared out of the foyer window at the sparkle of city lights on the other side of the harbour.

When Izzie had confided she'd been 'crazy about Glorion,' Rosetta had told her gently that in time she'd find someone else she would like just as much; that there was an advantage in getting older and meeting a few boys before getting too serious in any one relationship.

'Past romances help you see new romances in perspective,' she'd told her. 'They're sort of like a template.' What she hadn't admitted to was the invisible ink these templates seemed to be drawn in. Even with an extra twenty-three years' experience, Rosetta was still no expert. Being in love at thirty-eight was just as exquisite as it was at sixteen, perhaps more so because it wasn't all new and confusing. Perhaps less so. Maturity's learned cynicism tended to banish a good deal of illusory glamour. What would it be like to be in love again? Really in love? Her thoughts floated back to the night out with Matthew.

She flicked her head in annoyance and stared vacantly at the closed lift doors. Lately, without warning, stupid little memories would jump into her consciousness. She'd shoo them away, remembering the feel of the porthole window-glass when Matthew's car started up at Lena's. Tempting to touch but cold.

Whenever those sunken hopes arose, she'd involuntarily travel back to that magical night at Amaretti's when Matthew and she had talked like old friends, agreeing on just about everything, and locked spoons in a mini-war over the hazelnut gelato. But then she would hear the *ker-plunk* of her spirits as they plummeted, along with the echo of Matthew's amused words: *Elephant...Healthy appetite...Off her face.*

Inside her apartment on the fourteenth floor, Rosetta found on the black granite benchtop a shopping bag with a note from Izzie:

Gone swimming in downstairs gym. Royston's giving you this copy because he got himself another.

Inside the bag was the dark-blue copy of *Our True Ancient History*. Her heart lurched. The book she'd given Matthew had made its way back. She seized up the phone and dialled Royston.

'Yeah, he phoned me. Said he was ready to return it.'

'How did he know your number?'

'I write my name and number on the third blank page of every book I lend. Didn't you see that, love?'

'No, I didn't. Do you know if he'd read it?'

'Yep! He'd read it.'

Wanting not to seem too hooked on the answer, Rosetta paused and said, 'Did he like the book?'

'Didn't say. Just handed it back and thanked me for lending it.'

Rosetta couldn't deny she felt slighted that Matthew hadn't returned it in the way she'd suggested, via his stepdaughter and Izzie, although taking it back to its owner, rather than obeying the instructions of its curtly dismissive lender, was probably the more assertive option.

'And then?'

'And then he left.'

'Did he want to know anything about...' The words dwindled. Wanting to know whether Matthew had asked how her move had gone was juvenile. Egocentric. She changed the subject. 'How's Darren?'

'Very well. We're looking forward to seeing you at the poetry night on Tuesday. No excuses, Rosetta.'

'What about the excuse of not having a poem to read out?'

'Then write one. Before Tuesday. Ta-ta, lovey.' Royston had gone.

That night, she booked a flexi-fare online to Alice Springs. Seeing Craig's new Northern Territory house and finding out more about these intriguing crystals would be exciting. To breathe in the Red Centre night air that Craig had described with such enthusiasm. To see Uluru for the first time. But before deciding on the date of her flight she'd need to wait to find out when Craig would be there. For jet-setting Craig Delorey right now, staying at home wasn't an option. He'd been devoted this past month to tripping around the country with the aim of signing-up investors.

'This way please, ladies.'

Rosetta and her friends followed a white-jacketed waiter to a table situated against panoramic windows.

'I'm Vince, and I'm looking after you this evening.'

'Vince!' Rosetta said. 'You looked after me last time. I was here with my daughter.'

'Ah!' Vince passed round the drinks list. 'Rosetta. Of course.'

Eadie leaned forward in her seat to admire the city and harbour, 250 metres below, enclosed in a shimmering twilight.

Lena nodded across at a water feature near the centre of the revolving restaurant, an aquatically themed sculpture hovering above a cascade that jettisoned into a silver-lined pool. 'Love the dolphin,' she said. The sleek-tailed cetacean—a glimmering steel-blue—arched cheekily over swirling lotus images projected up through the pool via underwater lasers.

'It doubles as a fountain,' Rosetta said. A thin stream of water flowed from the dolphin's snout to form a continuous arc. 'So once you get thirsty, girls...'

'Nothing nicer than a glass of interhalogen compounds,' Lena said.

'What are *they*?' said Eadie.

'Components of chlorine,' said Lena. 'You can smell the stuff from here.'

'In that case,' Rosetta said, 'I think we should drink bubbly to be on the safe side. Either that or we get you to run home, Lena, to collect your water purifier. What'll it be?'

'Hmm' said Eadie.

'My water purifier does remove ninety-seven per cent of chlorine.' Lena pretended to look tempted.

Rosetta set down the drinks list. 'Could we have a really nice champagne, please, Vince?'

'Certainly, Rosetta.' Vince handed them each a menu. 'I'll return shortly, ladies, to take your entrée orders.'

Lena peered into the elegantly striped boutique bag from a Castlereagh Street designer. 'You're very naughty, Rosetta, insisting on buying us everything we admire.' She gestured to the fountain. 'And just in case you're considering it, my lounge room isn't spacious enough for that dolphin.'

'You deserve all those things,' Rosetta said. 'And I promise I won't get that water feature for your lounge room.' Vince returned to fill their glasses. 'I'll get it for your barbecue area instead.'

'What about you, Rosetta?' Lena said. 'You're heaping gifts on us, but I don't see you getting much for yourself.'

'I think I'll be fine somehow. But you're my *friends*. You guys are family! Don't think I've forgotten how much you've helped me over the years.'

'That was nothing like you're doing for us now,' Eadie said.

'What about when you all banded together and covered one of my home-loan repayments? I wouldn't call that nothing.'

Lena and Eadie looked modestly at the table.

'You've been absolute angels!' Rosetta lifted her glass and toasted Lena and Eadie. 'To my two kind guardian angels. Long live friendship and kindness.' She scanned the menu. 'I'm starting with the gazpacho soup. What do angels eat?'

Lena decided on the chickpea and quinoa linguine.

'And Eadie?'

'Um...can't decide.' Eadie looked up from her menu and spoke to Lena. 'Did Rosetta tell you about the guy I met at the singles lunch cruise we went on?'

'She texted me about your dinner date with him,' Lena said. 'So you'll have to tell me how it went.' She turned to Rosetta. 'And you weren't so lucky, this time?'

'You'd never hear the end of it if I was. Great for Eadie though. His name's Carl, and he's really sweet.'

'Rosetta received a fair bit of unwanted attention,' said Eadie. She took up her champagne glass and settled it back on the table. 'There was a rather diminutive violinist who followed her around all evening.'

'Oh, really?' said Lena. 'Sounds like perfect husband material, Rosetta. You could sing, and he could play.'

'I thought so too.' Rosetta folded her arms and pushed out her lower lip. 'But he got concerned about our height difference.'

'So what happened really?' Lena wanted to know.

'He was adorable,' Rosetta said. 'He entertained us all with his radical playing on the boat, and I realised I'd seen him before. I went up and told him that. From then on out he became my shadow, sneaking along behind me, just for fun.'

Eadie giggled riotously at the memory. Vince, topping up Eadie's water glass, eyed the dark-haired beauty-therapy graduate with un-masked interest. 'And every time a guy came across to chat to Rosetta, the violinist deliberately played something tuneless so that they couldn't hear each other.'

'So how do you know him?' Lena asked.

'It's funny actually. Do you remember the child minding position I went for?'

'Nope.'

'I applied for a fortnight's nannying role. Dette Weissler adver-tised it in the local paper. Dette was who Adam was cheating on me with.' Rosetta hesitated. 'Or was it that he was cheating on her with me? Glad I didn't know that back then.'

Lena looked blank.

'This woman was the one who threatened Adam with a gun. I went to dinner with her husband, and he...Remember the guy who held a pre-dinner drinks hour to head off his retirement dinner? The one I was chatting to—at the bar—who didn't know his wife was flirting with Adam?'

'Not...exactly,' said Lena. Confusion clouded the alert hazel eyes.

'The one whose stepdaughter is friends with Izzie.'

'All these tangled connections,' Lena cooed. 'Sounds like *Days of our Lives!*

In a low voice, Eadie said to Lena, 'Matthew. The recently separated guy.'

'Oh. *Matthew.*' Lena grinned and nodded. 'A real catch. Has a wayward wife. I remember now. Rosetta told me about him over coffee at Hansel & Gretel, not long after her date with Adam. What's Matthew got to do with the violinist?'

'Well when I was chatting to Matthew at the bar, we noticed a guy making all these amazing moves on top of the counter. He danced like a Russian.'

'And?'

'The violinist on the cruise was the same guy.'

'So Adam took you to a bar, and that's who was there on the boat. The violinist,' Lena said, simplifying Rosetta's long-winded account.

Nodding, Rosetta glanced to the side. What did Matthew have to do with all this anyway? She didn't even *like* Matthew. Didn't want to draw attention to him. What had she planned to bring up next? Aha! Amaretti's. Which, regrettably, also included Matthew. 'But that's not all, Lena. When I went to dinner with Matthew, he played the accordion.'

'Matthew plays the accordion?' Lena was intrigued.

'No, the violinist.'

'Versatility plus.'

'Yeah! I'm looking forward to stumbling across him again just to see what else he has in his showman's repertoire.'

'Fire breathing?' suggested Lena. 'Rabbits out of hats? Egyptian belly dancing?' Leaning forward in her seat, she said, 'So Matthew's divorcing is he?'

'Uh-huh. And I wish him luck in all his future endeavours.'

'Sounds all very formal, Rosetta.' Lena was trying not to smile. 'In other words, you're saying you don't want to keep up with him.'

'Why not?' said Eadie. 'Lena says he's a catch.'

'According to Rosetta he is,' said Lena. 'I've never met him.' She gave Eadie a knowing look. 'Sounds very nice though.'

Resisting their attempts to evoke a confession, Rosetta said, 'The man is cold.'

'Cold?' said Eadie.

'Condescending.'

Eadie and Lena said nothing.

Aware of the intensity igniting those words, Rosetta swiftly shifted the focus from herself to Eadie's forthcoming TAFE graduation ceremony, to Lena's goal of starting a neighbourhood vegetable garden, to their plans for EGS a.k.a Ending Global Suffering. Their conversation meandered through a variety of topics, then settled comfortably on astrology. Rosetta turned to Eadie and tried to sound nonchalant. 'I've got a question. What would you say is the most compatible? A man's Moon Sign the same as the woman's Sun Sign or the woman's moon and the man's sun both in air signs?'

'Both of them are fabulously compatible,' said Eadie. 'Who are we talking about here?'

'Er...me, and...someone I happened to get on well with once.' Rosetta hurriedly continued with her questions. 'What does it mean if a man has Venus in Scorpio?'

'What does it mean? Well, as you already know, in a man's horoscope chart, the Venus Sign indicates the type of woman he finds attractive.'

'So he's more likely to go out with a Scorpio then?'

'Not necessarily. A planet or two in Scorpio is probably enough, but his interest might be sparked by Scorpio traits that he's unconsciously projecting onto her.'

'For instance?'

'Well he might perceive her as mysterious and seductive. Exotic maybe. Even if she's straitlaced and no-nonsense.'

Unable to imagine how anyone could see her as mysterious or seductive, with that chatterbox tendency of hers, broadish childbearing hips and roaring laugh that embarrassed Izzie senseless, Rosetta circled a wineglass rim with the tips of her manicured fingers and said, 'Hmm.'

Eadie continued. 'And in a woman's horoscope, the sign Venus resides in indicates how she expresses herself around a man she finds attractive. If I remember rightly, you have Venus in Scorpio too.'

'So I express myself like a Scorpio when I like someone?'

'Exactly. So a Scorpio Venus guy is likely to be attracted to you, especially if his sun and moon are compatible with yours.'

'Interesting,' said Rosetta. Not that it mattered. A simpatico horoscope didn't make Matthew any less heartless.

'Mars of course,' said Eadie, 'is a man's masculine expression of attraction. And what a woman looks for in a man. What's your Mars in again?'

'Libra,' said Rosetta.

'So you like men with Libran qualities. Even-tempered, musical, fair-minded, romantic. Does the guy you're talking about have any planets in Libra?'

'The sun. He's a Libran.'

'Bullseye!' Lena winked. 'Go for him!'

'Ooh, um...I knew him ages ago. Ages and ages and *ages* ago.'

'Seek him out then,' said Lena. 'And if he happens to be single, propose. Who is this guy anyway? Anyone we know?'

'Er...'

'Aha!' Lena's grin was triumphant. 'I know who it is.'

Rosetta stirred her espresso with nervous zeal. Prattling on about the glittering city below in a bout of conversation-halting *oohs* and *ahs* did nothing to deter Lena from pointing at her accusingly and saying with a nod, 'It's Matthew.'

'Is it Matthew?' said Eadie.

Rosetta gave in. 'But it's not relevant now. I was really just wondering how Matthew could have been so charming and affable one minute, and then taunting and heartless the next.'

'Venus in Scorpio could be biting, I expect.'

'Well *I've* got Venus in Scorpio, and *I'm* not biting! Aw, Eadie, don't look at me like that. I was being ironic.' Rosetta reached into her bag and passed Eadie a horoscope constructed on an astrology site. Matthew had mentioned his age at Amaretti's, so Rosetta had asked when he'd be turning thirty-five—and had, days after she'd charged out of his car, keyed his birth date into Astro Logica's horoscope generator.

Eadie established that Matthew's Mars probably aspected his Rising Sign if he'd been born in the last stages of Cancer Rising. 'A first-house Mars connection sometimes adds aggression to the personality,' she advised, 'and a love of keeping fit.'

'Not sure about the aggression, but he swims a lot. Does laps each morning in his indoor pool.'

'Sounds great to me,' said Lena. 'Then why—'

'Remember the night of the rabbit apparition when I waved down that car?'

'Of course,' said Lena. 'Couldn't forget that. It was such a bizarre thing to happen.'

'Funny though,' said Eadie giggling, 'to the guy in the red car.'

'Do you have to remind me of that, Eades? The guy was Matthew.'

'Matthew?'

'Matthew was the guy in the cherry red Jag.'

'No way!'

'And he's been laughing about me ever since.'

Fuelled by Lena and Eadie's attentive sympathy, Rosetta launched into a dramatic account of her shock and humiliation when she'd realised Matthew's crazy lady grasping at the road had been her.

Almost, but not quite tearily, she stared into her coffee, feeling hugely and justifiably sorry for herself. 'Charades!' She fidgeted with her napkin. 'He thought it was some kind of senseless guessing game.'

'And he guessed you were being an elephant?' Lena said softly.

Rosetta nodded. 'An elephant. Or a frog, or a—' At the sound of muffled snickers, Rosetta looked up from her twisted napkin.

Lena was gripping the table's edge with her head bowed, shoulders shaking amid snorts of uncontainable laughter.

Indignant, Rosetta spun round to Eadie.

Eadie, at least, was making an effort to remain sober-faced. She took a swig from her tumbler and met Rosetta's annoyed gaze with an innocent half-smile.

And then Eadie, mouth uncomfortably full, lost control. The water escaped in a thin, arching stream. Rosetta glared across at the spewing-dolphin fountain, looked at giggling, snorting Eadie, and then back again at the dolphin. The likeness was uncanny.

Vince hurried over and dabbed at the tablecloth's puddles with a cloth, asking Eadie with an amused gleam in his eye if everything was okay with the Perrier, but the only answer he received was 'Ye...hee-hee-hee-*hee-ha!*'

'Admit it, Rosetta,' said Lena, emerging from her hysterics. 'It's funny. Really funny! Wouldn't you have laughed if you'd encountered something like that on your way home?'

Recalling how much she'd laughed with Matthew before the story became horribly familiar, Rosetta acknowledged that Lena was probably right.

'And what about when Matthew was just some dude in a Jaguar? A stranger?' Eadie said. 'We giggled heaps about that on the phone. You thought it was funny you'd made him laugh.'

In a flash of discomfiting insight, Rosetta reflected on her response to him. He'd treated her to a four-course dinner at a restaurant she'd loved, listened intently to her plans for EGS and went out of his way to drive her to Lena's place on the other side of town.

She'd been mesmerised, but now she would never see him again. 'Ah well,' she reasoned. 'Plenty more fish,' but her voice's forced brightness seemed only to emphasise the uncertainty she felt. 'Eadie, what would you like for your entree?'

Vince appeared at their table. 'Did I hear a plea for fish? Our soup of the day is trout chowder.'

Once Vince had taken their orders, Lena said, 'There may be plenty of fish, but it's quality you're after, not quantity.' Eyeing the water feature, she added, 'I wouldn't be letting *that* fish swim away.'

Rosetta gestured to the sculpture approvingly. 'Not a chance. He's pretty secure there on his pedestal.'

'I'm not talking about the dolphin,' said Lena. 'I'm talking about someone who does laps. Matthew. Mr Compatible. Don't let him swim away.'

Izzie followed Charlotte Wallace through a greenhouse lined with exotic blooms.

'It's too cold to go swimming,' Sara said, trailing behind. 'Maybe we should just go to the mall instead.'

'Wait till you try the water,' Charlotte said over her shoulder. 'Once you're in, you won't want to get out.' She reached up and pushed distractedly at a potted oriental lily pressing against her ear.

'You look like a Hawaiian dancer,' Izzie said, returning the flower to Charlotte's head.

In answer, Charlotte launched into a cartoonish fast-motion hula, then plucked the lily from its stem. 'And a yellow orchid for Izzie,' she said, 'to go with her red hair. And this one, Sara...' *Snap!* '...is for you. But don't tell Mum I took them from here.'

'Why brown though?' Sara whined. 'You know I hate brown. It makes me look anaemic.'

'Here then,' Izzie said. She tucked her orchid under a clip in Sara's pale hair, fastened the maroon flower into her own and followed Charlotte out to the Wallaces' pool.

They changed into their bathers in an enclosed gazebo at the other end of Diondra's rainforest garden and ran shivering across to the pool's descending steps. The water was comfortingly tepid.

'The pool at my complex is heated too, but it's nowhere near as warm,' Izzie commented.

'The one at Izzie's place is bigger,' Sara said, dog-paddling up to Charlotte. 'And the pool I had at Cabarita Heights was bigger than either Izzie's or yours, Charl. And much, *much* warmer.'

Charlotte and Izzie exchanged sad smiles. Although Sara hadn't talked much about the marriage break-up between her mum and step-dad, they could tell she missed her old home.

Before long, Sara brought up Tyson. 'He's captain of Silver Tongues now,' she said, floating towards one side of the pool. 'The guy who took over the debating team from Glorion Oster...the Prince of Perelda I mean, moved to Bathurst. I'm so sad the prince didn't answer your emails, Izzie.'

Charlotte was frog-kicking in the opposite direction. She took hold of the edge and turned to face Sara on the other side. 'But he told Izzie he was closing down his email address, and Izzie was cool with that, weren't you Iz?'

'I knew he wouldn't have got the emails,' Izzie said quietly, even though she felt sure he had.

'And he told Izzie he didn't want to drag her into all that publicity,' Charlotte added. 'So, what he did was actually really heroic. He was protecting her.'

'I guess,' Sara said, uncertain of herself now.

Izzie waved her hand through the water, watching her fingers turn to elongated blobs beneath the undulations. She would never admit to how devastated she'd been when she'd realised Glorion's communication had begun and ended with that single email. She'd been overjoyed at first to receive it, and then her mum had returned from New Zealand and suggested visiting Crete during the summer hols. Izzie had only wanted to see Wollongong, the coastal town south of Sydney to which the cab had nearly taken her and Glorion, but when Rosetta suggested she consider somewhere further away, she'd steered the conversation around to Perelda. 'I've heard so much about Sweden now,' she'd said. 'So do you want to go there, Mum? You've always dreamed of visiting the Scandinavian countries.'

Rosetta had agreed to it, although a little reluctantly, Izzie thought. When Izzie had talked about their trip the next day, Rosetta had said, 'Izzie sweetie, I hope you're not just going there so that...Ooh, is it five already? I'd better get across to the shops.'

Rosetta's unspoken concern about the trip being a disappoint-ment if it hung purely on a whim had Izzie resolving to give Glorion plenty of warning about her visit, but the painstaking email she wrote bounced back immediately. Since the other two emails hadn't, Izzie concluded Glorion would have received them before he'd shut down his Australian email address and that he'd either chosen to ignore her or was getting behind with his replies.

She'd then looked up the name of Glorion's royal residence on Wikipedia and wrote him a letter—Mrs Gunning, her correspondence-crazy English teacher, would have been so proud. Told him she was 'passing through' Perelda on her European tour and asked if he'd be free to meet up.

Rosetta hadn't known Izzie had contacted Glorion by mail. Izzie had been in the study one afternoon, absorbed in geometry homework, when she'd heard an excited squawk from the lounge room. 'Isobel!' Rosetta had shrieked. 'You won't believe what I found in the letterbox!'

Her mother had been all smiles when she'd handed over the envelope with its intricate Perelda Palace crest on the back. She'd hovered around Izzie in a restless dance while Izzie had silently read the three-sentence contents.

Dear Izzie, it had said.

Thanks so much for your letter to me. Unfortunately, I receive many letters from around the world and cannot endeavour to reply to each personally.

Thank you again for thinking of me. I wish you all the best for the future.

She had run to her room and thrown herself on the bed, shocked at the indifference of Glorion's reply and embarrassed at having posted him a whole four pages. The pillow was saturated with tears by the time her mother knocked on the door. Izzie had waved the letter about lethargically. '*This* is what Glorion told his assistant to tell me,' she'd said in a snuffly squeak.

Rosetta had sat at Izzie's desk and frowned over the five lines. 'It wouldn't have been him, Izzie,' she'd soothed. 'Glorion wouldn't have written this directly to you. It's a standard reply, something his admin staff just send out automatically.'

While not a cheering thought, Rosetta's revelation had lessened the sting of rejection. Still, since that day, Izzie had decided that she no longer wanted to visit Perelda and that she was tired of pining after a boy whose complete lack of accessibility almost deemed him mythical.

She then began to resent his farewell email. *Hold no candle for me* he'd said. Who did that guy think he was? Mr Perfect? Glorion needed to get over himself. And Izzie had needed to get over Glorion.

Izzie glided to the end of the pool, vaguely aware of Sara and Charlotte's unhurried chatter. 'What did you say you were seeing to-night?' Charlotte was asking.

'Me?' said Izzie.

'Yeah. You and Ben.'

'We're going to see the sequel to *Invasion of the Star People*. It's a movie they made in the 1950s.'

'Saw it,' said Sara. 'My stepda...I mean Matthew, took my sister and me to see it ages ago. It's not all that good.'

Ben Morris. Lena and Andrew's son and a shining star during those dreary post-prince days. The guy she'd chased after unselfconsciously during her childhood whenever they'd played Tag the Bunyip in his front yard had since become a worthy Spatchawokki opponent, and not long after that, a friend. Ben's quirky sense of the ridiculous always made her laugh, and ever since he'd completed his orthodontics, that smile of his had sent silly little quavers through her heart.

Their romance had blossomed the night Sidelta got herself stuck in a eucalypt outside the new apartment. Izzie had shone the torch while Ben climbed up and rescued the mewing bundle. He'd tried to pass tension-riddled Sidelta to Izzie, but Sidelta had scratched his bicep and leapt from his arms.

Izzie had voiced her concern about the scratch, and Ben had said, 'It's nothing,' and sidled closer. He'd put his arm around her...and that was it! The arm had stayed, and the owner of that arm hadn't abandoned her like Glorion had. And now...Ben took up all the space in her mind that Glorion once occupied. Ben was the best boyfriend any girl could ever have. And Glorion was welcome to stay where he was. Izzie had never liked princes anyway.

A shout rang out from the house. 'Whaaaaaat?'

Izzie and Sara looked at each other, then up at the windows of the Wallaces' three-storey home.

'Just Mum getting angry,' Charlotte said.

Another bloodcurdling shout. 'How *could* you? How *could* you?'

A worried line appeared across Sara's forehead. 'Is she upset you're home, Charlotte?'

'Nope. She doesn't even know we're here. I didn't tell her we left Sports Day early.' To avoid further questioning, Charlotte dipped under the water.

'How *could* you?' Diondra repeated. '*How* many million?' Her voice was scratchy and demanding. 'Answer me! Answer me now.'

Izzie cringed for the person Diondra Wallace was yelling at. She'd always been more than a little scared of Charlotte's glamorous and crotchety mother.

'How. Many. Million.'

The voice that answered her was a man's, high and indignant, Charlotte's dad sounding like he'd been dragged into a wrestling match with an uncompromising banshee. 'Only three,' he called.

'Oh, fabulous. Only three, he says. Only three! Look what you've done to us! Look what you've done to *me*.'

'So you think it's all my fault, huh? You think I'm the one who goes around squandering all my hard-earned dough?' Dominic's tone had a murderous quality to it now. 'Well, think again, lady, and take a good, long look in the mirror.'

'You're meant to protect me and Charlotte,' Diondra bellowed. 'And now you've sent us to the poorhouse!'

Izzie did a quick check of the water. Much to her relief, Charlotte had dipped under once more and hadn't yet surfaced. She had no idea what the poorhouse was, but it sounded similar to the Women's and Children's Refuge dorms where her mum volunteered.

'Go on, Diondra. Go on. Do your best. Shift the blame to me, as you always have throughout this pathetic joke of a marriage. Don't bother to admit to your insatiable expenditure. You and your obsession with looking as well-off as Dette. But we have to keep up with the Weisslers, now, don't we?'

Izzie spun round to Dette's daughter. Sara's eyes were round and startled.

'You had to have the Audi. Same make and model. Got to keep up with the Weisslers.' Dominic's voice had launched into a vindictive sing-song. 'Oh, yes. Got to keep up with *them*. You had to have the three-storey Georgian. You had to have a Jacuzzi that rivalled Dette Weissler's heart-shaped one.'

'Oh, you *know* what type of tub Dette has, do you? Ah, but I'm forgetting you know a lot more about Dette than that.'

'What in Christ's name are you getting at?'

'Don't think I haven't heard what's been going on there! You chased her to Vanuatu. Thought you'd fooled me, didn't you, with your Port Vila Real Estate Convention fairy tale. You would have found out soon enough that Dette wasn't alone.'

'I...I...I don't know wha—'

'Ha! The shame in your face is proof enough! Mimi from tennis saw the two of you last September. Down at the surf club drinking macchiatos! What do you say to that? Huh? Drinking macchiatos at the surf club one morning, and then Dette tells me in the afternoon that she's spent her entire day at her city beauty spa. What do you make of that?' Diondra's screech lowered to a brutal treble. 'I've found you out, Dominic. I know you've been sleep—'

'La-la-la, la...' Izzie launched into the beginning of a Boyd Levanzi song in an effort to shield open-mouthed Sara from the revelations about her mother. Words failed her. She couldn't remember a single lyric. What was that song about people meeting innocently for coffee? Or was it tea? 'Coffee...for...two...just me and you.' Izzie tried desperately to improvise. 'Which is quite okay because...we're just enjoying the day.'

Sara shushed her and turned back to the house.

'How long have we been in the red?' Diondra demanded. 'How long have we been spending air? How long have you hidden your business going bad?'

'Don't act like you haven't known we were in trouble. How many times did I have to tell you we were living on credit? But did my excuse for a wife ever ease up on the designer wares? Of course she didn't. She just sent us all broke quicker. Just wanted to look like a Weissler.'

'Better than looking like a Wallace,' Diondra bit back. 'Matthew Weissler would never drag his family into bankruptcy.'

Dominic echoed Diondra's last words, mimicking her defiant shrill. 'And by the way. How *is* Matthew-Baby? Isn't he the guy you truly-wuly love?'

'*What* are you *talking* about?'

Charlotte, having emerged from the pool's depths, was watching Sara helplessly. Charlotte's face, Izzie noted, had turned the colour of the beetroot soup in Rosetta's Rasputin Recipes book. 'Let's do some underwater races,' she suggested brightly. 'Come on Sara. Izzie?'

But Izzie, like Sara, was clinging to the rocky edge like a starfish, unable to tear herself away from the awful accusations. Sara was hanging onto the flat rocks with one hand. The other was cupped firmly over her mouth.

'*What* am I talking about?' Dominic was firing now. 'What am I *talking* about? I'll tell you what I'm talking about. I'm talking about that tragic little phone call you made to Matthew Weissler, when his wife was away. To tell him that you loved him. Loved him!'

A shriek from Sara.

'Uh-oh,' Izzie whispered to herself. Could it be true that Sara's stepdad and Charlotte's mum had actually met up in secret?

Diondra's voice lowered again to brutal and threatening. 'So you're eavesdropping on me now, Dominic? You were meant to be downstairs.'

'I was! Do you have any idea how loud you are when you're drunk?'

Dominic and Diondra's shouts had changed direction several times, having moved from the left side of the house to the right. Diondra's voice sounded nearer than ever now, like she was pacing beside a door to the back garden.

Charlotte had given up on urging Izzie and Sara away from the explosive disclosures and was swimming back and forth like an anxious seal eager to win an imaginary race against imaginary competitors.

'The solution is obvious.' Diondra was hoarse from all the screaming.

'Oh?' Dominic's voice was closer now too.

Their voices had reduced in volume, from super loud to moderately loud.

'Sell your secret love nest.'

'My secret what?'

'Don't play daft with me, Dominic. My private investigator told me all about it.'

'Ah! So you're spending money we don't have on P.I.'s! What a very smart thing to do.'

'Sell it.'

'Sell what, Diondra?'

'The place you take your tarts. The place you've taken Dette. The place you've taken your secretary and God knows who else. That renter woman, probably.'

'Who, may I ask, is the renter woman?'

'Isobel Redding's mum. Californian Bungalow.'

Now it was Izzie's turn to clamp her hand over her mouth. She waited tensely.

'Rosetta *rents* the Cal Bung? I don't think that's right. She owns it. I'm sure she does'

'Nuh-uh. Definitely rents. I've seen the sleazy looks you've given her.'

Dominic said something that Izzie couldn't hear.

Diondra's voice rose up. 'Whaaaaaat? You sold it in January?'

No reply from Dominic.

'And we're *still* three-million dollars in debt?'

The screen door squealed open. Diondra appeared in the yard, the violent clash of her green leather shirt-dress and flaring red cheeks reminding Izzie of the plastic holly berries that livened up Yuletide marzipan.

Dominic appeared behind her, his hands flapping about like confused butterflies.

Sara and Izzie promptly ducked their heads beneath the edge of the pool. They could hear Diondra stomping down the garden path. Dominic's footsteps were hurrying behind her. 'Just to let you know,' Dominic sang. 'I'm divorcing you.' Victorious snort. 'Should have done that years ago.'

'Fine.' Seething pause. 'Which of us gets to keep my eyeshadow?'

Izzie clung to the pool's edge with trembling, pruney fingers, not daring to move. *Please don't let them see us*, she prayed. *Please save them the embarrassment.*

'What'll I do now?' Diondra's voice had become frail. In that moment, Izzie couldn't help feeling sorry for Charlotte's mum. 'What'll happen to us? What'll happen to *me*? What are people going to think?' The footsteps were stumbling now. 'I'll have to get a job,' Diondra was saying.

'Shame Myer aren't advertising for vintage models,' Dominic sneered.

Seeming not to have heard him, Diondra continued her shocked and panting self-talk. 'I'll have to go out to work! I'll have to slave away at some menial task each day, just to put a roof over our heads. I'll have to rent.'

She'd reached the pool now, her head shaking side-to-side. 'Where would I get a job?' she wailed. 'Where?' At that point, Diondra's eyes, pink from crying and hazed over with desperation, settled gloomily on Izzie. Her gaze swept across to Sara, then back to Izzie again.

Dominic, not far behind, drew to a dramatic stop and gaped at his daughter and her two apologetic guests.

'Where?' Diondra said, still shaking her head, seemingly unconcerned about the three pairs of ears that had taken in all she'd uttered. She was staring at Izzie vacantly. 'Where would I get a job.'

Izzie wished she could disappear beneath the water like Charlotte had earlier. But Diondra seemed to have directed the question at *her* and now she was obliged to come up with an answer.

'There's a job going at the bakery in Concord,' she suggested in a small voice.

Diondra continued to stare.

Feeling she hadn't been helpful enough, Izzie added, 'I think it might be fifteen dollars an hour. The full-time shop assistant left last week.'

L

Maleika's time had come. Her life in the forest had thankfully been harmonious. Throughout her brief existence on the earth, she had managed to avoid being harmed by gold-skins—plenty of sprites were far less fortunate—and, along with raising children of her own, had taken care of orphans, the vulnerable mites whose parents were victims of the Grudellan Palace. As their Clan Watcher, she nurtured their soul-missions and plied them with Remembrance Essence each evening to ensure they remained aware of their work in the Dream Sphere and was ever delighted to teach them of other worlds.

She now lay in the heart of Elysium Glades, cushioned by moss and smiling across at the spring sprites seated around her, who had ceased their work on the flowers now in bloom. Croydee was there too, her chestnut-clad nephew, as was Kloory, her airy-eyed son: two Brumlynds who had faithfully walked the path of earthly life alongside her.

'You have had a good existence in this dimension, Maleika,' Kloory told her. 'We shall look forward to seeing you again at your Wake.'

'And what a revel it will be,' said Croydee. 'We shall celebrate this incarnation so uproariously, all residents of the Dream Sphere will have cause for complaint!'

Maleika chuckled. 'I look forward to this, dear companions. I now leave my earthly life with gratitude and embark on my sojourn in the Dream Sphere.'

Rosetta opened a document on her new computer and tapped out a piece to recite at Poets' Garret. Reading it almost made her blush. Mawkish passion with a thunderous rhythm, a downward spiralling portrayal of an eclipse of the sun and moon and their subsequent combustion. Hardly entertainment.

She checked the clock. Not long until Craig's arrival. Half-an-hour to write another! *A whirlwind visit,* Craig had said, *before I fare-well Sydney for good.* This time she wrote about the positive aspects of regret—likening them to spider webs glistening on apple trees, diamonds dancing on a windscreen, frost on a bottle of chilled red wine—and tailed it off with an uplifting conclusion, using light as a metaphor for hope. Reciting this on Tuesday night would be far less distressing than belting out a maudlin lament inspired by a man whose Moon Sign matched her sun.

The intercom buzzed. 'You gonna let me in Fortnighter? I'm pacing your lobby like a croc on a hunger strike.' Craig, freshly arrived from his flight, would be staying at Lena and Andrew's for three nights before heading back to his Alice Springs enterprise.

Rosetta pressed the button by the door and said, 'Come on up, Fortnighter! Can't wait to hear all your news on the crystals,' then rushed across to the kitchen to make tea.

They talked about his not-so-secret project, Craig lolling on one of the apartment's plush lounge suites, Rosetta cross-legged on the floor. He told her he'd had the crystals valued. The International Mineralogical Association deemed them low in value due to their similarity to mica. 'We were told they couldn't be compared to anything much,' Craig said, 'because the IMA hasn't encountered this sort of mineral before. They said the structure most resembled scrap and flake silicates and that the crystals could probably be processed to form drilling fluid.'

'Who are you supposed to sell drilling fluid to?' Rosetta asked. 'Hardware retailers?'

'Nah, you sell it to the big mining guys so they can drill more wells. But what the IMA can't assess, of course, is the energy these stones contain. If I were in it for money alone, I'd whack a huge price on each of the crystals and talk about their astounding capabilities.' Craig's gestures had taken on a youthful exuberance. He sat up, swung his legs over the edge of the lounge and leaned forward. 'But my whole aim here is accessibility to anyone who wants to experience them. I want the healing properties the crystals contain to reach as many people as possible, so I'm charging a token fee, the same price your Crystal Consciousness boss charged for a coin-sized rose quartz. Minus overheads of course.'

Craig, Conan and Jim had agreed to accept donations from any-one unable to afford the given price. 'Even if it's a couple of silver coins from one of the Aboriginal kids whose families are poverty-stricken,' Craig said.

'Why not just *give* them to the kids?' Rosetta said. 'It's not as if you're profiting with a few cents here and there.'

'We've discussed all that, but we feel it's important an exchange takes place, no matter how small. People are more likely to value something they've purchased, and we want these stones to be respected.'

'Fair enough. I see the logic in that.'

Craig told her about the reports he'd received concerning the im-pact the crystals were having on people's wellbeing, both physical and emotional. A broken leg healing at phenomenal speed, resistance to a potentially lethal snakebite, an eradication of violent aggression.

'The leg fracture happened to a friend of Conan's,' Craig said. 'He fell from the roof of a house he was building. Once the medicos set the bone, the guy taped one of our crystals to the plaster.'

The doctors couldn't give an explanation for the leg's rapid recovery. His shin-bone knitted fully within three days.

'They'd put it down to the guy's physical make-up. Told him he had outstanding recuperative powers.'

The poor unfortunate snakebite victim was a child of six. Craig described the phone call from the child's neighbour, a woman who had purchased a crystal from Jannali Dalesford two days before. 'She told me she ran home to get a blanket for the boy and snatched up the crystal from her dressing table.'

Her young neighbour held the crystal for no more than thirty seconds before allowing it to fall to the ground. He then shook off the blanket and jumped to his feet. By the time the ambulance arrived, he was scampering across to his swing-set.

'The medicos treated him of course,' Craig said, 'but couldn't understand him having zero indications.'

Rosetta shook her head at the stories. 'Utterly brilliant! Something like this could change the world.'

'Yeah, I mean, so far it feels like the sky's the limit. We're still cautious of course. Since we've made them available we've been getting a good number of stories about the crystals' effects. Some are a bit hard to believe.'

'Such as?'

'One guy claimed one of our crystals brought his father out of a coma. The bloke had been unconscious for days. Things like that. I'm guessing not everyone phoning in with testimonials is completely truthful, but we're most of the time keeping an open mind.'

'So tell me about the success you've had with aggressive behaviour.'

'Ah, yes! I was down the main street in Alice Springs, and this bloke I've known since childhood—Fred McAlistair is his name—was up further ahead, bullying his wife as usual. I've never been able to stomach seeing that, 'cos I've always felt so helpless. And we're not supposed to interfere in domestics are we?

'So there's Fred, yelling at Lola. He's grabbed her shoulder and pushed her into one of the shops. All I can think to do is get a crystal across to him somehow. So I go up to him, say, "Hiya Fred," and slap his back with the crystal against my palm. Naturally, the crystal fell to the ground, but it took only a second to work.'

'So what happened?' Rosetta was intrigued.

'It was surreal. Fred just turned to Lola, really slowly. She's just crying and cowering like she usually does. But Fred's watching this like he's seen it for the first time. And then he says in a shocked voice, "Lola, I've hurt you!" Next thing I know, Fred's clasped her hand, and he's saying over and over, "Lola, please forgive me. I am so sorry." I slipped the crystal across to Lola and continued on my way.'

'And what happened to them? What's going on with Fred now?'

'I hear through the grapevine that he's turned his life around. He's disgusted with himself for the way he's treated Lola, and now he's doing all he can to atone for that.'

Rosetta clapped her hands together and dabbed at the tears that had sprung to her eyes.

'Anyway, changing the topic for a sec,' Craig said, 'I haven't yet asked you how you're enjoying your money. What's it like being a rich bitch?'

'Craig!'

'Just stirring, sweetheart. I had no idea you were planning to outdo me in the wealth stakes. How does it feel to be more affluent than yours truly?'

'I can't even begin to tell you, Craig, how incredible it is. Beyond words!

'Sure is.' Craig threw her a wink.

'Daunting though.'

'Daunting? What's the matter? You suffering from poverty nostalgia?'

Laughing, Rosetta shook her head.

Craig regarded her with affection. 'Interesting reaction to inheriting a half-share in royalties from your mother's songs. All evergreens of course. Each one set to bump up the old bank balance every time it's played on air.'

'Not to mention the fortune from Daniela's estate. But I can't explain this feeling. It's surreal. I mean, before the inheritance my lack of money fenced me in.' She took a sip of her tea. 'It was almost as though the fences were guidelines. They acted as boundaries. I knew my routine, and I knew my limitations. But now...' She turned to him. 'I'm actually really confused.'

'So you want those limitations back?'

'Not at all, but money's seductive in its own way. I'm scared I'll get side-tracked by all the things I can buy for myself.' She hesitated. 'You know me, Craig, I'm a Sagittarian! I do everything on a big scale. I'm in severe danger of becoming hopelessly decadent!'

'Well, from what our friends are saying, Rosetta, you're more in danger of giving all your money away than frittering it on yourself.'

Rosetta couldn't help smiling at that. 'You make me sound like Mother Teresa. I've hardly given them anything.'

'So you're saying the new car for Lena and Andrew, and Eadie's new patio, is basically nothing?'

Rosetta reminded Craig she'd bought herself a car just like his. 'And did you notice where I'm living now?' She swept a hand out to emphasise the apartment's lavishness. 'I'm treating myself pretty well, Craig.'

'It is a rental though,' Craig reminded. And then, in a good imitation of his grandfather's Irish lilt, 'Splash out! Go buy yourself something pretty.'

'That's the plan. Izzie and I are looking around for something permanent, but I'll only purchase once I've had the chance to look at a few. I actually *love* all this spending. And that has the potential to be a problem.'

'So you're afraid you'll become like the body kings.'

'Pretty much.' She told Craig about the echo of parental voices that were never far away. Mama's suspicion that the rich were both selfish and impossibly glamorous; Baba's insistence that money didn't buy happiness. 'They couldn't imagine me ever having more than a modest sum. Baba thought my only hope of becoming successful was to marry someone well-off.'

'We've both had similar upbringings,' Craig said, 'but as you know, my family were poorer than yours. And they got me believing self-denial was a virtue.' He shook his head, curls bobbing lightly. 'And then when I became the high-flying lawyer and entrepreneur, I felt completely unworthy. I've been there, Rosetta, so I know what you're going through.'

Contemplating this, Rosetta peered into Craig's cup. 'Ooh, you've finished your tea. I'll get you another.' She rose and wandered across to the kitchen opposite, telling Craig she'd baked galatopita that morning.

'Galato what?'

'Galatopita. Greek custard cake.'

Since Craig sounded suitably tempted, Rosetta served it to him on one of Mama's antique plates and went about refilling the teapot.

When she returned to her mulberry-toned lounge suite with their cups and a plateful of biscotti, she settled into the three-seater opposite Craig and continued to voice her concerns. 'What I want to know is how extreme wealth fits in with the Currency of Kindness. I didn't even earn this money! And others have so little. It just doesn't seem fair.'

Craig only viewed this with amusement. 'Of course it's fair! How perfect is it for playing your part in Ending Global Suffering? How else are you going to get EGS up and running?'

She told him she'd previously pictured doing that in a more measured way. 'Finish my degree, become a lawyer with a reasonable salary and then start small with EGS in the hope of expanding out over time, but what happened was—'

'Lady Luck snuck up and stole your boundaries.'

'You *could* say that, yes! But I had it all worked out, and then suddenly this future dream leaps into my present, and I'm totally unprepared.' She shrugged and smoothed a hand over one of the velveteen cushions. 'I'm way out of my depth, Craig. Achieving something as important as EGS feels unrealistic. It'll probably take me years to work out how to set it up. I don't want to waste Daniela's legacy on fizzled schemes.'

'Your mother's money is in good hands,' Craig said. 'And you're a born philanthropist. You just need some help to get started. But I reckon your definition of the Currency of Kindness is a tad too sacrificial. Too stringent. In my view the Currency of Kindness is as much about being kind to yourself as it is about being kind to everyone else. So kill the guilt.' He reached for another pistachio-studded biscotti. 'And as for getting EGS started, you don't have to do it all on your own.'

She told him Lena would help her too.

Craig was doubtful the two of them could achieve the results they envisaged. 'If it's just you and Lena attempting to tackle the endless red tape, it actually will take years as you say, only because neither of you has any prior knowledge.

'Look, Rosetta, the last thing I want is to see you falling prey to con artists. You need an additional person, someone with expertise.' He took a final swig of tea and set his cup aside. 'You mightn't know this, but I've got heaps of contacts through work. I've had a lot of experience in setting up charities for organisations and various foundations, and so...' He sat forward and drum-rolled the lounge suite. '...I'd be delighted to partner you in this venture.'

'Aw, Craig! Really?'

Pieces of the puzzle were clicking into place with surprising ease. Of course he would help them! How could she have forgotten how their friendship began? Their first conversation at the community law centre she'd visited, when tracking Angus down for Izzie's maintenance payments, had revealed family lawyer Craig to be passionate about ending world poverty. And now he would channel that productiveness of his into the cause that initiated their friendship.

'How could I not want to help you?' Craig said. 'You're playing a giant part in financing my crystals cooperative.' He seized up a cushion and pushed it behind his head. 'Conan Dalesford reckons wealth is to be enjoyed and shared. He says: "Let it flow *to* you and *through* you".'

'I like that.'

'I knew you would.'

'Craig, you know me too well.'

'You forget I went out with you.'

'That's a long time ago.'

'Feels like yesterday to me.' Craig caught her eye.

She turned and busied herself with collecting the empty teacups.

LI

*W*hen dawn rumbled drearily into the sky, a conglomeration of angry clouds and splinters of lightning, each sprite attending the sad farewell lay down to sleep, near to Maleika, who would not be waking at dusk.

Maleika could hear their thoughts; was able to resonate with the mild sense of loss they were doing their best to ward off. While managing without their Clan Watcher might disconcert them at first, they would be comforted by the knowledge that here was yet another forest dweller they might visit, in that same world they returned to in the day.

She was taking on her soul form now. Her spirit was becoming part of her heart, was beginning as tiny, very tiny, a spark of purple springing swiftly into the silver cord that connected the core of her physical being with the Dream Sphere.

Travelling through this silver cord was a downward falling rush through darkness, a thundering whirl through a tunnel devoid of light.

At the end of this rapid journey through enveloping blackness was a spectacular dazzle of pearls. Luminous flashes of gold and silver. Falling softly into Maleika's consciousness was the awareness that she had arrived at the Devic Great Hall and had transformed from a lilac hued flash of flame to a replica of her expired self.

Alcor was standing beside the rose-cherubs' pearlescent gateway. 'Do you remember these gates, Maleika?' he asked. 'Do you remember who you were when you left this realm to become a forest elf?'

<hr/>

Rosetta met up with Craig for an early morning power-walk around Lavender Bay. They'd stopped for a break and were sipping hot take-away coffees on the ferry wharf, foggy air curling through their words.

Craig ambled to a stop. 'So what's next, Rosetta, now that you're a woman of substance? A lifetime soulmate?'

'You still think there's such a thing as soulmates? Wow, Craig, if I could bottle and market that optimism of yours...' Rosetta wouldn't tell him about that last fiasco. She'd already confided too much to the girls. A stray pebble rolled under the sole of her shoe. Softly, she kicked it away. It fell through the gaps in the beams of wood, landing in the water with a *ker-plinker-splish*. 'We're never satisfied are we?' she said. 'It's like we get one thing, then we want another.'

In answer, Craig whistled a tune: 'Money Can't Buy me Love'. Rosetta gazed out at the sparkling blue and hummed along to Craig's trills. The Beatles were spot-on about that. She'd thought it would be easy now that she could afford to go places. Her horizons had expanded but her prospects hadn't. The singles events she'd gone to had led to being asked out by a few, each of them decent and attractive, none of them able to make her feel the way the man who'd taken her to Amaretti's had. 'Mama might have been right after all,' she'd told Eadie. 'I probably am too fussy.'

She sat down on the edge of the wharf.

Craig's whistling dwindled. 'Do you know what I think?'

Rosetta turned to him. 'No, what do you think?'

'I think you're amazing.'

'Me?'

'Yeah, you.'

'There's nothing too amazing about me. Why would you think that?'

Craig, contemplating the harbour beneath, said quietly, 'Just do.' He drew in a breath and said, 'Your strength over all these years. That's amazing in itself.' He settled himself down on the edge of the wharf. 'No matter how many times you get knocked down, you're up and fighting again.' He was sitting directly beside her, so close, she could feel his breath on her cheek. For some reason, Craig's voice sounded pained. Craig's hand was now on her shoulder blades, pressing firmly against her back. 'But you're more than that. I'm sure you already know how I feel about you, Rosetta. You can't be friends with someone for fourteen or more years and not know how they feel.'

In a flash of insight, Rosetta said, 'Oh!'

The tone of their friendship had suddenly taken on an uncomfortable seriousness.

'And...uh...I've never actually told you this...'

Rosetta's only thought was *Don't*. She didn't want Craig making any embarrassing declaration. She had to protect him from that.

Rising abruptly to her feet, she searched for something to say. 'Wonder where a bin is. Ooh, wow, the wind has sprung up. It's suddenly so cool. Have you finished with your cup?'

Ignoring this, Craig rose from the wharf, looked at her fixedly and said, 'I never stopped being in love with you.'

Aware she was gaping at him in surprise, Rosetta looked away. Patted his arm.

She'd only ever seen his compliments and lingering glances to be signs of a random restlessness. Impersonal flirting, she'd thought, a playful familiarity that diminished whenever Craig got serious about someone. Poor, beautiful Craig. His vulnerable confession almost made her cry.

'Craig, I had no idea. I thought we were buddies!' She tried to make light of it without injuring his feelings. 'I didn't think buddies fell in love.'

'They do.' Craig clasped her hand for a second, an unusually solemn expression in place of his zany smile. 'Would you ever consider rekindling our relationship?'

Not knowing how to respond, Rosetta frowned down at the wharf boards. 'You're not even in Sydney anymore. Why would you want to—'

'Because I don't mind travelling. I can be down here for a couple of days each week if you decide to go ahead with seeing me again. Being back in Central Australia is good. Really good. It's a great place to live, but I've missed you.' Craig stared at her with pleading eyes. 'You don't have to give me an answer straight away. Think about it, okay? You've got to admit, though, that the two of us get along like a house on fire.'

'So much to talk about,' Rosetta conceded. She'd been hoping to add a 'but' to this. Craig, however, was already agreeing wholeheartedly.

'For sure! We're both intrigued by the idea of soul travel and other dimensions. And you've even warmed to the Aboriginal belief of reincarnation. Despite your traditional Greek-ness! You even said it once, that you and I are spiritual soulmates.'

Rosetta bit her lip. The emphasis had been on the word 'spiritual'. Whenever it was that she'd apparently said this, she should have said 'spirit siblings'. Never could she have imagined that the guy with the gregarious demeanour, who she'd come to rely on as one of her most treasured friends, could ever have seen her as more than she'd seen him. It was ages since they'd decided they weren't great as a couple. She would never have believed the decision they'd agreed on hadn't been entirely mutual.

Rosetta began with, 'Craig, much and all as I adore you and your friendship, it wouldn't be right.'

'I *said* think about it.' Craig's voice had tensed. 'Don't make any decision until you consider it thoroughly. You're lonely Rosetta. So am I. And being just your friend is turning me into a crazy-man.'

He picked up her empty cup. 'Finished?'

'Yep.'

'I've got to catch up with a mate of mine.' He kissed her forehead in a way that was a little too lingering for her liking. 'So I'll say goodbye until tomorrow.'

Rosetta sat back down on the wharf, quietly watching Craig's lanky form as he meandered up the shaded lawns to the car park. For a long time after he'd left she gazed into the harbour's depths, envisaging what life would be like if she started seeing Craig again.

It's not that Craig's in any way uninteresting, she thought. And he's a beautiful guy. Not cruel or condescending in any way. I can't see how he'd ever be capable of hurting me.

She tossed a small pebble into the harbour. Ripples corrupted the aquamarine smoothness.

While it might have been mild, there was certainly an attraction between the two of them, the reason she'd wanted to go out with him all those years ago. Craig's clinginess had been her reason for ending it. She'd wanted freedom, and Craig's devotion had felt stifling. A lot had happened since then of course. They were no longer young and starry-eyed, or intolerably definite about the ingredients of a good relationship. Both of them had learned a lot through life and love.

Perhaps devotion was what she needed now. Wasn't she tired of all that uncertainty? She'd only the other morning resolved to stop falling for men whose only apparent purpose in her life was to surprise and disappoint.

The seasons were dwindling so fast! Spring was around the corner. Another birthday in summer, and then she'd be one year off forty, more than likely galloping towards singledom with stoic resignation, reflecting on the 'could have beens' and smiling courageously at weddings and dinner parties.

Craig Delorey with the strong brown hands and contagious laugh. Could it be possible Craig was the ideal partner? That Rosetta might search the world only to find the love of her life had been there in her backyard all along?

And Craig was one of her very best friends. She could do a lot worse than Craig.

Epiphany concludes in Book 3

E p i p h a n y – THE SILVERING

'A riveting adventure from start to finish...'
Veritas Vincit "Bill"—USA

'The great writing style/mystery/fantasy was more present than
ever...and I actually enjoyed this one [the most.]'
Karen Ruggiero—USA

'Everything I hoped it would be and more...The layered plot is
clever and unfolds nicely as each revelation comes to light.'
LA Howell—USA

'I could never have guessed at or expected the reversals and
outcomes. They fell into place in a most incredible way, completing
plots and tying up loose ends from the first book.'
Elf Dreaming—Australia

Acknowledgements

In my third *Epiphany* novel, *THE SILVERING*, I acknowledge in detail those who have helped to bring about the *Epiphany* series. Here I wish to thank these same lovely people for their contribution to both *THE GOLDING* and *THE CRYSTALLING*.

My utmost gratitude goes to each of my obliging beta readers: Amanda Earley, Vikki Warren, Kim Jagers, Rose Pollock, Filiz Niyazi, and Robyn Kelly for comments and positivity; structural editor Deonie Fiford for smoothing out the intricacies of a complicated plot; copy editor and manuscript assessor Abigail Nathan of Bothersome Words for providing perceptive guidance; and to my highly talented international associates who helped with the book's production: Jesh Designs and Sergey Nivens for the magical cover of *THE GOLDING*; Kim Dingwall and SelfPubBookCovers.com for the glowing heart cover of *THE CRYSTALLING*; Lorie DeWorken of Mind the Margins for designing the spine, front cover text and back cover of *THE GOLDING;* MiblArt for creating the spine, front cover text and back cover of *THE CRYSTALLING;* and Rachael Cox for consistently excellent advice and conversion of the paperback files, which I typeset and formatted for printing.

I owe a great deal of thanks to my parents for their continued support and encouragement. If it hadn't been for their optimism and unceasing belief in my writing, the *Epiphany* books would neither have been published...nor seen by this reader. Yes, *you*—the one who arrived at this page! Don't quite recognise you from here, but feel sure I know you. Maybe we've met in the Dream Sphere!! Thank you for purchasing *Epiphany – THE CRYSTALLING* and for taking the time to read these acknowledgements.

A final thanks to Kate O'Donnell for critiquing the first chapters of the series, and to Tom Flood, Alex Davis, Karl Monger, Jessica Augustsson...and Code Name:EM657 of Scribendi (you know who you are!) for advice concerning the first few pages of the initial draft.

Did you enjoy the second book in Sonya Deanna Terry's
Epiphany series?

Would you consider recommending

Epiphany – THE CRYSTALLING

in a sentence or two on Goodreads
and/or the online retailer you purchased from?
Your opinion matters!

About the Author

Sonya Deanna Terry was born in Melbourne, Australia.
From the age of six she developed a passion for writing, and
throughout her childhood, teens and twenties wrote novels for
children. *Epiphany* is Sonya's first major work for adults.

Sonya worked in the advertising division of a leading Sydney
newspaper for several years before moving north and now lives in a
quiet but friendly coastal town where she is completing an arts degree
majoring in communications.

Sonya can be contacted via her website at:

www.SonyaDeannaTerry.com

Glossary

Our True Ancient History

Backwards Winding
A journey back in time. Gold's Kin sorcerers engineered the Backwards Winding to move the Grudellan Palace to a previous century.

Beauty-Creation
Earthly sprite magic fuelled by Kindness Merits. Will only work if used benevolently.

Bewitchers
Faeries enslaved by courtiers of the Grudellan Palace and drained of their goodly beauty-creation powers.

Century of Ruin
The century in which Pieter and his clan were born.

Clan Watcher
The leader of a sprite clan, such as Maleika.

Crystallings
The equivalent of modern-day christenings. An infant-naming ceremony wherein twelve former faeries bless a royal child with the palace's crystal-crowned wands.

Devas
Those of the devic realm, including:

> Earthly dwelling *Sprites*
> (Elves, faeries, undines, pixies, dryads, gnomes)
> and
> Dream-Sphere dwelling *Angels*
> (Cherubs, Passed-over sprites, Dream Masters)

Dream Sphere
The dimension sprites visit in their slumber (via their dream bodies). Sprites return to the Dream Sphere once their lives on Earth are complete.

Ehypte
Egypt (pronounced Ee-*hip*-tee)

Elysium Glades
A part of the Elysium forest in which Maleika's Brumlynd clan dwell.

Gold's Kin
(Referred to as 'gold-skin' or 'body kings' by the sprites).

A hierarchical race who enforce gold as a means of trade in favour of the sprites' Currency of Kindness.

Their native blue-grey colouring has changed to pale-gold because of the dragon blood they consume. It is for this reason the sprites they enslave mistakenly believe they refer to themselves as 'we of gold skin'.

The less respectful term sprites use for these tyrannical interlopers is *body kings*—a disgruntled reference to the conceit with which Gold's Kin regard their own physicality.

Grudellan Palace
Residence of Gold's Kin, the Grudellan empire, set on a treeless plane near to the sand dunes where sprites are forced to mine gold.

Grudellans
Smaller-sized flightless pterodactyls who serve The Solen.

Kindness Merits
Credits sprites earn in the Dream Sphere for helping another gain wisdom. The Kindness Merits transform into sprite magic (beauty-creation) in their earthly lives.

Magic-Robbing Ceremony
The draining of sprites' beauty-creation. Eagle-winged Crystal Keepers store the stolen beauty-creation in crystal vials, which they ship across to a faraway southern land, to avoid the crystals' *silvering* effects.

Norwegia
Prehistoric Norway

Pre-Destruction Century
A century occurring before the Century of Ruin, and the place in time to which the Backwards Winding has transported the Grudellan Palace.

Remembrance Essence
Water the sprites source from The Wandalobs and infuse with crystals. Consumed soon after rising from sleep, the potion clears the amnesia that accompanies Dream Sphere returns and allows sprites to recall their slumbering journeys.

Season cycle
One year

Silvered
To be silvered is to receive the heart-healing frequencies of the Grudellan Palace's silver-pink crystals. The crystals are formed from sealed crystalline vials containing an ethereal heart elixir, the beauty-creation powers Gold's Kin steal from sprites and handle with caution. Gold's Kin who are inadvertently silvered (Eidred and Storlem, for example) possess the much-despised sprite qualities of warmth and kindness and gain a deep respect for all living things.

The Silvering
A predicted time in the far-off future when a new species known as humanity (a sprite/Gold's Kin hybrid) will see an end to the Cycle of Suffering. As Maleika describes it in Book 1, *Epiphany – THE GOLDING:*

> "The Silvering is a time of repair in the extreme future. It is expected to occur when the gold-tainted illusion of *greed* equalling *lack* and *lack* equalling *greed* has multiplied to an unbearable point."

The Solen
Gold's Kin ruler of the Grudellan Court in Norwegia.

Soothsayer
Grudellan Palace fortune teller. An aged bewitcher.

Undines
Water sprites such as Zhippe and Carlonn (pronounced *Zzship*-ee and Car-*lon*).

*Unlike books funded by a publishing company, the **Epiphany** series was edited, printed and marketed at the author's own expense.*

*If you resonate with both books in the series and would like **Epiphany** to reach more readers such as yourself through increased distribution and promotion, we invite you to view the **Patreon** details on Sonya Deanna Terry's website.*

www.EpiphanyTheGolding.com